THE
FLYCASTER

THE
FLYCASTER

R.K. BLESSING

Boyle
&
Dalton

Book Design and Production
Columbus Publishing Lab
www.ColumbusPublishingLab.com

Print ISBN 978-1-63337-067-8
E-book ISBN 978-1-63337-066-1

Printed in the United States of America
1 3 5 7 9 10 8 6 4 2

To everyone who helped make this book possible.
Thank you so much.

I 'm high in the mountains, sitting in silence beneath the evergreens and hardwoods. In front of me, a healthy stream snakes its way through the underbrush, winding effortlessly like a ribbon before flowing into a deep pool that's crystal blue like the sky above me. On the opposite edge of the pool, riffles sparkle in the early afternoon sunlight as the water babbles over pebbles and small rocks before continuing on its way down the mountainside. I'm hoping for some sign of life but, like myself, many of the trout have receded to the banks to avoid the afternoon sun.

When a gust of wind comes up, I happen to see an insect whipped off a nearby branch. After landing in the pool, it dances about on the surface film, trying desperately to stay afloat. Out of habit, my eyes scan the water and sure enough, I spot the shadowy form of a fish surfacing from the depths.

It glides up beneath the insect like a ghost, and a gentle slurping sound echoes over the pool. The insect is gone. Soft ripples radiate across the surface while the trout swims in lazy circles, searching for another meal. When the shadow of a large bird soars overhead, the trout disappears and everything grows quiet once more.

I smile and close my eyes. Much like the river flowing down the mountainside, beautiful memories float through my brain. But just like the shadow of the osprey flying over the pool, darker memories glide along the fringes of my mind as well. They will always be there, haunting me forever. Even when my eyes fly open, I can see them like a waking dream…

I wasn't snobby or rich. I wasn't refined by any means and I certainly didn't live a life of prestige. I was just…me, Brody Allen, the poor kid hiding under the worn-out, piece-of-shit bed that I'd slept on since I was out of my crib. There was a tangy, metallic taste in my mouth as blood oozed from my cracked lip. My cheek was on fire from my father's heavy hand, and as the adrenaline wore off I felt bruises setting in all over my body.

My father had just beat me. Like many nights before that one, he got drunk, and as usual after a good beating, he got high and passed out on the recliner in the living room. Thankfully, that night was the final straw for the next door neighbor, sweet Mrs. Murphy. She always gave me cookies, but not that night. Instead Mrs. Murphy called the cops.

I was still whimpering amongst the dust bunnies when

they busted through the door of the house. I'll never forget how loud it was. The door frame cracked like thunder when they broke through the lock. It scared me so bad I clamped my hands over my ears, figuring my father was starting his next rampage. Next came the shouting and heavy footsteps. I had no idea what was going on. Their voices reverberated through the tiny house, and I laid there trembling. By the time they hauled me out from under the bed, I was a cowering mess covered with dust and dried blood.

My dear father was so wasted that he never even woke. He was arrested on possession and domestic violence charges. I was only twelve, but I was smart enough then to understand what that meant. In the end, he was sent to prison.

Where's my mother in all this you might ask? She's dead. So guess what? No parents or relatives meant I was put into the system. By the age of twelve, I was a ward of the State. There was no one else to take care of me, so I bounced from house to house—a foster kid, and all I had to my name was a duffel bag. You get used to it though, being alone. The things you enjoy most about your life—friends, hobbies, emotions in general—they all become memories you hardly enjoy because the only thing that matters is taking care of yourself. Making sure you wake up the next day.

It gnaws at you. Sometimes the families are nice and sometimes they aren't. Sometimes the parents are just in it for the checks, and that's depressing. So in the end, I left. The last family I had was nice, though. They helped me get my driver's license, but I didn't have a car, so it didn't make much of a difference. There was still that sense of freedom, though; after acquiring my GED at sixteen, I struck out on my own.

I wasn't going anywhere in particular, because I didn't know where to go. All I knew was that there were a lot of places I could go, but sadly, most of the really cool, interesting places required money, which I didn't have much of. Stealing was an obvious choice, but if I got caught, I would more than likely end up back in the system, if not somewhere worse.

Thankfully, I was able to scrounge up some work as I moved from place to place. I was a cook six times, and that was actually pretty fun, especially since I usually got a free meal every shift. I did landscape work and held positions on a couple golf courses.

One time, there was this greens keeper I worked for—a country guy out in Michigan who was one of the hardest working people I've ever met. His passion for cutting grass and keeping that course meticulously groomed knew no bounds. I called him Chief and he called me "a deluxe human being," which never really made sense to me. In any case, he was more than just a superb greens keeper. He was one of the funniest guys I've ever met, and God knows I could use a little humor in my life.

If only people knew what happens on golf courses after dark. I'll never forget the night when I came back to the golf course hoping to crash in one of the storage buildings. Apparently there was an anniversary party for the course that I'd forgotten about, and there were all sorts of people making a hell of a ruckus. Chief had turned the gentle sweeping hill of a small par-three behind the clubhouse into a giant slip 'n' slide. While he was roasting food on the grill, the crowd was laughing and cheering as person after person slid into the lower valley of hole number six. Eventually I had to move on—it was rare for a job to last more than a week.

If there's one thing I learned during that time, it's that farmers are always busy, which was great for me. I cut wood, shoveled shit, pruned trees, disked, sowed, and harvested fields. It was hard but rewarding work. Sadly, farming gets pretty quiet toward the end of the year, and I had to move on again.

Since staying warm sounded more appealing than freezing to death outside, I took up janitorial work for a time. I was a heavy lifter for a box company. I even worked out in the oil fields in the Dakotas, and let me tell you I don't miss that one.

I shake my head and focus again on the crystal blue water. While I wait for the bite to pick up again, I'll just sit here on the riverbank, thinking about the last year of my life, the day I made it to the west coast, and how it led me to somewhere I never dreamed of being.

The twinkling stars were beginning to fade as the morning sun illuminated the horizon. Beyond the window, the neon sign for a little diner near Boise glowed through the remaining darkness: *The Griddle*. A cheerful jingle filled the diner as a tired couple made their way inside.

"You can sit anywhere you like," a hostess called out from behind the counter. It wasn't long before a waitress meandered over to their table, pouring them cups of freshly brewed coffee. I inspected the new patrons from behind my bowl of oatmeal. The girl's pronounced dimples made the fella's freckly cheeks get pink, and they shared some nervous laughter and yawns once their order was placed. Before their arrival I'd been sitting quietly, listening to the soothing sounds of clinking dishes back in the kitchen while debating my next course of action. But now their conversation was distracting me from those thoughts, and I was faced with another dilemma. Being alone.

Wholesome country folk. I stared at them with tired eyes and a glum smile before shifting my gaze back to the plate in front of me. Since I wasn't sure when I'd have another chance to eat, I'd splurged and got some bacon as well, but only because I knew I needed the calories. When the steady rumble of an engine brought my attention back to the window, I noticed a pickup pulling into a parking space at the far end of the diner. Soon the door jingled again, and a rugged man walked in and took a seat at the counter. He broke into conversation with the waitress, and I continued eating while he droned on about his trips through the mountains. Neither the waitress nor I could keep from smiling as bits of egg and grits collected in his burly beard.

When his tales became more elaborate and exaggerated, I tuned him out until I heard him mention Oregon. My ears pricked up and sure enough, he mentioned that he was driving out to Portland today. I grinned to myself. Maybe I would make it to the west coast after all. After paying for my meager breakfast, I left the diner and very casually and discreetly climbed into the back of the man's truck. Thankfully he didn't find me, and it proved to be a good ride. The steady rumble of the engine actually put me to sleep after a while.

We made it to Portland later that night. The truck driver must have been a regular diner guy, because he made a pit stop at another delicious-smelling eatery. I waited several minutes after he went inside before hopping out of the truck, and I waited even longer for the driver to leave the restaurant so there wouldn't be that awkward second encounter. By then my stomach was growling painfully, so I decided to splurge on dinner.

While waiting for my meal, I welcomed the sounds of the diner as I traced the rim of my water glass with my finger. I thought about my ever-thinning wallet, hoping I had enough left to buy some shampoo and wash my clothes at the laundromat. Then a more worrisome thought strutted to the front of my head. Summer would be giving way to fall soon, and I knew that I needed to find something stable.

Just as I was getting too hungry to think straight, the waitress appeared, but instead of an appetizing plate of dinner in her hands, there was only a heavy foam container. There was no tab either. I looked up in confusion.

"I didn't order this to go," I said. She glanced up at me without saying a word. Then her eyes briefly flew to another spot in the room. I turned to catch the eyes of a few patrons. They were giving me a weird look and quickly bowed their heads. *What? You've never seen an eighteen-year-old with a ratty sweater and holes in his jeans?*

"Fine," I said. "How much do I owe you?" At first I thought she didn't hear me over the fountain machine, but then she sat a cup of soda next to my dinner.

"Nothing. Have a good night," she said with a wry smile.

I sighed. It wasn't the first time I'd been turned away from a restaurant, but it was irritating all the same. I chose not to say anything. It wasn't worth ruining my appetite. All I wanted was to enjoy my dinner in peace, so after leaving the diner I crossed the street and slipped into an alley. I narrowly avoided soaking my boots in a stream running from the gutter of a long building with thick, wood siding. A dumpster loomed out of the darkness, and after walking past I found a nice porch attached to the building—it even had an awning over the top.

I climbed the steps and took a seat beneath a window at the far end of the porch. Not five minutes after sitting down, a steady rain began falling from the sky. *Perfect.*

So there I sat, eating my greasy patty melt and fries, sipping on cola. Eventually I fell asleep listening to the late summer rain as it drummed away on the sheet-metal roof.

"Hey," the voice said. "Hey. Wake up. Are you dead?"

I groaned painfully when I felt something jab against my ribs. "No, I'm not dead. I'm sleeping. Or I was sleeping."

"You scared me."

"Sorry." Then I started coughing. They were painful coughs, and when they finally subsided I could feel my eyes watering. When I opened them, I found myself staring at a woman about my age with long hair pulled back in a ponytail. The morning light hadn't made it back to the alley yet, and all I could see from behind my heavy eyelids was that she was wearing boots, jeans, and a pullover of some sort. I coughed again as my body began to shiver.

"Are you okay?" she asked. "And why are you asleep behind my shop?"

"I'm not sure. I'm freezing though. I fell asleep back here after dinner." I managed to motion toward the empty take-out container a few feet away before I started coughing again.

"Are you homeless?"

"No, not exactly. I prefer the term vagabond."

The woman tipped her head. "So a Gypsy then?"

"No!" I snapped. "I'm not a Gypsy."

"A drifter?"

"No."

"A nomad?"

"What are you? A walking thesaurus?" I coughed. "Where am I anyway?"

"Chill, dude. You're in Eugene, Oregon."

"Not Portland? I thought I was in Portland."

"Nope. Eugene."

"Hmm." When I tried to stand up, the cramped muscles in my body stung. I groaned, and the girl pointed the handle of the broom at me again.

"Relax," I managed before the coughing fit returned once more. "My name's Brody. I'm not going to hurt you. Just give me a minute and I'll get lost." I tried again to stand, but the coughing fit only got worse and I slumped back to the ground. My lungs felt like they were on fire.

"No," she said. "You promise you won't hurt me?"

"Why would I hurt you?" I said. "You're the first person that's held an actual, meaningful conversation with me in days." I closed my eyes and tried to focus on the gentle pitter patter of raindrops dripping off the porch roof. When the urge to cough subsided somewhat, I opened my eyes again and the girl smiled.

"Meaningful, huh? Come on, you need to get warm." She helped me to my feet and led me inside. The store was dark, but she brought me to a back room where there was a little couch, table, and a kitchen that smelled of coffee and cinnamon. There was a comforting, warm glow coming from a pair of lamps tucked under the cabinets that hung from the walls.

"Would you like some coffee or tea?" she asked. I gaped at her. Only minutes before she was ready to beat me with a broom, and now she was offering me a hot beverage.

"What? Really?"

"Yeah," she said. "I like tea. Prefer it actually, but most of the folks that work here prefer coffee, so I'll drink coffee if I have to." She was nervous, that much was clear to me. Whoever she was, she kept staring and talking fast. I couldn't blame her. I'm sure I looked pale and gaunt from being cold and not having enough to eat. It probably didn't help matters any that my clothes were worn out and dirty. There were holes in my jeans, and the cuffs of my hoodie were starting to fray terribly. I resisted the urge to run a hand through my unkempt hair sprouting out from under my cap, and instead rubbed the scraggly brown stubble that covered my face.

"What are you having?" I asked.

"Tea with two sugars. Maybe a little milk."

"Then I'll have that too…please. I don't want you to go

to any trouble for me." She gave me a strange look after I said that. A moment later she set a warm cup in my trembling hands and then gently prodded me toward another door.

"Where are you taking me now?" I asked before coughing again.

"I'm sorry, Brody, but you look and smell like shit and you need to get warm, so go shower. There's a shower in there."

"Seriously?" I hadn't showered in days.

"Yes, seriously. I'd prefer if you didn't die in the alley behind the store. Not exactly good for business."

"Who are you?" I asked, feeling more grateful by the second.

She didn't answer right away, but instead gently pushed the cup to my lips. "Drink. My name is Isabel. What size do you wear?"

"Excuse me?"

"What size?" she repeated, and tugged on my shirt and pants.

"Um, large shirt and thirty-four thirty. Maybe thirty-two. I haven't looked in a while. That's what the belt is for."

She grinned and shook her head. "Go shower. There's soap and towels in the cupboard. When you're done, just stay in here, okay? I made some oatmeal. Feel free to have some. Please stay in here."

I nodded like an obedient child. "Alright. Thank you."

"You're welcome," Isabel said, and disappeared out the door. I lingered for a moment to see if she would reappear and tell me I had to leave, but she never came, so I carried the tea with me into the shower. The warm, honey flavor was soothing on my throat, and the hot water felt amazing on my body. Not long after climbing in the shower, I heard the door to the bathroom open and close, but when I peeked there was no one. Instead, a pile of brand new clothes rested on a shelf by the door.

Despite loving the piping hot water, I had no intention of upsetting Isabel and overstaying my welcome, so after a few glorious minutes in the shower, I left the sanctuary of warm water and got dressed. The new clothes she'd given me were the nicest things I'd ever seen. There were thick cotton socks, light-brown denim pants, a thin long-sleeve undershirt, and a thicker green flannel that made me feel like I was wrapped in a blanket. *This has got to be a joke. Why in the world is she doing this for me?*

In the kitchenette Isabel was leaning at the counter, taking small bites from her bowl of oatmeal. All the while she continued to stare at me, so I stared back at her now that I could see clearly enough. The hair that I saw pulled back in a ponytail was dark brown, and a few locks of it hung down, hugging her cheeks. Her pale complexion was offset by her bright green eyes, and at the moment she had the tiniest smile on her face, as if she couldn't decide how to feel about the situation.

"Are you feeling better?" she asked.

"Yeah, and thanks for the clothes," I said.

"You're welcome. I can get you a short-sleeve shirt if you like. I think it's going to be warm today."

Out of habit I tugged gently on the sleeves. "No thanks. These are great. I prefer long sleeves."

"Okay. Are you hungry?" she asked. I nodded eagerly since I was always hungry. "Come here. Have some oatmeal. There's brown sugar there and some milk in the fridge."

"Thanks," I mumbled.

"So. How long you been sleeping on my porch?"

"It's not your porch."

"How do you know?"

"Because not many people our age own their own businesses," I said.

Isabel's emerald eyes bored into me. "What if I'm the exception?"

"Well I'd give you the benefit of the doubt, except your bag on the floor kind of gives you away." A little tag hanging off one of the zippers read Eugene High.

"Fine. You win. This is my uncle's shop. I was going to do my homework if I wasn't too busy today." Isabel tilted her head. "Our age?"

"Yeah. Our age. I didn't really peek in the mirror, but I'm not as old as I probably look," I said.

"Really? Because you look like you're at least twenty-five, if not older."

My wheezy laugh was caught between more coughs.

"How old are you then?" she asked.

"Eighteen," I said. "You?"

"Seventeen."

I nodded and glanced around the room again while eagerly spooning oatmeal into my mouth.

"And what sort of shop did I have the pleasure of falling asleep next to?"

"A fly shop."

"A fly shop? Is this some sort of strange bug pet store that also has really nice high-end clothing for sale?"

Isabel covered her mouth, holding back a giggle. "No, it's a fly shop...for fly fishing?" I gave her my best vacant expression. "You have no idea what I'm talking about, do you?"

"Not a clue," I answered. "But I do know about oatmeal, and this is good stuff. Thank you."

She laughed again. "It's just oatmeal."

"Maybe to you, but this was made with TLC, and the raisins and brown sugar make it even better."

"Well, you're welcome," she said. "Just hang tight, alright? I gotta go open up."

I nodded, and she walked from the room again. For several minutes I sat in peace on the little couch, eating my oatmeal, but curiosity got the better of me and I went to peer into the shop. Isabel was walking around flipping on the lights, and all of a sudden I was staring into the most mesmerizing big-kids toy store of all time. My legs were moving before I could stop them.

Every inch of the shop was dedicated to fishing merchandise. The walls were decorated with all sorts of fancy clothes, fishing poles, and other gear that I assumed was meant for fly fishing. Even the ceiling was used as advertising space. From the rafters hung small kayaks and float tubes. When the phone rang, I glanced at the counter and saw Isabel twirling her finger aimlessly around the cord. She looked irritated. I looked away when I caught sight of a mounted fish on the wall, but her voice carried through the empty store. "Yeah…Alright…Uhuh… Okay…Alright, thanks for calling." When the phone clicked in its cradle, I heard her footsteps and turned to see her going to the back room. "Hey, Brody?"

"I'm over here," I said.

"Oh," she said. "Hey."

"Hi. I'm sorry. I know you said stay put."

"Actually I said hang tight, but it's no big deal. Don't worry about it. Are you…"

"Busy…Leaving soon…" I suggested. "I won't stay long. I'm sure I'll just be in the way if I hang out much longer anyway."

"No, actually, if you wanted to stay, I've got some homework to finish and a paper to write. The other person that was supposed to work just called and bailed, so I could use the help," she said.

"Um—alright," I said.

"I mean, unless you want to get going."

I shook my head. "It's nice here and I'm enjoying this oatmeal," I replied. Although "nice" was an understatement. I hated being cold, and the warmth of her uncle's shop was a godsend.

"Help yourself to more," she said. "Come see me when you're finished."

I wandered around the shop, eating two more bowls of oatmeal in the process. With each lap, I wove through the maze of wire racks and displays, noticing more items of intrigue that I'd missed previously. Fancy-looking pliers and handcrafted nets, spools of thread and wire, books, and gleaming reels that appeared to have been fashioned out of pure silver or gold. The list went on and on. Whenever I came close to the register, I averted my eyes from Isabel. I knew she was watching me, probably trying to make sure I didn't steal anything.

When the bowl was empty I went to see her at the front counter. Isabel's expression was neutral when she gave me a page of discount stickers.

"Where should I put these?" I asked. Isabel pointed back to a section of the shop where a vast peg board held all sorts of craft materials.

"Any of the tying materials made by Fly Tie Co. get a sticker," she said.

"Okay. Sounds easy enough."

"Wait," she said. "Where did you come from?"

"Out east," I replied, making my way toward the peg board.

"Come on. You gotta give me more than that."

I looked back at her, wondering if she really cared. Not many people cared about a nobody, and I didn't like when people pried. "I'm from Portland, Maine."

"Ah, so the whole going to Portland, Oregon—you're on some sort of trip or something?"

I sighed and raised my eyebrows. I had no idea what to say. "Something like that."

Without another word, I started posting stickers. It was definitely one of the simpler jobs I'd had, and for several minutes the shop was silent. All I could hear was her pencil scratching away as she did her homework, so I started whistling. Apparently Isabel didn't like this.

"You're whistling. I'm trying to concentrate."

"Sorry," I sighed, and kept posting stickers. Within seconds though, I was quietly humming.

"I can still hear you," she said.

"Sorry," I chuckled. "I'll stop that, too."

She started to say something else, but a customer walked into the store, deterring further conversation. When I was done tagging the various items, I came across a wall of photographs. Faces of numerous anglers stared back at me as they held up their trophy catches, and it wasn't long before I spotted a familiar face. I looked back to the counter only to find Isabel staring at me. She quickly looked down at her homework.

"Is this you?" I asked.

Isabel left her post behind the counter to come stand next to me. "Yep. That was the first fish I ever caught. My uncle said it was one of the biggest bluegills in the pond."

"That's cool." I tipped my head slightly as I continued to stare at the picture. Isabel couldn't have been more than seven or eight in the picture. Her clothes and face were streaked with mud, but nothing could stop the grin on her face as she held up her fish. She was so happy.

The hairs on my neck prickled and I knew she was staring at me again, so I looked at her.

"What?" she said.

"You're all dirty."

"Yeah. I slipped on the bank before I caught that fish."

That made me smile. It was difficult to picture the girl standing beside me all dirty.

"What?" she said again.

"Nothing." I shook my head and wandered off to peruse the store.

"Tell me." Isabel walked up to me again. "Do you think it's stupid that—"

"You were a cute kid."

Her cheeks grew red and I wandered over to a rack of fly rods, wishing I had more oatmeal to eat. Normally I couldn't have cared less about fishing, but there was something different about them compared to other poles I'd seen. They were less clunky looking, less mechanical. It was almost as if each one had the potential to have a personality of its own. From the corner of my eye, I noticed Isabel coming to stand near me yet again. Her soft footsteps also carried along the pleasant smell of her perfume.

"Did you find your pole yet?" she asked. Many of the tall, slender rods reached almost to the ceiling, but other than some being shorter, I had absolutely no idea what the difference was.

"I don't know," I said. "Is there one in particular that I should use?"

"Depends what you're fishing for."

"A big fish."

"Of course you would say that."

"What's wrong with that?"

"Nothing," she answered. "Steelhead or salmon?"

"Sure. What about this one?"

"No," she snapped. "I mean—sorry, not that one. It's too short."

My eyebrows raised and I reached for a different rod. "Okay. What about this one?"

"No. That's a three-weight rod. Way too light."

I smirked and shook my head. "Why do you like this kind of fishing anyway? It seems complicated. What's wrong with a regular pole and a coffee can of worms?"

Isabel huffed and reached for a pole herself. "First of all, this is the pole you want. A seven-weight at nine feet. You can cast heavier flies with this, and the fight will still be wicked because the pole isn't too stiff. Secondly, there is nothing wrong with fishing with a spinning reel except that it's lame."

"Lame?" I repeated.

"Yes. Lame. Fly fishing is elegant and beautiful. Watching someone who is good at casting is like watching a dance. It's about timing and gracefulness. Good casters can make a fly land on the water without leaving a ripple." Out of nowhere,

Isabel whipped the rod past my nose and a mischievous grin crossed her face.

"Not to mention when you hook a ten-pound steelhead, it's one of the most exhilarating things ever—there's no way it compares to a spinning reel."

"Uhuh," I said. "I'll take your word for it."

"You'll see," she said, and walked off with the pole. I doubted nearly everything she said because, first of all, in my recent experience some of the most beautiful and elegant things were food and a safe place to sleep. Secondly, I would probably never get a chance to fly fish. Something was bound to happen within the next day or so and I would be off on my own again, trying to find a way to Portland.

Yet hearing her say *elegant* and *beautiful* resonated somewhere inside of me. Then she turned and gave me a wink as she pulled a reel off the shelf. I allowed myself a smile and decided to follow her to the counter. Her class work was pushed off to the side opposite the till. Amongst all the knick-knacks at the front of the counter was a donation jar half full of cash and coins. On the front was a big sticker that read "TU."

"What's this?" I asked. Her eyes flitted between me and the jar.

"A donation jar for Trout Unlimited. It's a non-profit group that helps support fisheries."

I nodded and glanced around the shop again. When I returned my attention to Isabel, the donation jar had vanished. I withheld a sigh, but the words I was thinking still slipped out.

"You can put that back. I'm not gonna take any." She stopped fiddling with the reel, looking more embarrassed than anything else. Then, very casually, Isabel produced the jar from under the counter again.

"So what are you doing there?" I asked.

"Putting backing and fly line on this reel."

"I'm sorry if I'm annoying you," I blurted out.

"You're not."

"It's just...I know absolutely nothing about fly fishing."

"I suppose it's a good thing you're asking questions then, huh?" Isabel gave me another sleek smile.

"Yeah. I suppose. What's backing then?" I asked.

"Backing is what you put on the reel first in case you hook a big fish that takes out all your fly line—you'll still have the backing, just in case." The polished aluminum reel glinted in the early morning sunlight. "This is called an arbor knot. It's how you usually tie the backing to the reel."

"And when you connect it to the fly line?" I asked.

"A blood knot. Hang on, I'll show you." She tied the first knot and wound several yards of backing onto the reel, then grabbed the end of the fly line.

"What's the difference between the backing and the fly line besides it being fatter and bright green?" I asked.

Isabel huffed. "There's nothing that special about backing. It's just a high-stress line used for backup. The fly line is the special stuff. This kind floats. That's what the 'F' means on the box." I glanced at the string of letters and numbers on the corner of the box. "Some lines float, some sink, and there's different weights and tapers. It all depends on what kind of fishing you're planning on doing."

"Alright. And why is it bright green?" I asked.

"So you can see it. Why else would it be bright green?"

I think I blushed more then than I had in my entire life, and I spent the next few minutes keeping my mouth shut. Isabel made the task of connecting lines seem effortless. Her fingers danced and twisted with a dexterity and grace that I didn't know was possible.

"See?" she said. "Pull." We each took a side and pulled. To my surprise, the knot held.

"What if it breaks?" I asked.

"My knot won't break. But if it does, you'd probably be witness to one pissed-off angler."

I laughed. *Confident, too, apparently.* "What's that loop for?" I asked, pointing to the end of the green fly line.

"That's where you tie on a leader."

"A leader?"

"Yep. That's the stuff that looks like regular fishing line." She held up a plastic envelope with a coil of line inside.

I shook my head ever so slightly.

"What?" she said.

"I'm telling you, Isabel: complicated."

"And I'm telling you, Brody: I've done this all my life. It's absolutely worth it."

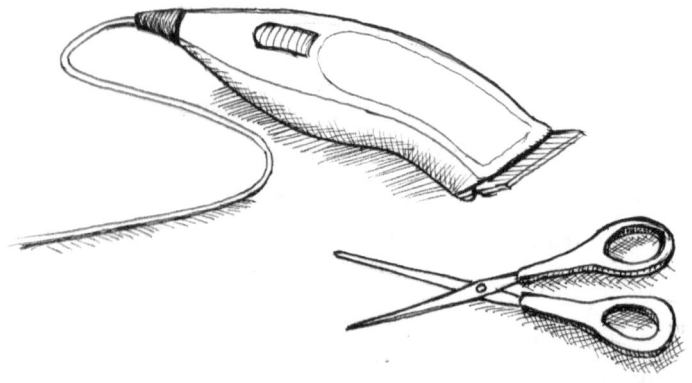

"So that's that," Isabel said, flipping off the last bank of lights. "A day in the life of a fly shop." We were once again at the back of the shop where the day had begun.

"Thanks a lot, Isabel. This has been really great. Best day I've had in a while, actually."

"Good. You're welcome. So, where are you going now?"

"I'm not sure." I shrugged. "Maybe try to get a bus ticket to Portland."

"Really?"

I had lied my way out of so many situations in the past, but as I stood there with her it didn't feel right. "Probably not, actually. I don't have enough money left."

Isabel continued to stare at me and I wondered if her heart was beating as hard as mine was. People who were normal and had friends would be able to hug or whatever, but I wasn't exactly normal and I wasn't sure if Isabel and I were friends at this point. I just stood there awkwardly, wondering how to say goodbye.

"Well, did you have any actual plans tonight or tomorrow?" she asked.

"Do I really look like one to be making plans?"

"No, I suppose not," Isabel said after an uneasy laugh. "Seriously, what are you going to do tonight?"

"Well, most nights I would scrounge for some food and find a nice place to crash. Seeing as how your back porch was so nice, I was seriously considering crashing here again. Listening to the rain back here last night was kind of beautiful."

Isabel bit her lip while rocking back and forth on her heels. "How about you make some plans with me?"

"Really?"

"Yeah. Why not?"

"I guess," I replied. "I don't have much else to do."

With a quick smile, she pushed open the door and walked onto the porch. I wanted to follow, but instead I lingered in the entryway. "What?" she asked.

"Are you just messing with me?"

"Do you think I would have given you clothes and food today if I was messing with you?"

I shrugged. My father had lured me back with lie after lie. I wasn't keen on repeating that process.

"Come on," she insisted. The first few minutes of our

walk down the sidewalk were awkward and quiet. Without the distraction of the fly shop I had no idea what to talk about. What she said next blew my mind.

"I was thinking that you could stay at my house tonight on the couch, and then tomorrow, if you want, you could help out at the shop again. My uncle is gone until tomorrow afternoon guiding a trip, and it was really nice having your help today. I actually got some homework done, and I'm sorry if I sounded grumpy."

I raised my eyebrows. "So you actually like the whistling and humming then?"

Isabel gave me a playful shove. "Get over yourself. Seriously, what do you say about tomorrow?"

"Well, I had a lot of casual vagabonding scheduled, but I think I could fit you in."

Her cheery laugh filled the early evening air. It wasn't too often that I got to make someone laugh or smile. It made me feel useful in some way. The phone in her pocket jingled, but she didn't answer it.

"So, you're from the other side of the country?" she asked.

I nodded.

"What's it like? Do you remember it much?"

My gaze dropped to the pavement and I half expected a giant, gaping hole to open up in the sidewalk and consume me. *Sadly I do remember it, Isabel. Those were the worst twelve years of my life.* But I refrained from saying that. What was the point? "Yeah. Portland's really beautiful—on the ocean and everything. The salty air. The different seasons. There's a really big lighthouse I used to love visiting on Cape Elizabeth. It's all white, and the roofs are all bright red, and on sunny days it looks perfect against the ocean."

"That sounds nice."

I replied with another nod, wondering once again why she wanted to talk to me.

"Where did you come from last?" she asked.

"Boise."

She slowed to a stop. "You don't say much."

"You ask a lot of questions," I countered.

"Can you blame me?"

I shrugged.

"Well, are you like the brooding silent type who thinks your problems are worse than everyone else's?"

I bristled, knowing I could tell her things that would probably bring her to tears in seconds. "How about me and my problems just go?" I said.

When our eyes met, the harsh defensiveness in hers had vanished. There was only worry. "You don't have to go. I'm just trying to make conversation," she said.

"I know. I'm sorry," I said.

"So…" Whoever this Isabel was, it was clear that she was going to be persistent, and maybe that was all right. After all, she had helped me get cleaned up and given me food and work for the day.

"I actually picked up a couple shifts at a library in Boise."

"Really? That's cool." A tiny smile appeared on her face, and then we started walking again. "How'd you end up here then?"

"I hitched a ride on some dude's truck."

"Like, *Hey mister! Can I have a ride?* Or you just literally hitched a ride?"

I let my silence speak for itself. Her eyes widened and she remained silent while we continued down the sidewalk. Old oaks and maples towered above us like giants, sheltering the neighborhood. We came to a stop in front of a small, two story house. It had dark green siding and shingles thick with moss. A series of steps led up to a porch that ran across the front, with a door centered between two windows.

"So," Isabel said. "This is my home."

"It's nice looking. I haven't been in a house in a while." I sucked in a breath. *Why did I say that?*

"Do you promise to be good?" she asked.

I frowned and tilted my head. "I'm not a dog. I'm a potty-trained human being."

Tiny wrinkles formed as her eyebrows raised incredibly high. Then she started laughing. "I just meant that I'm letting you into my home, so don't steal anything."

"I won't. I promise. Listen, Isabel, it's been really nice hanging out with you. You know, listening to you hash out your fishing knowledge to dudes has been wonderful and all. I wouldn't want to ruin that."

In a flash, she swatted me in the stomach. "Are you making fun of me?"

"What? No. I meant that mostly as a compliment. Or did you mean that as a rhetorical question?" I laughed, figuring she was going to swat me again, but instead she gave me a cool smile and dashed inside. I took a deep breath and followed her up the steps.

Once inside, Isabel shed her jacket and skirted off through the house, flipping on lights as she went, leaving me to stare. It had been well over a year since I'd been in an actual home. Much of my time had been spent in restaurants, workshops, and warehouses. Isabel's home was beautiful—much nicer than the place I'd grown up in anyway. It was clean, neatly trimmed, and rustic. The initial feeling of confinement made me want to run, and yet the longer I stood in the entryway, the more the waves of anxiety dissipated.

Her home even smelled how I hoped a real home would smell. My father's place had been musty and rank from all the booze bottles. Mrs. Murphy's had been better, but it was stuffy and the smell of her perfume lingered like a cloud. Isabel's home, on the other hand, held a wonderful smell that made me feel happy and safe. I slid off my boots and bag and walked farther into the house.

Many of the walls were adorned with shelves that carried the weight of pictures, shells, and dishware. There were also paintings of wildlife, beaches, forests, and lighthouses. As I continued walking, the paintings transitioned to photography, and my heart was gripped by a pang of jealousy when I spotted

Isabel in pictures with other members of her family. She had both parents and a sister. I did my best to bury those feelings before they could become an issue. A little farther on, I found another photo hanging proudly on its own. Her father was apparently serving in the military.

"Hey, Brody! Would you come here?" Isabel called.

"Sure." I drug my eyes away from the photos. As I neared wherever she was in the house, the sound of music got stronger. There was also the steady on-and-off pulse of something buzzing.

"Are you going to taze me? I said I wouldn't take anything."

"No, you dork. Come here," she said. When I peered into the kitchen, I saw that Isabel was now dressed in comfy clothes, and on the counter was an array of hair grooming items.

"Isabel—"

"No. I'm sorry, but you need some TLC. That's a condition of me letting you stay here." The kindness in her words eased my worries.

"Alright," I said. After sitting down on the stool in front of her, she tugged gently on my shirt.

"Do you want to take this off?"

"No." I shifted uncomfortably on the stool, tugging on my sleeves.

"Are you sure? I don't want you to get itchy."

"No. It's fine. I'll be all right."

"Suit yourself." She draped a towel around my shoulders.

It was fluffy and warm and smelled of spring.

What is going on? Was that patty melt laced with something?

"Okay," she said. "I won't take all this off. But definitely a lot."

"Go for it. I think I've known you long enough to let you cut my hair."

Isabel laughed. "Just relax, alright?" I knew she could feel the tension in my shoulders as she gently moved them so I was sitting properly for a haircut. "You're lucky my dad isn't here. He'd shave you bald."

That got a nervous chuckle out of me. "The military man," I said.

"Yep, the Sarge," Isabel mused, and I chuckled again.

"How long has he been gone?"

"Almost a year."

"I'm sorry. That must be hard."

"Yeah. You get used to it though. Hang on. Tip your head." I did as she asked and fell silent in the process, while chunks of my hair dropped to the floor around me.

"The worrying never goes away though," she added.

"I bet. I'm sure he misses you."

"Yeah. You know, I'm sorry I said you smelled like shit earlier. That probably sounded mean."

"Ha. Don't worry about it. I'm sure I smelled funny. I do wear deodorant, you know. I just haven't had a chance to wash my clothes in a few days."

"Well, we'll get you cleaned up. Just relax, okay?" Her

fingers gently ran through my hair as she cut off the longer, gnarly strands. I had no idea how much her touch would affect me. Every now and again, her hand or arm would brush against my shoulders, and the resulting tingles were like an electric shock coursing across my body. The more hair she cut off, the more I could feel her fingers running along my head and neck, and the more intense the tingles got, so much so that I finally had to stand up.

"Hey, what's wrong?" she asked.

"Nothing. I'm good. It's just…your hands feel really good." I was stuttering and could feel myself getting red. *How embarrassing.*

Isabel started laughing again. "Good, I'm glad. Now come here. You look kind of ridiculous."

I reached up and brushed a hand through my hair. One side was neatly trimmed while the other side was still long and scraggly. "Oh my goodness," I breathed.

Isabel was apparently enjoying this immensely as she tried to hide more laughs behind her hand. "Please, let me finish. You're almost done."

"Okay." I sat down again and she continued trimming. I tried to distract myself from the wonderful feeling of her hands by enjoying the music playing on the radio, but it was often interrupted by her gentle humming, which I also found oddly soothing. *I must be dreaming. Is this like one of those fantastic dreams guys have? What the hell was in the patty melt?*

"Do you like this song?" Isabel asked.

"Yeah. It's got a fun beat," I said. "I haven't kept up on music much in the last few years though."

"You haven't missed too much. Don't worry, I'll catch you up." She ran her hand affectionately across the top of my back.

"Okay," I said, glancing again at all of my hair piling up on the floor.

"Alright. I'm no pro, but what do you think?" Isabel held out a mirror for me. It was certainly different. Normally, all I saw was my dirty gruffness in the reflection of windows while walking down the sidewalk. But now I didn't look so gruff any more. In fact, I actually resembled an eighteen-year-old again.

"Wow," I said. "I think it looks okay. I look my age again, anyway." The scraggly locks of near shoulder-length hair were gone, exposing more of my freckle-covered face. "Thank you."

"You're welcome. You should go shower again and shave. I'll make something for dinner."

I couldn't take it any more. Nobody I'd run into was as nice as Isabel. There had to be a catch of some sort. "Why are you doing this?" I asked. "Taking care of me, I mean. You're being super nice."

"Because."

"Because...why?"

"Just go shower, you dork. Down the hall."

I slid off the stool and started for the bathroom, but I only made it to the doorway of the kitchen. When I turned back, Isabel was retrieving a broom from the closet. She paused when I walked back into the kitchen.

"You're not gonna hit me with that are you?"

She glanced at the broom and laughed. "No."

A nervous smile crossed my face as I reached for the broom. "Really. Let me. I am sort of a pro at this. There must be something that I could do or help you with. I feel like I need to say thanks as much as possible."

Isabel laughed again and gave me another pensive stare that I'd already seen so many times that day. "It's not a big deal, Brody."

"So, are you saying you help all the stray dogs you find behind the shop then?"

"No. Do you like mac 'n' cheese?"

"Sounds delicious. Seriously, Isabel…"

"Call me Izzy."

"Okay, Izzy. You've made this day incredible. There's got to be something that I could do to return the favor." I could only imagine that I looked like the ultimate goof ball, standing before her with my new haircut and an awkward amount of facial hair, holding a broom and a dust pan full of my hair. *I really hope you say something, Izzy…*

"You any good at math?" she asked.

"Definitely."

After enjoying my second shower of the day, I joined Izzy in the living room where we had mac 'n' cheese, carrots, and cucumbers. It was like I'd died and gone to heaven. The mac 'n' cheese was piping hot, creamy, and delicious. While it cooled off, I crunched on the crisp veggies like Bugs Bunny and gazed around the living room, wondering what it was like to grow up in a real home.

"Brody, you're chewing with your mouth open."

"Sorry," I mumbled through a mouthful of carrots.

"It's okay. What do you like to do? Do you play sports or anything?"

I shook my head. "No. Not really."

"Seriously? Like soccer or baseball?" I shook my head again.

"Water polo?"

I couldn't help but laugh. "Do I really look like someone who enjoys a good game of water polo? I don't even know what that is."

"Well, what do you do?"

"I work as much as possible," I answered. Then I pointed to a strange picture on the wall. It was a drawing of hands drawing hands. "What's this?"

"Oh, my mom has a thing for M.C. Escher. There's a couple of his pieces around the house. He draws all sorts of wacky stuff like that."

"Gotcha."

"What did you do before the library job in Boise?"

"I rode around with a trucker for two weeks." I turned away from the drawing to find her staring at me.

"You've got to give me more than that. And before you say I'm prying—I'm not prying. It sounds interesting." She gave me a half smile and returned to her homework.

"His name was Sammy," I offered. "Big Sammy. Huge guy. Full beard, baseball cap. He reminded me of an old-time lumberjack. We met at a delivery station up in North Dakota."

"What were you doing there?"

"Filling a couple shifts on an oil crew. I got let go, so I was looking to pick up a few hours at a diner, but the manager said he didn't need anyone. I guess Sammy heard me and found me outside. He offered me a job helping him unload his shipments since he had a bum leg or something. We left North

Dakota and went all over the states in that area."

"Sounds like one heck of a road trip," Izzy said.

"Yeah, it was pretty neat. After a couple weeks though, he said he was heading back east, so I stayed in Idaho." Before she could ask anything else, I shoveled another bite of dinner into my mouth.

Izzy continued to stare at me from her seat on the floor between the coffee table and the couch. "Okay, seriously, Brody. What are you doing?"

"What?" I replied after swallowing a mouthful of mac 'n' cheese.

She set her pencil down and continued to gawk at me.

"Did I spill something?"

Izzy laughed as I frantically checked my shirt for runaway noodles, but there was nothing. "Why are you sitting like that? You look like you have to use the bathroom."

I was sitting on the edge of the cushion and leaning awkwardly into the arm of the couch. For the past twenty minutes, I'd been using it as a makeshift table, as well. I shrugged. I didn't want to admit how nervous I was. "I don't know," I said.

"Well, come sit closer. I don't bite." Izzy picked up her pencil and resumed working through a problem. I consented and casually scooted closer, this time using the whole cushion. "Better?" she asked.

"Yes. Are you sure about this though? I don't want to get you into trouble with your mom."

"Don't worry about it," Izzy said. "My sister gave her

so much grief. If this is the worst thing I ever do, she will be thrilled."

I nibbled on a carrot, debating whether I should ask the next question. "Are you gonna tell her where you found me?" The scribbling ceased.

"For right now…no. We'll cross that bridge when we get to it," she said. "I just want you to rest and get something to eat."

"Thanks. This mac 'n' cheese is really good, too."

"You're welcome. I'm glad you like it." When she blew the hair out of her face in frustration, I couldn't help but smile. Then she groaned in dismay after punching the buttons on the calculator. "I don't know what I'm doing wrong, Brody."

"Let me see." Izzy handed me the paper and I skimmed through her work. She had beautiful handwriting, delicate and precise. It was easy on the eyes and it didn't take me long to find the problem. I leaned forward with a smile on my face.

"I think you forgot a couple steps—here, and here." I pointed to a sample problem in her textbook. Izzy eyed me cautiously like I might be duping her, but she did as I instructed. A moment later, there was a whoop of joy.

"I got it! Thank you!"

"You're welcome. Glad I could help. So, where is your mom, anyway? Is she a nurse or something?"

"No, not quite. My momma is a librarian and a substitute teacher. She's taking night classes so she can become a full-time teacher."

"Oh, very cool."

"Yeah. I'm proud of her," Izzy said. I wasn't sure what to say next, but thankfully Izzy kept talking as she leafed through the pages of her calculus book. "How do you know all this, anyway? I thought you said you were a vagabond."

"Are you mocking me?"

"No," she said, and giggled when I nudged her shoulder.

"I really liked math when I was in school."

"Were you valedictorian or something? I mean, you seem wicked smart."

"Thanks, but no. I wasn't. I didn't graduate."

"Did you get kicked out or something?"

"No. I probably should have, though. I got into enough fights with stupid kids. I don't really want to talk about it though if you don't mind."

Izzy sighed and returned to her work. I looked at the bowl of macaroni in my hand and suddenly felt bad again. She was being so nice to me and I kept clamming up. "I got my GED a couple years ago, before I started all my traveling."

Her pencil stopped moving again and she turned to look at me. "You got your GED when you were sixteen?" she asked.

I nodded, hoping it was enough for the time being. Her eyes narrowed for a moment, then she slid the paper across the coffee table so I could read through her steps.

"Looks good to me," I said. "That's the last one, right?"

"Yeah. Thanks so much."

"No problem. I'm glad I could help." Just when I was

starting to get comfortable her phone started ringing again, so I quit talking. She peered at me and set the phone down.

"Just answer it, Isabel. It's fine. Especially if it's your mom."

"It's not my mom," she said. The phone jingled again, and from the corner of my eye I saw a name flash on the screen: *Derek R.* There it was, the disappointment I was worried about.

"I won't talk long," Izzy said, but there was a pained expression on her face as she left the room. I sighed, picked up our empty plates, and carried them to the kitchen. After doing the dishes and stowing them in a drying rack, I grabbed the toothbrush from my shabby bag and went to brush my teeth. As I stared at my face in the mirror, I tried to remember the last time I'd shaved, but being worried and alone made the days blur together. All I could come up with was several weeks before.

She still wasn't back in the living room when I was finished, so I curled up on the couch. Part of me thought about leaving. I had clean clothes, I was actually full, and she'd given me a haircut. I could probably pick up a job somewhere now, and a good one at that. It would be so easy to slip away. But another part of my brain was keeping me rooted to the spot. There was something special about Izzy. Her warmth and compassion was so foreign to me, and already I didn't want to lose it, so I wrote her a quick note on top of her homework. *Thank you again, Isabel. Dinner was great! You're the best.* Then I stretched out on the couch, eager for a peaceful nights rest. I had no idea my body could shut down so fast, but within seconds I'd dozed off.

When Izzy sat down on the couch again I woke for just a moment, but I kept my eyes closed while Izzy read the note to herself. Another gentle wave of perfume washed over me as she leaned closer to pull a blanket over me.

"G'night, Brody. I'm sorry I took so long." Then she went to bed.

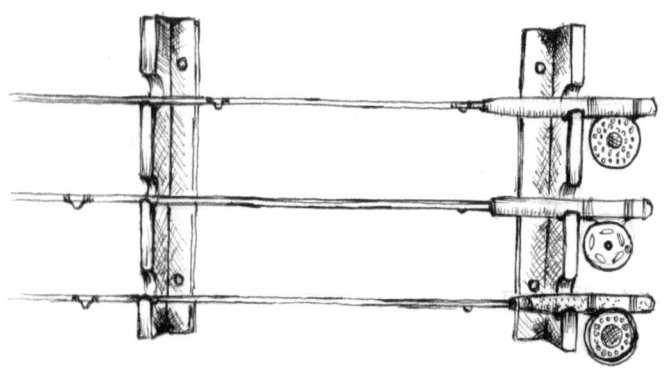

When I woke the next morning I wondered if I was still dreaming, because the house was dead silent and I had absolutely no idea where I was. You'd think I'd have gotten used to that feeling after waking up alone in so many random places. Maybe some people do, but I didn't. I still woke with a pounding heart as the oppressive silence threatened to engulf me.

From behind closed eyes I took a few deep breaths, feeling more rested than I had in several months. As sleep wore off, memories of the prior day flitted through my brain, and my pounding heart subsided.

Wow. This is amazing. I knew I could have slept several more hours, but I was determined to do something nice for Izzy, so I slipped off the couch and tiptoed into the kitchen.

After carefully and quietly rummaging in the closets, fridge, and freezer, I found enough ingredients to make Izzy and her mother some breakfast.

While a burner heated up, I gripped the handle of a frying pan. The clanging, bustling sounds of past kitchen jobs came to mind, and I wished that I could find a good cooking job of some sort. With a smile, I cracked eggs into a bowl and started whisking. Then I prepared a hearty helping of pancake batter. Everything was going fine until I came face to face with Izzy's mother.

I couldn't remember the last time I yelled or screamed in surprise, but when I turned from the stove to find a spatula in one of the drawers, I yelped at the sight of a woman wrapped in her bathrobe, holding a broom like a long sword. She was by no means silent either.

"You're not Henry!" she exclaimed.

"No, I'm Brody."

"Who the hell is Brody?"

"I'm Brody!"

"No, who's Brody?" she asked again.

"I am. I'm Izzy's friend," I said.

The woman's exhausted eyes narrowed. "Do you have any idea what time it is?"

"No."

"It's six-thirty in the morning!"

"I'm sorry—"

"What are you doing in my kitchen?"

"I'm making you and Izzy breakfast."

Her mouth hung open, but no words came out. Instead, she turned and left the kitchen, still carrying the broom. Muffled voices echoed through the house, and it wasn't long before there was a parade of footsteps on the stairs. Izzy appeared in the kitchen, followed closely by her mother. It was hard not to laugh. Although her mother's hair was a bit messy, Izzy was suffering from a severe case of bedhead, but it did little to dampen her cheery mood.

"Morning, Brody," she said, poking me in the side playfully. "What are you doing?"

"Making you guys breakfast. I thought that would be okay." I leaned in toward Izzy's ear. "I think your mom's mad at me."

"I can hear you, Brody. I'm standing right here," she replied, and I winced.

"Of course you can. I'm sorry. Are you mad?"

"No way. I love pancakes and bacon," Izzy interjected. "Are you mad, Momma?"

"No. I guess not. Just really startled. I thought my brother was sleeping on the couch, and it turns out to be a boy I've never seen before."

I barely glanced at Izzy. I could feel her eyes locked onto me, expecting an answer just as much as her mother. I said the first thing that came to mind, not wanting her to confess anything about me yet. "Yeah, we're friends from school. I needed a place to crash this weekend, and your daughter was gracious enough to let me stay here last night."

"*Gracious*?" her mother repeated.

"Yes." I handed her a plate of hotcakes and scrambled eggs.

"And you cook?"

"Yeah. I love to cook." From the corner of my eye I saw Izzy beaming at me, and I loved the way it made me feel. "Here you go." Izzy continued grinning as she took her plate and sat down at the counter.

"How long have you two been friends?" asked her mother, poking at the pancakes with her fork. "These are pretty good!"

I sucked in a breath, not knowing what to say, but thankfully Izzy jumped in.

"He just moved here, Momma. We met at the end of school this week."

Sunday went better than I could have expected. After fashioning a deceptively clever white lie to distract her mother, Izzy kept me busy at the fly shop. If I was lucky, I normally managed one or two days—sometimes even a week—at any particular job, and that was only because I was filling in for hours that other people missed. Izzy, however, insisted that I could stay and help longer if I wanted.

At the end of the day we walked back to her house, and she told me a little more about fly fishing. We shared a quiet dinner together, but it was clear to me that Izzy's mother, Heather, was still nervous about my presence. Several times I noticed her peering suspiciously at me, and just as many times that evening I considered leaving.

But every time I glanced at Izzy she smiled at me, and that kept me anchored to my seat. When Izzy went to shower and get ready for bed, I tried to express my thanks as much as possible to Heather, but she seemed cautiously indifferent. In the end I retreated to the living room where I was out of the way. To my surprise Izzy stayed up with me for several hours that night, and I explained how I ended up in Eugene instead of Portland.

"You rode in the back of a truck for eight hours," she said.

"Yeah, vagabonding to the extreme. It was good most of the day until we got closer to Oregon. The sun started to go down, and that makes for a pretty chilly ride when you're up in the mountains."

"How come you didn't just ask the guy for a ride?"

"I've found that a lot of people are really skeptical of folks like me."

"You mean hitchhikers?"

"Yeah, I guess." I held back a sigh. "Some people are nice, but sometimes it's easier to just be kind of sneaky."

"Wow. I couldn't imagine." Another yawn escaped her.

"You can go to bed if you want. I know you have school in the morning."

"I feel bad that we didn't get to talk much last night after I finished my homework," she said. "I like talking to you."

"Don't worry about it. We got to talk tonight. Besides, I don't want to get you into trouble with your mom. I'm not sure she likes me being here."

"Don't worry about it. She's just being Mom." Izzy's grin was very cute—that disarming type of cute that could make even the grumpiest person crack a smile. I was coming to realize I was a sucker for it.

She gave me one last cheerful wave and a hearty yawn before tromping upstairs. With Izzy gone to bed, I shut off the living room lamp and stretched out on the couch. The peaceful silence of their home was comforting, but unlike the night before, sleep eluded me. I was tired, but part of me was still nervous that my apparent luck in Eugene might be too good to be true.

The next morning, there was a little note on the table from Izzy telling me to just relax and make myself at home. Her signature was a smiley face, which left me feeling strangely happy. After making some breakfast I took the spare key she'd given me, locked the house, and wandered into town in search of a library. Before long I was sitting at a table sifting through books. But in my excitement from the previous evening, I had forgotten one minor detail.

"Hello, Brody," said a familiar voice. I glanced up to find Izzy's mother staring intently at me.

"Oh, Mrs. Cooper. Hi. That's right, you're a librarian…"

"Yes. And you aren't in school."

"No. Not exactly. I, uh, was reading up on this fly fishing stuff. I wanted to see why Izzy likes it so much."

"I see. Well, I think we need to have a little chat this afternoon when I get home, because I'm very curious to know why you're not in school."

"Okay. Am I in trouble?"

"I don't know. I guess we'll see," she said. "Depends on if you tell the truth or not."

"I will," I blurted out. "I promise."

"I hope so, because I don't like being lied to."

"Mrs. Cooper—"

"Save it, Brody. I don't know what's going on, but I have to go back to work. We can talk about this later."

"Well, would it help if I made dinner?" The fight or flight instincts were starting to fire, but I wasn't ready to give in.

"It might. I'm not sure how serious this will be," she said with a whimsical smile. "But I like spaghetti."

"With or without garlic bread?"

"With," she said. "I don't mind if you stay here to read, but you best explain yourself later. Both of you." Mrs. Cooper walked back to her desk, and I bowed my head in disappointment. My palms were sweating like crazy, and the joy of reading had disappeared entirely. With one last sigh, I scooped up the books and returned them to their spots on the shelves. Then I found a back door and left the library.

It was the last week of August and the air was sticky and muggy, which only amplified the discomfort I was feeling. A nearby street sign read Eleventh Avenue, and I started walking. My head was a swirling pool of doubts, and for once my appetite was gone.

I groaned and kept walking, block after block. After crossing a highway, I came upon the University of Oregon campus. It was a pretty place, and all the students strolling about looked happy and content with their lives. I sighed again and continued on my way. On the opposite end of campus, I found a bike path that crossed a gorgeous river and disappeared into a park. I wandered the various trails, stopping occasionally to stare at the river, which a plaque said was called the Willamette. I spent much of the day sitting in a vacant outdoor amphitheater, replaying my encounter with Heather that morning.

All I could see was the pained and worried expression on her face. It was stretched across my mind like a spider web, stopping me from thinking about anything else. The more I thought about her, the more I considered leaving just so Heather could come home and not have to worry. Izzy would be there safe and sound, and I would be long gone.

The only problem was that I was starting to like Eugene. After all the traveling I'd done, it was one of the few places that I found appealing. It carried a certain charm: the rivers and greenery, the mountains in the distance, and so far the pleasant people. It was also so far away that my father would never find me.

I wanted to apologize to Heather and explain myself to her and Izzy, but that would mean opening up, and I wasn't good at that. A soft breeze blew through the amphitheater and I closed my eyes, trying to figure out what to do...

"Hey. You all right?" I woke to someone tapping on my shoulder. When I opened my eyes, the afternoon light glinted off of something shiny. I blinked a few times and realized it was the last person I wanted to see. A police officer. Adrenaline flooded into my system as I tried to keep calm.

"Yeah. Yeah…I must have fallen asleep," I said.

"Yeah? You sure?" The officer's eyes were hidden behind a pair of dark lenses, and I could feel my insides shrinking.

"Yep, I'm good," I said.

"You sure? It took me a couple tries to get you awake. You're not on any drugs are you?"

I managed to force a laugh. "No, no. I'm just tired. I was out walking this morning and then I came to sit down for a break. These are cozy chairs."

"Hard plastic seats?"

"They were comfy when I sat down. A little awkward now that you mention it." To my surprise the cop actually cracked a smile.

"You sure you're all right?" he asked.

"Yep. I wasn't planning on falling asleep, though. Do you have the time?"

The cop removed a phone from his pocket. "It's a quarter to three."

"Right! Well I better get going. I've got dinner plans. Thanks for checking on me!" Carefully I got out of the seat, and the cop held his distance.

"You're welcome. Have a good day, sir," he replied.

I nodded and stepped past him, eager to get as far away as possible. I was so tired of running. I just wanted a regular life. On my way back to Izzy's house, I stopped at a grocery store and emptied my wallet buying ingredients. I was going to make the best spaghetti I could muster.

"Brody?" Izzy's voice echoed through the house.

"Yeah, I'm in the kitchen."

"Is everything all right?" she asked.

"I'm not sure really. I mean, I'm okay, but—"

"My mom's mad, isn't she?"

"Yeah…I sort of forgot about her working at the library and I ran into her today, and she was expecting me to be at school. How did you know she was mad? Did she call you or something?"

"Yeah, she sent me a message." Izzy gave her phone a solemn wave. Then she let her bag slump to the floor. "Dad and I always make spaghetti for her if she's upset. It's the only time she likes it."

"Kind of picked up on that." I dumped an entire box of noodles into a pot.

"It smells good."

"Good. I hope your mom likes it." When I glanced at Izzy, her brow was furrowed with worry.

"Brody, what's really going on?"

"I'll explain when your mom gets here. I promise."

"Okay. Well, do you want any help?"

"Sure. You want to mix up the spread for the garlic bread?"

"Oh, you're going all out, huh?" Izzy grinning at me made things feel a little better.

"Yeah. I like it here. Not exactly keen on hitting the road again."

"Good. Do you mind if I put on some music then?"

"Nope. Go ahead." I was expecting her to leave the kitchen to get a computer or a radio or something, but she just continued standing by the counter.

"Do you dance, Brody?"

"Excuse me?" I nearly dumped an entire jar of seasoning into the pot of pasta sauce. Then I accidentally touched the hot pan.

Izzy giggled. "Do you like to dance?"

"Do you?" I asked. "For some reason I got the impression you don't dance much, Isabel."

She shrugged and walked away. After a moment, the sounds of jazz music filled the kitchen. I froze at the stove. I hadn't listened to jazz since my time spent in the south and my palms started to sweat again as I wondered what was about to happen. *Maybe I'm dreaming*. I touched the hot pan again. It was still burning hot.

I tried desperately to run through everything that had happened in the last few days, but before I could come up with anything, she reappeared and carefully slid her hand around my forearm. The thick flannel I was wearing did nothing to stop more tingles from shooting across my body. She eased me away from the stove and into the middle of the kitchen.

"Do you like jazz?"

"Yeah," I managed. "I listened to it all the time when I was down south."

"What were you doing down south?"

"Working. Restaurants and box companies."

Izzy's head moved up and down as she started taking small steps around the kitchen.

"I was in a movie, too," I blurted out.

"You were in a movie?"

"Yeah, but it happened by accident." I was nervous that I sounded dumb, but Izzy didn't seem to mind, since the smile never left her face. "I haven't danced that much though…like ever."

"You worry too much, Brody. I haven't either." Her smile was intriguing, so I followed her lead. When she started swaying to the mellow harmonies I tried to replicate her movements, but I felt awkward and gangly. Izzy was persistent though, and guided me through the speedy rhythms until my tensions dissipated.

The hard hitting notes of the trumpet and saxophone taunted me playfully until I finally slid my hand into hers. Unlike my hands, which were rough and callused, Izzy's were smooth and warm. Her slender fingers gave mine a gentle squeeze, so I chanced spinning her around. For someone who'd never danced before, this was an experience I would never forget. I was caught by the fragrant net of perfume cast by her hair as it flew out around her face. I was ensnared by her dazzling smile that lit up the room. It was like she was daring me not to stop, but I couldn't help my nerves.

"I'm not sure if I'm doing any good," I mumbled.

"I think you're doing great."

I spun her around again and when she came in close, her hands clasped around my neck. There was nowhere to put my hands except her waist, and Izzy grinned. "You look nervous," she said.

"What? No. Me, nervous? I just don't want to step on your feet."

"Uhuh." Izzy laughed. "I thought about you today."

"Did you now?"

"Yeah. Mom texted me and said we needed to talk. Then she said you disappeared. I wondered maybe if you left."

"I thought about it."

"Why didn't you?"

A variety of answers flew through my head, but it was hard to focus on any of them with Izzy so close to me. "I wanted to apologize to your mom. I don't want her to worry or be angry with you."

Izzy nodded. "Are there any other reasons?"

A stupid smile crossed my face and I spun her around again. "Well, I'll probably need another haircut again soon, so…"

Her cheeks grew pink as the song ended. I stepped away, hiding my nerves and giddiness by stirring the steaming pot of boiling noodles. Izzy's hands fell to her sides. When I glanced at her again, she looked hopeful. The sounds of be-bop filled the kitchen as another song started.

"I wouldn't mind trying that again," I offered, and Izzy's fair cheeks grew rosier still.

"Me either."

I'd lost track of the number of songs we danced to by the time Heather got home. In between tracks, Izzy and I had set the kitchen table with food and drink. There was steaming pasta, a bowl of mouthwatering garlic bread, and a cheerful green salad. All I could think about now was Izzy's smile as we continued dancing merrily around the kitchen.

"Hello, you two," Heather said. Immediately our laughter ceased and we separated with guilty grins on our faces. Heather dropped her purse on the counter and headed for the fridge. "Brody, you must think you're in some trouble if you made all this after we talked this morning. But it's been a long day and I just want some answers."

I glanced at Isabel, hoping for her smile, but all I received was a vacant stare. She clearly wanted answers as well.

"Where should I start?" I asked.

"Wherever you want," Heather replied. "I'm going to

start with a glass of wine. I love jazz, too, by the way. Good choice." Despite the tension in the room, Izzy and I both laughed. Heather shifted uncomfortably while she poured the glass. Her silence was making me nervous.

"Well, first of all, Mrs. Cooper, I hope you're not mad at Izzy. I may have allowed a bit of a white lie the other morning."

Her gaze grew very stern. "Did you get my daughter pregnant?"

"What? No!" I said.

"Mom!" Isabel exclaimed.

"Well, I'm a mother. I have to ask these things. I know teenagers have sex."

"Mom!" Izzy's cheeks were redder than I thought possible.

"It's all I've been thinking about all day. I'm sorry, but I'm not ready to be a grandma."

"Oh my God, Mom. Please stop!"

"How about we sit down," I suggested.

Heather nodded and took a sip from the glass in her hand. Her eyes flitted about frantically and I felt just as awful as I had that morning. "Did you really make all of this?" she asked.

"Most of it. Izzy helped me when she got home."

"I made the garlic bread," Izzy added.

"How do you know how to cook so well? Most teenage boys I know can barely dress themselves."

"I've worked in a lot of restaurants over the last couple years."

"Okay. So, you were at the library today and not in school because…"

"I was at the library because I wanted to know more about fly fishing."

"Oh really?" Izzy said.

"Yeah." I'd been planning on keeping that a secret because I wanted to impress Isabel. "I wasn't in school because I'm not in school any more. I graduated early."

"Are you some sort of genius?" Heather asked.

"No, not that I know of. Just determined I guess."

"He got his GED," Izzy chimed in.

"Really?" asked her mother.

"Yeah." We all fell silent for a moment while piling food onto our plates. I was too nervous to eat, and I watched Izzy's mother poke at her dinner, hoping for her approval.

"Where did you go today? You left the library in a hurry," Heather said.

I shrugged. "Wandered around town. I ended up in some park on the other side of the university."

"That's a couple miles away," Izzy said.

"Yeah. I like walking."

Heather nodded and finally took a bite of her dinner. "This is really good, Brody. Are you sure you didn't get my daughter pregnant?"

"Mom!" Izzy repeated, and this time I started laughing. *I may have a shot at this.*

"Yes, I'm sure," I said. "All right. I'll just say it I guess, but it's probably going to sound weird to you guys. Being with you two for the past few days is the closest thing I've had to anything resembling a family in almost three years. I was a foster kid, and I ditched the last family I had when I was sixteen. I've been making my way across the country ever since."

"Oh." Heather stopped chewing and her jaw tightened.

"Really?" Izzy said.

"Yeah." Out of habit, I bowed my head, too afraid to look at either of them. Then there was a poke in my side and I found Izzy smiling at me. When I glanced at Heather, she waved her fork between Izzy and me.

"Wait—so how did you two meet then?"

I opened my mouth to speak, but Izzy cut in. "I found Brody sleeping on the porch behind Uncle Henry's shop. He was on the verge of getting sick, so I brought him inside, and he hung out at the shop with me all day."

Heather took a big drink from her glass after hearing that one. "Well, I'm glad to know that I raised a good girl. And to think I spent the afternoon thinking the worst. I almost called your father, you know."

"Oh, please don't call Dad," Izzy said. "He'll get all worked up over nothing."

"I'm not going to call him, Isabel. Not right now anyway. Brody?"

"Yes?"

"You are welcome to stay here as long as you like, but no more lies." I nodded vigorously. "Izzy told me that you're eighteen, so it's your choice as far as I'm concerned, but I hope that you'll stick around for a little while at least. So far, I'm quite fond of your cooking, and I think Izzy is pretty fond of you in general."

"Mom!" Izzy exclaimed. I blushed and bowed my head again, but not before catching the wink that Heather gave me.

"Are you really serious about learning this stuff? Because we should totally go practice tomorrow if you are. There's a pond not far from the shop that's loaded with bluegills," Izzy said.

I laughed and took one of the books she handed me. "I would like to, yeah. If you don't mind teaching me."

"Not at all."

"I don't have anything, though."

"Brody. I work at a fly shop."

"Yeah that's true. What's this?" I flipped the book over in my hands.

"This is a book, Brody, and it's better than what you'll find at the library." She grabbed a couple more off the shelf and then pulled me over to a couch where we sat down together. The first book I opened was like one of her magazines on steroids. There was page after page of colorful diagrams, wondrous landscapes, and stunning photographs of brightly colored fish. For a moment I thought that I'd stepped back into a science class, only this one was way more interesting.

"So this book is kind of a general guide to fly fishing. It talks a lot about reading the water, knowing the most likely places to find fish, yada yada yada," Izzy explained. Then she motioned to one of the others. "This one is a little different. It covers more about the flies themselves—you know, how to make them and where they came from. A bit stuffy in terms of history, unless you're into that sort of thing, but the pictures are great for practice."

When I looked up from the book, her face was mere inches from mine. My heart started to beat fast again, just like the night she'd cut my hair. There wasn't a blemish on her face, just her beautiful skin and bright eyes. Her wavy, dark hair that smelled like summer hugged her cheeks, and for mere moments I allowed myself to imagine what it would be like to nuzzle my nose against hers before kissing her sensational lips…

"You okay, Brody?"

I sucked in a breath and glanced back at the book. "Um, practicing what?" I stuttered, and Izzy's cheeks reddened ever so slightly.

"Tying. Making these flies," she said.

"You can make these?"

"Yeah, I make a lot of them for the shop. Hang on." Izzy jumped off the couch and ran upstairs. A minute later she flopped back onto the couch, clutching a plastic case in her hands. She bit her lip, looking hopeful and excited. "Are you ready for a crash course in fly tying?"

"Absolutely."

"Alright, so, these are dry flies," Izzy said, pointing to several rows at the top of the box.

"Is the name kind of self-explanatory?"

"Yeah. They're supposed to sit on top of the water when you fish with them, but most dry flies have some sort of hackle."

"What's a hackle? Sorry."

Izzy giggled. "It's fine. That's the fuzzy stuff you wrap around the hook. Usually it's chicken feathers, but you can use partridge and duck, too. It's what helps them float."

"Even with the weight of the hook?"

She nodded. "Yep. There's actually different types of hooks, too. The ones for dry flies are lighter."

"Okay. Is there such a thing as wet flies?"

"Yeah, that's these here," she said, pointing to several rows below the dry flies. "They're meant to imitate younger bug forms, so there's usually less hackle and the bodies have more thread and dubbing."

"Dubbing?"

"Dubbing is finely cut up material used to create a hairy looking body on a fly. It can be natural or synthetic, like cut-up squirrel fur or wool or little threads of shiny plastic."

The flies at the shop were displayed on a giant wooden shelf that was divided into miniature cubbies. Every time I passed by, each cubby looked like it was full of colorful craft materials. But the flies in Izzy's tackle box were neatly displayed, allowing me to see all the subtle intricacies that made them so unique.

"It seems like you could really get into the study of bugs with this."

"Oh yeah," Izzy said. "Some people take this super seriously. They catch bugs in the river so they can match color and size or whatever."

"Do you do that?"

"I have a few times, but I'd rather spend time hiking and fishing."

I moved my head up and down as I stared at the next rows of flies, which lacked hackle or wings of any sort. "What about these?" I asked.

"These are nymphs. These are meant to be the baby forms. They're usually small, with beads and shiny stuff to make them look like they're just starting to grow legs and wings. Some tyers get really into it and use epoxy to make it look like air bubbles are trapped on the body."

"Wow."

"Yeah," Izzy said. Then she tucked the tackle box against her chest. "I hope you know that I'm not expecting you to get super into this if you're not interested."

"No, no. It's not that. I just… I haven't had the time or money to actually pick up a hobby," I said. "I think this has the potential to be really cool, and I really appreciate you showing me all this."

"Yeah?"

"Yes. Really."

Izzy handed me the box again and I flipped it over.

"What are these big ones?" I asked.

"Streamers. Big flies for salmon and steelhead, but you can use them for other fish, too. Mine are kind of rough, but some people can tie super fancy streamers."

I nodded and plucked one from the box. "Izzy, this looks like a mouse."

"It's supposed to be a sculpin—a big minnow thing." The soft smile that crossed her lips left my cheeks burning and I returned to the tackle box, pretending to study the flies. But then she leaned in closer and her hair brushed across my shoulder, causing the burning sensation to spread throughout my entire body. "That's rabbit fur."

"Get out of here."

She laughed as I ran my finger along the soft fur.

"These are really amazing, Izzy."

"Thanks," she said.

A sudden knock caused us both to look up from the tackle box. Heather and a man were standing in the living room doorway. He was about my size, with dark hair and a full beard. His messy hair was hidden under a cap, and he looked tired and windswept.

"May we interrupt?" Heather asked. I turned to Izzy for an answer, fearing for an instant that Heather had called social services. But then again, I couldn't remember anyone from social services wearing tall mucking boots.

"Hi, Uncle Henry." She got off the couch to give him a

hug, and I stood up as well but remained where I was, since my stomach had sunk to my ankles. *I don't know what's worse…*

"Hi, sweetie. How are you?" he asked.

"Pretty good. Did you have some spaghetti? There's a bunch left."

"No, not yet. It smells good, though," Henry replied.

"Izzy, I was wondering if you could come with me for a minute," said her mother. "We'll fix Henry a plate."

"I, um, sure…" When she glanced back to me, I gave her the tiniest shrug, wishing she would stay. But she walked off with her mother, leaving me alone with her uncle.

"So, you must be Brody," Henry began.

"Um, yeah. It's nice to meet you, Mr.…" I stepped forward with an outstretched hand and nearly stumbled over the coffee table in the process.

"Henry. You can call me Henry. Are you all right?"

"Yeah, I'm fine. It's nice to meet you, sir."

"You too. So, I heard that Izzy found you sleeping on the porch behind the shop."

A puff of air escaped my lips. *Word travels fast around here apparently.* "Yeah. Sorry about that. I'll try not to do that again, but for what it's worth, it's a very nice porch."

To my surprise Henry chuckled. "Don't worry about it. I'm just glad you didn't keel over back there." He motioned to the books resting on the coffee table. "Do you like it? Fishing?"

"I haven't gone that much," I confessed. "But it seems cool."

"It is. It's a lot of fun when you get out there. Especially when you hook a big one."

"Yeah, that's what I've heard." I tried to smile, but I was busy waiting for the passive aggressive threat. I could feel it coming, and sadly I was already planning a subtle exit strategy.

"So, I have a question to ask you," Henry said. He took a seat on the recliner and I found my spot on the couch again. "Do you enjoy spending time outside?"

"Is that some sort of joke? Because, you know—I'm sort of homeless."

"No. Of course not. I'm sorry. No. Wow. Shows how good I am at this sort of thing. I'll just cut to the chase then. I told Heather that I had to let one of my employees go today, which really put a damper on things. Now I'm in need of another person, and it just so happens that she has a capable young man hanging around the house."

"Excuse me, but are you offering me a job?"

"I am, if you're interested that is."

I shook my head and stood up as a wave of anxiety washed over me. Usually I had to beg for work. Nothing was ever handed to me, let alone on a silver platter.

"Why are you all being so nice to me? No one has ever been this nice to me."

"Well, Heather and Izzy are two of the nicest people I know. It's in their nature," Henry replied.

"I agree with you there," I said.

"Yeah, and I do my best to keep up with them. So what

do you say?"

I sat back down and picked up one of Izzy's books again. It was hard for me to picture a life other than the meager one I'd been living, and yet, the allure of the photography awakened my imagination to a life well beyond anything I'd ever dreamed before.

"What would I have to do?"

"Well, I heard that you already helped out at the shop, and did a good job by the sounds of it. You could keep doing that when Izzy and Jack aren't available, and then you could come out on trips with me. Help folks with their gear and such."

"You understand that I've spent most of the last few years working just so I had something to eat, right? Those aren't usually the best jobs. You're saying that you'd pay me to go on fancy trips with rich folks and carry their shit? No offense."

Henry laughed. "None taken. Believe me, some of these folks are very wealthy and can be a bit...snooty. Most of them though are just really passionate about fishing and love being outside. But yeah, that's more or less it. Plus you'd get to fish, of course."

I was in disbelief. So much so that my insides were prickling with a hint of anger. "Are you messing with me? Because I really don't—"

"I'm not messing with you, Brody. None of us are."

My head was beginning to spin. *What is happening?* "But you don't even know me..."

"Well, I don't really know any of my employees till we

have a little interview and they start coming to work. So what do you think?"

I shrugged. "Why are you doing this again?"

"Because I'm trying to be helpful. Heather said you might be sticking around for a while, and I'm just trying to help, too." Henry pushed himself out of the chair. "Let me know what you think, alright? You know where to find me."

It was too simple, too easy. Nobody in my life had been this nice, and I knew there must be a catch of some sort. But then I thought of Izzy, and how she brought about a plethora of intriguing emotions every time she was around me.

"Hey, Henry," I said.

"Yeah?"

"If I said yes, would you show me how to make these, too?" I lifted up the tackle box Izzy had left behind.

"Are you saying yes?"

I wanted to say yes. Desperately. But in the past two years every yes had just led to me being cut loose with little to show for it. And yet, it was those past yeses that had led me to this moment. I ran my finger across the smooth lid of the fly box, wondering if Henry really cared—if any of them cared. When I looked up, he was leaning in the doorway, silent and expressionless, but still staring at me. My heart thumped loudly in my ears as I contemplated the possibility of not having to run any more. If there was even a remote chance this could work, I knew I had to try.

"Yes."

"Great." Henry clapped his hands together. "I would suggest asking Izzy. She's the one with the delicate fingers. See you tomorrow, Brody."

"Alright. Thank you," I replied.

Henry left the room grinning, and it wasn't long before Izzy returned to her seat next to me on the couch. She was also smiling from ear to ear. I had already accepted the fact that she was beautiful, but that night every part of her face seemed to smile: her eyes, her dimples, and her mouth. It made her more breathtaking than I could have imagined.

"You're in a good mood," I said.

"Well, yeah. Looks like we'll be working together on occasion and I hear you want to learn how to tie?"

"Possibly. Didn't I say that earlier?"

She gave me a shove and continued reading through the books with me. As I flipped through the pages, Izzy made comments about certain places or gave me the names of famous tyers, none of which I was familiar with, but it was ten times better than reading street signs and cheap restaurant takeout menus. After a while, I quit reading when I realized her commentary had ceased.

For several minutes I stared at the peaceful expression on her sleeping face. I watched the hair flutter against her cheeks each time she took a breath. I battled with myself. *What if something bad happens? Getting attached only means that it will hurt that much more.* Once again, part of me thought about leaving, but I couldn't without waking her since her legs were stretched across my lap. That brought a smile to my face, and I couldn't help but think there was just a small chance I was meant to be here. I read for several more hours before falling asleep where I sat with the thick paperback book open in my lap.

Early the next morning, I woke to the sound of water gurgling through the coffee maker. The startling sound gave way to a pleasant aroma that wafted its way through the house. It was soon joined by the mouthwatering smell of something being toasted. To top it off, I was warmer than I'd been at any time in the last two years. It was literally a dream come true.

I eased back into the couch, eager to savor the warmth and continue sleeping, but then I realized my pillow was moving. The morning grogginess vanished and I slowly opened my eyes. The living room was nearly pitch black except for the soft glow of light coming from the kitchen. The rise and fall came again, and I realized that I'd fallen asleep next to Izzy.

My head was resting on her stomach while one of my

arms was around her back, the other around her legs. I tried to take a few deep breaths and enjoy the fact that I'd at least had the chance to be this close to a lady, but strange thoughts and worries began racing through my head as I wondered what would happen when Izzy finally woke. Would she be mad? Happy? Maybe she'd kick me out.

Then she stirred briefly and everything in my head disappeared. I held my breath, pretending to be asleep in hopes of keeping things less awkward. But she never said anything. She squirmed about for a moment, and then to my surprise, her hand brushed across my back in a very affectionate manner. Soon Izzy fell back to sleep, and I got up wishing I could stay on the couch with her. But Heather drove that thought from my mind as soon as I stepped into the kitchen.

"You two looked cute this morning." She was sitting at the counter eating an everything bagel while browsing through class materials about teaching English.

"Oh my goodness, Mrs. Cooper. I'm sorry."

"For what? I said it was cute."

I nodded and pulled a sweater over my head.

"Aren't you going to eat something?" she asked.

I shrugged. The last thing I wanted was for Heather to think I was going to eat them out of house and home, but the smell was making my mouth water. "I don't know."

Apparently that's not the right thing to say to a mom. Heather shook her head. "Come here," she insisted. I stepped toward the counter and she handed me half of her bagel. "Take this with you."

"But—"

"Take it. I can make another one for Izzy and me."

"Okay. Thank you—for everything."

"You're welcome. Have fun today. My brother's a good guy, Brody."

"Yeah. I got that. Would you mind telling Izzy I said bye?"

Heather grinned. "Yeah, I can tell her."

"Alright. Thank you, and thanks for breakfast."

She gave me another smile and returned to her books. I made for the entryway and the door shut silently behind me.

The walk to work was quiet; not even my footsteps echoed in the darkness. Just like always, I found myself counting the lines in the sidewalk. Every day since I was little, maybe six or seven, I would count the sidewalk lines until I got home to my father's house. Every day after school, four hundred and forty-seven sidewalk lines until I got home, and always there was the potential for pain and suffering. But now that was gone and I walked in silence, counting the sidewalk lines. Each time I passed under a street light, I wondered if someone could see me before I slipped back into the darkness.

Then I lost track of the sidewalk lines. All I could feel was Izzy's hand running along my shoulder and the warmth from being asleep next to her. I couldn't remember a time when I'd been so warm. I forgot the sidewalk lines completely and peered up into the early morning sky. A few of the strongest stars were still showing, but there was a faint glow on the horizon, and I knew that soon they would be gone when the sun rose to its place in the sky. *I wish that this could all work out. I think I might like it here.*

I met Henry at the shop before anyone else got there. He was standing at the counter, flipping through a magazine, sipping from a cup of coffee. It was quiet like the day I met Izzy, but this time there was no smell of cinnamon, which I missed. There was however the smell of new things, and the smell of *new* was good too.

"Did you walk here?" Henry asked.

"Yeah, why?"

"Well, it's still dark out. I could have swung by to get you."

"Oh. Don't worry about it. I'm used to it. So, what would you like me to do?"

"Well. You want some coffee or something to eat first?"

My stomach growled for more food, and I stared blankly back at him.

"Seriously, grab whatever you want," Henry said.

"I wouldn't mind some oatmeal. The stuff Izzy made was really good."

Henry laughed. "Yep, she likes her oatmeal." Before Henry could say anything more, a loud jingling caused me to turn around, and I came face to face with an excited dog barreling toward me. Its paws skittered across the wooden floor as it tried to come to a stop. The tail was wagging furiously, and when I knelt down to give a few pats, its warm, slobbery tongue splashed across my face.

"Oh, my goodness," I said. "What's your name?"

"That's Molly," Henry said. "I'm sorry. I completely forgot about her. She comes with me to the shop all the time."

"Don't be. I love dogs."

"Well, be careful. She could kill you with kindness."

I laughed and kept petting her. Molly's fur was long, soft, and a mixture of black and white with black dots in random places. Her muzzle was compact and white except for the nose, which looked like it had been dipped in black paint. She had floppy, black ears decorated with curly fur, and her kind, brown eyes pleaded for more attention.

"What kind of dog is she?"

"An English Springer Spaniel," Henry said proudly.

I stared longingly at the toothy grin. "I wish I had a dog sometimes. How long have you had her?"

"About five years. One of the other fellas who works here, Jack, had a dog just like Molly. Her name was Sadie, and Izzy fell in love with her when she was little. Whenever she came to the shop with me, Izzy would take Sadie on walks around the store and outside to pee."

"She didn't have a dog?"

"No, her sister's allergic to dog hair, so they couldn't have one in the house. When Sadie passed away I decided to keep up the tradition, and I must say I love having her around. She's good company."

"I bet," I said, watching Molly trot off to her bed.

"Well, I was thinking maybe you could help do some inventory work this morning if that's all right. I got a few boxes of new tying materials and fishing equipment I need scanned in and sorted. Then I could show you how to fill out the online orders and package them to send."

"Sounds good to me," I said. "Can I ask you something?"

"You bet."

"Why did you fire the last fellow? You didn't just hire me because you feel sorry for me, did you?"

"No. I hired you because my sister was worried about you, and if you're going to be staying with her, she wants you to be able to take care of yourself. I also needed a hard-working, capable person who I can trust. I let the last fella go because he'd been bailing on shifts, and during the last outing, he tripped on something and broke three of the rods used for the clients. It goofed up the entire day, trying to keep those folks happy while another guy ran some more poles out to us."

"Ouch! That stinks," I said.

"Yeah. I was mad, but then I just felt bad because that guy wasn't terribly into the sport. His dad was just hoping to get the kid outdoors more."

It made me chuckle, but inside I sighed. I was so worried I'd be useless to him. "Well I haven't had many opportunities to fish lately, so I don't know how useful I'll be."

"Don't worry about that. You'll get plenty of chances to go out. We have a trip scheduled this coming weekend. I'll take you along."

"Really?"

"Yeah, definitely. If you don't already have plans that is…"

"Not that I know of. Why do you say it like that, Henry?" A thin smile peeked out from behind his cup of coffee. "Henry?"

His silence quickly gave way to laughter as he made his way out from behind the counter. "Come on, Brody."

"Hang on, Henry. What's so funny?"

"Oh, nothing. My sister may or may not have sent me a message saying that you and Izzy were cozied up on the couch this morning." Henry wandered away with his cup of coffee, leaving me staring aimlessly at the ceiling, freshly embarrassed.

I found him back in the storeroom, and when I got inside my jaw dropped. Remember how I said I liked libraries? Well, imagine an old-fashioned library with one of those cool roller ladders that people dream about playing on as kids, except modernized. Instead of books, each shelf held tubs and containers of fly-tying supplies, fishing equipment, and brand new clothing: boots, socks, pants, jackets, gloves, and whatever else people who fished needed.

"I get to play in here?" I asked.

"Yep. When stuff runs low out front, we fill the shelves from here, and this is where we fill the online orders from," Henry said. "That's what that computer station is for over there, and there's empty shipping boxes and envelopes on that shelf behind you."

"Doesn't sound too bad."

"Nah, something tells me you'll pick it up pretty quick. Enjoy your oatmeal. I'll see you in a few."

"How'd your first day of work go?" Izzy asked.

"It was good," I replied. "It was nice being able to enjoy your uncle's shop without the worry of getting in trouble."

"Did you meet Molly?"

"Yeah I did. She almost licked me to death."

Izzy laughed. "So, you like dogs then?"

"Oh yeah. I love dogs."

I was so used to people being indifferent to my opinions (or my presence for that matter). But after class that afternoon, she picked me up from the shop and took me to a nearby park for my first fly fishing lesson. She seemed genuinely excited to see me, which I was happy about, but I didn't want to seem too eager, either. The result was a lot of awkward laughing when we both started asking questions at the same time.

"How was your day?" I asked.

"It was good. You know, just class and stuff, wishing I was working at the shop. How about you? Anything else cool or funny happen?"

"Yeah, your uncle made fun of us for sleeping on the couch together."

Izzy laughed. "Yeah, my mom did, too. She must have

told Henry."

"Yeah." I gazed out the passenger window, lost in thought. After spending much of the morning daydreaming about Izzy in the store room, I was excited to fish with her, but laying on the couch again sounded even better. When I turned back to her, she was staring at me. Out of habit I tugged gently on my sleeves. Thankfully, she didn't seem to notice.

"Let's go, Brody. It's time to fish." She flashed me another radiant smile.

"You must have some faith in me."

"Hey, if you can cook the way you do, I think you can learn to fly fish."

Despite it being early in the fall, it was another muggy day, and Izzy told me a couple times during the ride that it would make the fishing a little better. From the parking lot, it was easy to see the big pond that Izzy intended for us to practice on.

"What's in here that we can catch?" I asked.

"Bass and bluegill, and I've heard people say there's some trout, but I've never caught any."

When we got out of the car, Izzy opened the back hatch of her Jeep, exposing a wide variety of fishing equipment. There were a couple of poles, a crumpled-up pair of waders, and a bag that held a few tackle boxes of flies.

"You come out here a lot then?" I asked, watching her put a pole together.

"Yeah, this is kind of my go-to place."

"It's nice here."

"I'm glad you like it," she said. The pond was calm like glass and gleamed when the sun broke through the blanket of clouds. I watched a trio of ducks paddle along the edge and disappear behind a wall of bushy cattails.

"Bluegill, huh? Is this the same pond in your picture at the store?"

Izzy grinned. "Yep. Uncle Henry used to bring me here all the time."

"Do you still remember where you slipped in the mud?"

Izzy gazed at me from behind her aviators and I wondered if my question had insulted her. Then a smile crossed her face and she pointed to a spot on the bank not far from a tree that had fallen in the water long ago. "We're gonna go over here and start out on the grass," she said.

"Not on the water?"

"Nope, this is the way Henry taught me, and it will be the way I teach you." We walked out to a spot free of trees in the lawn. "So, fly fishing," she began.

"Fly fishing," I repeated. "You're so cute by the way." I blurted the words out before I could stop myself.

"Brody!"

"Sorry. Fly fishing." I was definitely embarrassed, but not even her long, brown hair could hide her flushed cheeks.

"The idea behind fly fishing is that you're trying to trick the fish with a fly that looks very much like something they would actually be eating. That being said, there's not much weight associated with anything. You saw the flies I made at home," she said.

"Yeah, super tiny."

"Yep, they don't weigh much of anything and that's why a lot of them will float on the water."

"Alright, makes sense."

"Okay, so to cast then, you have to use the weight of the line," she said while peeling line off the reel. "Now, you want to pull some through like this…" Izzy threaded the line through the ferrules spread out along the length of the pole.

"And you have to do this every time?" I asked.

"Only if you take apart your pole when you're finished like I do. It gets really fluid when you practice enough, though. Anyway, then you're ready to practice your cast. You want to hold the rod in one hand and the line in the other. Keep your arm tucked against your body and then start a back-and-forth motion. It might help you to follow the line with your eyes to get the timing down…"

I watched carefully, trying not to get distracted by the cute, determined expressions she made. With each complete casting motion, she let a little more line slide through her fingers. The arc got longer and longer until, with a final flick of her wrist, she sent thirty feet of line unrolling perfectly on the grass.

"Wow. You make that look so easy."

"It's not so bad," she said, handing me the pole. "Just takes some practice."

"Easy for you to say. You're a pro."

"Ha! I don't know about that. Just try not to go too fast.

It's not worth it, because you'll just get frustrated. Just take your time."

"Okay. Are you going to make fun of me?"

Her lips pursed and her eyebrows raised. "Maybe a little bit."

I grinned and commenced my first ever casting motion. Despite trying to heed her instructions, my first attempts were nothing short of a disaster. The line and leader tangled up around the pole, and after getting that matter situated, my next practice casts caused the line to unroll awkwardly into a coiled mess on the ground. I was so embarrassed.

"No, no, not like that." Izzy took ahold of my elbow and upper arm. To anyone watching nearby it looked like we were doing the funky chicken dance in the lawn. Every time I resisted, she pushed harder. "Keep your casting arm tucked against your body."

"Okay."

I watched in amusement as she readjusted my shirt. "Sorry about that," she said.

I just smiled and shook my head. I tried casting again with some improvement, but the line still tangled when I made the final forward cast.

"Nope, not like that either." Izzy grabbed my arm again, leaving me feeling like a marionette. "You don't need to go back or forward that far. It's all in the wrists. Only go all the way forward on your final cast... What's that look for?"

"Nothing," I said. "I'm just worried that as soon as a fly

goes on there, I'm going to hook myself in the ear or something."

"Nah, you'll be fine. If you do though, I'll get you a sweet earring."

"Oh really? A nice diamond one?"

"Pshh. No way. I'll make you one. Maybe a nice long zonker, or maybe a little Copper John." I had no idea what she was talking about, but we both started laughing when she flicked my ear. "Come on, keep trying."

"Alright." After several more attempts, I finally had the general casting motion down.

"Not bad, Brody. Think you're ready for the water?"

"Bring it on."

"Okay, let me see that."

Instead of giving her the pole, I whipped it playfully in front of her face like she'd done to me at the shop.

"Watch it, Brody."

"Or what?"

"I know where you sleep at night. That's what."

I couldn't help but smile as I tipped the pole in her direction. Izzy's delicate fingers threaded the leader through the eye of the hook and began tying something to the end of the leader. When I looked closer, I saw that it was a foam fly that resembled a spider.

"How long have you been doing this anyway?"

"Since I was little. Seven or eight probably. Uncle Henry got me hooked early."

"Hooked. Nice."

She grinned. "I've been waiting for a chance to use that one. You ready?"

"Yeah! How do I catch the fish though?"

"Keep ahold of the line in one hand and the pole in the other, and when you get a bite, pull on both. It's kind of a timing thing, and you don't want to let go of the line. Just give it a shot."

It took a minute to get a good casting rhythm going, but eventually I sent a decent cast out over the water. The little foam spider flopped into the water and went still. "Now what?" I asked.

"Just watch."

Before I could reply there was a big splash where the foam spider had been.

"What the…" I yanked on the line, but there was nothing there.

"That's why I brought you here first. Bluegill are fun to catch and they're very gullible, which means they make for great practice. Try again."

I retrieved the rest of the line and cast out again. This time I didn't look away from the water, and when I twitched the line in hopes of enticing a reaction from the mysterious fish, I heard Izzy giggle behind me. There was another ripple and splash, but this time I was ready. As soon as the foam spider disappeared, I tugged on the line and pole like Izzy instructed. The pole immediately bent toward the water.

"Go, Brody!" Izzy said. "You don't have to use the reel either. You can just pull on the line."

I nodded feverishly, barely hearing what she said. Whatever was on the end of my line was tugging with all its might, having realized too late its dinner wasn't dinner at all. With each second that passed, I could feel the exhilaration and anticipation growing as I watched the line dance about in the water. I didn't want to lose it and embarrass myself in front of Izzy. Finally, exhaustion set in and I lifted the fish from the water, letting it dangle by the hook.

"That's it?" I blurted out.

"What are you talking about? That's a good one," she said. "It's pretty!"

The hefty bluegill was as big as my hand with a dark back and bright yellow breast. From its mouth radiated a series of beautiful electric-blue markings that arced along the saucer-shaped body.

"Yeah," I said. In one swift motion, I grasped the fish and plucked the foam spider from its mouth.

"Wait! Wait! Don't chuck it yet," she said. "Let me get a picture." Izzy fished a phone from her back pocket. A few clicks later, I tossed the fish back in the water, and she leaned in to show me the images on the screen. It seemed like a good picture, but that didn't stop me from sighing.

"What's wrong? You don't like it? I think they look good," she said.

"No, it's not that. I think they look good too. It's just…

Those are the first pictures anyone has taken of me since I got my license."

"Oh. Well, in that case, we should probably take another." Izzy leaned into me again. I barely had time to smile before she snapped a picture of us together.

"Izzy…"

"How 'bout that? I think it looks great," she said, pretending not to hear me.

"Me too." While I watched Izzy fiddle with her phone, I tried to savor the fact that I'd just taken a picture with a beautiful girl, something I thought might never happen. In fact, I had assumed that my next picture would be a mugshot once an act of severe desperation caused me to do something I regretted.

"Keep going," she said. "I'll be right back."

"Alright." I cast out again, but I ignored the bites of several bluegill as I glanced back to see Izzy heading toward her car. After a couple minutes, there was still no sign of Izzy, so I decided to go check on her. I was worried that I'd upset her somehow, because when I found her she was crying.

"Hey, you all right?" I asked.

Izzy sniffled and glanced up at me. "What? Yeah, yeah. I'm good. Thanks. Just got something in my eye."

My eyebrows raised instantly, because clearly something was wrong. "Uh huh, or maybe you hooked yourself in the ear?"

She laughed and shook her head. "Really, I'm all right. I just came up to get the other pole so I could fish with you."

"Alright. But if something's wrong I'll have to try and cheer you up, and I don't know how good I am at that. I've never had anyone to cheer up before."

Izzy smiled and took a deep breath. "You've done a good job so far. Come on, let's keep fishing."

We fished until it was nearly dark, and then it started to sprinkle. After returning home, we had dinner with her mother and took up residence in the living room. I kept catching Izzy staring at me, and I waited for her to ask me more personal questions, but all she did was ask about calculating derivatives.

Eventually, her yawns became too distracting and Izzy called it a night, leaving me to peruse magazines on the couch. Heather, who had been working on her classwork, retreated to the bathroom downstairs for her evening shower. This left me in a bit of a predicament, because after a while I really had to use the restroom and the last thing I wanted to do was cross some unknown boundary by going upstairs.

When the discomfort was too much, I decided to risk it and stepped quietly up the stairs, figuring that Izzy had long since fallen asleep, but I was wrong. A long thin slit of light cut through the darkness of the second floor, and despite knowing that I should respect her privacy, curiosity got the better of me. From behind her door, I thought I could hear voices, which made me sigh. *She's probably talking to that guy.*

I stepped closer and peered through the crack. To my surprise, Izzy wasn't on the phone at all. She was kneeling next to her bed, praying. Her eyes were closed and her fingers were interlaced, resting against her forehead as she muttered her prayers.

"God, please keep my momma and Henry healthy, and please keep Daddy safe. I love him and miss him so much…"

I bowed my head and stepped back away from the door. The only thing I'd ever prayed for was for my father to be taken as far away as possible, and so far that had been the only prayer that had ever been answered. My gut rolled over threateningly, but I didn't move because then I heard *my* name.

"What about Brody, God? I've been praying for my dad for years and I think you're listening. I mean I know he's okay, but I wished so many times that you'd bring him home and instead you suddenly bring Brody into my life? I've never had many friends and I've been alone and now there's Brody. God, I think something bad happened to him, but I'm scared to ask him…"

No longer interested in the bathroom, I quickly and quietly retreated downstairs.

ach morning, I walked to the fly shop, counting the lines in the sidewalk, plagued by the anxiety and worry that haunted my dreams. I never would have thought when I was four or five that I would still be scared of my dreams when I was grown up.

Yet, by the end of each day, those repressed emotions and twisted memories that presented themselves while I slept were beat back a little bit further. It was a big relief for me, except for the fact that I was very familiar with the phrase "All good things must come to an end." A couple days after Heather said I could stay, those words were already taunting me.

I was sitting on the couch when I heard the front door open. A jingling followed and Molly was soon pestering me for attention, which I was happy to give, but curiosity got the better of me. *What's Henry doing here?* I got off the couch and tiptoed toward the kitchen.

"Hello, Henry," Heather said.

"Hey, Sis. How's it going?"

"Fine, just trying to work on some homework for my teaching class."

"How's that going?"

Heather stopped writing and a silence filled the kitchen. "It's going good, thanks," she finally said. "What's up?"

"Is Izzy or Brody around?"

"Around me? No. Izzy's showering and Brody's reading magazines in the living room I think. Why? Is something wrong?" Her voice dropped to a whisper. "Did he steal something?"

My stomach dropped.

"What? No!" Henry said. "No. Brody's fine. He's great actually. That's why I stopped over. Do you have a few minutes?"

"Yeah. What happened?"

"Nothing but good things, Heather. Relax. Who is this kid anyway?"

"Your guess is as good as mine, Henry. I know his last name is Allen though."

From my spot outside the doorway, I heard Heather get up from her seat and open the fridge. Then there was the crack and hiss of a pop can opening.

"Thanks," Henry said.

"Yeah. I don't want to pry too much though. Clearly he hasn't been getting enough to eat. He looked so gaunt the morning I met him."

"He really must have been on his own then."

"Yeah," Heather said. "What happened though? You came over for something—"

"Everything is fine. I just wanted to see how he's doing with you. I haven't had as much time as I thought to check on him since I've been rotating more into the guide schedule with Jack and Tim. But he works really hard. He's already managed to clean and sort a ton of the merchandise for me."

"So you want him to stay?"

"Hell yeah, I want him to stay. That's why I was making sure everything was going okay with you."

Heather let out an uneasy laugh. "So you like him?"

"Yeah, don't you?"

"Yeah, so far I like him. I guess. Aside from the ruse he and Izzy pulled when he arrived, he seems very honest and I appreciate the help he does around the house."

"But…" Henry prodded. I was waiting for the *but* as well. I knew it was coming.

"But Henry, what if…he's a drug addict? Or what if he hurts Izzy? They've been spending a lot of time together. What if they have sex and he gets her pregnant?"

My stomach sunk even further and I didn't bother to wait for Henry's reply. I slipped out the back door and walked into the yard. Between the awful feeling in my stomach and the throb in my head, I thought for sure I was going to puke. I had no idea what to think. I slouched against one of the large trees in the yard, taking deep breaths of the evening air to clear my head, but it wasn't doing much good. Darkness was settling in around me, but I didn't care. I was used to the darkness. After a while the back door opened and the sound of Molly's jingling collar met my ears as she ran around investigating the yard.

"Brody?"

"Hmm?" I was too annoyed to say anything, even to Izzy. Her footsteps barely made a sound as she came across the yard, stopping just short of me. She was in her night clothes: sweats and a hoodie.

"I have proof that Molly likes you," she said.

"Oh really."

"Yeah. When I came downstairs, Mom and Henry were wondering where you went. I found Molly sitting by the back door. Can I sit down?" Her voice was kind and soft and I knew that I should have been more excited, but I was so worried and frustrated.

"It's your yard, not mine."

"Somebody sounds grumpy." I didn't like people being condescending or patronizing, but when I looked up to offer another bitter reply, she kept me silent with her nervous smile. "What's wrong?" she asked.

"Maybe this is a bad idea, Izzy."

"What's a bad idea?"

"Me being here. Maybe I should just go."

"Why? So you can go find some other porch to get sick on? Brody, that seems stupid."

I picked a fallen branch off the ground and snapped it in half. Then I tossed the pieces for Molly to chase.

"Well, maybe I'm not the brightest person."

"That's not true, Brody, and you know it."

"How do you know? You hardly know me."

Izzy's smile faded. "Fine. Stay out here if you want. Or go wander off somewhere. I don't care." Without another word, she got up and made for the back door.

"Wait. I'm sorry," I said, but Izzy kept walking toward the house. "I'm sorry, Isabel."

At the last second, she turned from the door and came to join me under the tree again. "So you gonna tell me what's bothering you then?"

I listened to the evening breeze whistling through the tree branches above us, wondering if Izzy had any idea what it was like to have people talk about her behind her back. "I heard your mom and Henry talking about me. Izzy, your mom thinks I'm a drug addict."

"Is that actually what she said?"

"Well, not exactly. She's *worried* I'm a drug addict."

"Are you a drug addict, Brody? Do you smoke weed constantly or have needle marks on your arms?"

"No!"

"Good. Neither do I. Glad we got that cleared up."

For some reason I started laughing. I don't know why, but

it just seemed funny to me. Somehow she'd made me feel silly about getting upset. "Izzy…"

"Brody. She's my mom. You're a guy she hardly knows. She's going to worry. Just give her reasons not to. I'm not saying go inside and spill your guts, but just be honest. Be yourself."

"I'm trying," I said. "But I'm kind of a loser. I don't have much to offer."

"That's not true and you know it." She got up and called for Molly. "If you're hungry, they made tacos for dinner."

I wasn't sure what to think or say, but as Izzy tried to get Molly back inside, I couldn't help but recall that only a few nights before, Izzy had left me on the couch to go talk with some guy. Now here she was trying her damnedest to make me feel better.

"Why do you care?" I asked.

"Why are you still here?"

Before I could answer, she disappeared inside, leaving behind the hint of a smile. I shook my head and glanced up at the tree we'd been sitting under. The low-hanging limbs would have made it easy to jump the fence and disappear into the night. But with everything they'd already done for me, leaving now seemed almost cowardly, so I finally went after Izzy. I was half expecting there to be an awkward moment in the kitchen, but there was nothing.

"Grab some food you guys," Henry said.

Izzy and I dished up our plates and joined Henry and Heather at the table. The food was delicious, but the conversation seemed a little forced. Whenever there was a lull in conversation, I found myself glancing at Heather. It was hard not to imagine her thinking I was a drug addict. Then Izzy broke through the drivel swirling between my ears.

"We should play a game."

Heather looked confused and nervous. Henry, on the other hand, seemed so amused that I thought he was going to start giggling. Izzy was clearly determined to make the evening the best it could be.

"A game?" Heather repeated.

"Yeah. Hang on." Izzy left the table and started digging through the drawers of a nearby cabinet. When she returned to the table, there was a deck of cards in her hand. My nerves kicked in and tiny beads of sweat formed in my hairline. I didn't know any card games except the ones Mrs. Murphy taught me: Go Fish and Old Maid.

"What are you doing, Izzy?" Henry asked.

"I want to play a game with you guys—get things a little livelier in here. I feel like we've just been to a funeral."

"Are you sure this is a good idea, Izzy?" Heather asked. "Henry probably has to get going soon."

It took everything for me not to bow my head. She wanted away from the table. I could feel it. I was probably making her really uncomfortable.

"Hang on, Sis." Henry paused from wolfing down a taco. "I like a good card game. Let's hear it, Izzy."

Izzy beamed at all of us as she began dealing cards around

the table. "Alright…"

And so began a very long game of Egyptian Rat Screw. Thankfully it was an easy game to pick up. The object of the game was to collect all the cards, and the first player to slap the pile whenever doubles showed up took all the cards. I noticed that Heather was hesitant to slap down, especially when I went for the pile. By the end of the evening however, our forgotten dinner plates and silverware were clanging together as we pounded down on the table. Our laughter echoed throughout the house, and everyone's hands were red from getting hit so many times. When Henry finally called it a night, he gave me a kind nod on his way to the door. Heather retreated to the study to read material for her class, and I carried dishes off to the sink. At the sound of a gentle knocking I turned to find Izzy lingering near the kitchen counter.

"You glad you didn't leave?" A thin smile appeared on her face and once again I was scrounging for words. In the end, I nodded.

"Goodnight, Brody."

"G'night, Izzy."

It had been a week since my arrival in Eugene. I still had a place to stay that was warm at night, and the company was great. Ever since we played cards, Heather's demeanor toward me had improved significantly, although I still worried that she was going to kick me out for the sake of Isabel's well-being.

But when I walked into their home after work on Friday afternoon, that was the last thing on my mind. The kitchen table was an absolute mess. It looked like a group of kindergartners on a sugar rush had gone haywire with craft supplies.

"Wow," I gasped. "What's all this?"

"My tying supplies," Izzy replied. I gave her a strange look. Everything at the fly shop was neat and organized in its tidy packages, but this was nuts. Spread across the table were containers of dubbing, wax, feathers, spools of thread, hooks, beads, and various other tying materials. "Yeah. I know. It's kind of crazy. Did you bring that practice vice home from the shop?"

"Yep." I lifted up the bag in my hand. "Where should I put it?"

"Next to mine."

"You're really excited about this, aren't you?" I asked while clamping the vice to the table.

"I am if you are." After we each took a seat, Izzy handed me a huge steel hook. The chemically sharpened tip was insanely threatening. "What?"

"Are we going fishing for small sharks?"

Izzy laughed. "Maybe. This first one might look like a mangled squid or something," she said with a devious smile. "The reason I gave you such a big hook is so we can practice easier. I didn't think you'd want to start with a size twenty-two hook."

"Tiny?"

"Look at the box." Izzy motioned to one of the containers she had carefully labeled. As the numbers got larger, the hooks got smaller. The size fourteen hooks, for example, weren't much longer than a pinky nail. When I reached the space marked *Dry Fly – 22,* Izzy laughed when my eyes widened.

"You tie something on that?"

"Sometimes," she said.

"You'd need a magnifying glass!"

"I've got one here somewhere." Izzy started digging

around in the various boxes. "These are for when I'm feeling extra nerdy." She slid the strangest looking space-age visor onto her head.

"Those are classy, Izzy." I laughed.

"I know right?" She set them aside and picked up a bobbin and thread. "You ready for your first lesson?"

I nodded, and for the next several minutes Izzy explained the techniques used to attach the wide variety of materials to a hook. At first it was like listening to someone on fast forward. Her words were going into my head so fast that they barely had time to register—I felt like a bogged-down computer.

"You all right, Brody?"

"I just…I like this. I really like doing this with you. I just…"

"If I'm going too fast, just tell me to slow down. We're not in any rush." The worried smile on her face made me chuckle.

"Okay," I said. "Could we maybe glance over some of that again?" After that, everything slowed down to the perfect pace and I listened in earnest, craving every word she said. Izzy knew so much about fly tying—much more than she let on initially—and after the first hour I realized I was getting to enjoy something that people had enjoyed for generations before me.

"What material do you like best?" I asked.

"I like the beads, sparkly dubbing, and the hackle feathers." Izzy picked up a pair of hackle pliers and effortlessly twisted a light brown feather onto the hook. By the time she was finished, the fly closely resembled a dark fuzzy caterpillar.

"What do you think?" she asked.

"That's neat."

"It's the first fly Uncle Henry showed me how to tie. A woolly bear caterpillar. It's been a long time, but it's still one of my favorites."

"Does this one float?"

"The smaller ones will. This one is probably a little too big. Check out what you can do with deer hair though." Izzy removed the first fly from the vice and replaced it with a fresh hook. Quickly and effortlessly, she tied on a feather to imitate a tail. From the pile of materials on the table, she produced a spool of silver tinsel. Carefully, Izzy wrapped a piece around the shank of the hook to make a shimmering body. Another feather was added to make a dorsal fin, then she pulled a chunk of deer hair from an envelope and snipped off a pinch. Very delicately, Izzy pressed the hair against the hook with her finger and began winding the thread through the hair. As she applied more pressure, the hair flared out, becoming a nearly perfect sphere around the eye of the hook.

"That's bad ass," I said. "What's next?"

"Usually you pack on a few more clumps of hair and then you can take a razor blade…" Izzy shaved the deer hair as if she were trimming hedges in front of the house. Slowly, she formed the hair into a cone shape. "Give it a little haircut and you've got yourself a Muddler Minnow."

"You're really good at this," I said. "Do you think I'm

ready to try a real recipe?"

"Recipe, Brody? Are you planning on cooking these when they're done?" We both laughed. "They're called patterns."

"A real pattern then?"

"Yeah, let's give it a shot. We'll do a simple one first. It's called the egg fly, and it's really popular with steelhead and salmon." Izzy handed me several pieces of thick, brightly colored egg yarn.

"So, is this your job?"

"Yes and no. Henry and I have a deal where we trade flies for tying supplies. I only get paid when I work at the shop. But sometimes he gives me a few extra bucks if a lot of my flies sell."

I wanted to answer, but I was too busy watching her cinch the yarn to the hook. It looked like an unruly mess, but then she used the scissors to cut away the extra yarn, leaving behind an orange egg shape.

"I'd rather have the materials anyway. I like tying, and I get to practice with a lot of the new stuff." Izzy shrugged, and the conversation dwindled as we both got into a good rhythm. It was an easy pattern to learn, and it wasn't long before there was a neat pile of bright orange, pink, and red egg flies stacked up between us. Rain drummed away on the roof, and from the corner of my eye I saw Izzy watching me. Then she shivered.

"You're cold," I said.

"A little."

My brain whirled into hyper drive. *Here's your chance,*

Brody. Do something nice for her. "Hang on. I'll make hot chocolate." I left my bobbin dangling from the vice and headed for the stove. After clicking on the burner, I poured water and cream into a small pan. When Izzy finished her fly, she joined me by the simmering pot.

"Where did you learn to do all this cooking?"

"I worked in a lot of restaurants."

"Yeah, but how come you didn't stay? I mean, clearly you have a knack for it."

"I got fired."

"What? Why?"

I didn't answer right away. As I stirred the contents of the pot, I remembered arguing with a chef who had an outrageously squirrely mustache. Spittle flew from his lips as he yelled at me for one thing after another. "Well, one time it was because I was snitching food. But the rest of the time, it was because I was having too much fun. The bosses didn't like when I was changing their recipes all the time or using up their food making new dishes."

"That's lame. So what are you doing here? You don't just use the water and packets?"

"No, my old neighbor used to make it this way. It's really good."

"What was her name?"

"You know, I'm not sure. I always called her Mrs. Murphy. A great name for a neighbor I suppose. Very non-descript. She made good hot chocolate and cookies though."

Izzy giggled. "Did you ever figure out her secret?"

"I don't know." I shrugged, thinking back to the days when I dreaded having to leave Mrs. Murphy's to return to my father's house. "I always thought it was real chocolate, but I suppose it was the TLC."

"Yeah..." She leaned into me slightly and watched the mixture of cream and water come to a gentle boil. Then I ladled the liquid into mugs she set on the counter. Izzy gleefully yanked open the fridge door and soon a steady whooshing sound filled the kitchen as she topped the mugs with whipped cream.

"I hope you like it," I said.

"I'm sure I will. Come on. Let's go sit down." Instead of reclaiming our seats at the kitchen table, Izzy led me to the couch in the living room. We exchanged a quiet toast when she raised her glass to clink gently with mine. When the creamy goodness met her lips, she immediately glanced at me, unaware of the whipped cream mustache she had.

When my laughter died away, I realized how lost I was. I hadn't thought much past the hot cocoa, but she leaned into my shoulder and stayed close to me. I wasn't used to people being so close—not that she made me uncomfortable. On the contrary, I was delighted by Izzy's close proximity and I didn't want her to go.

"Can I ask you something?" she said.

"Sure." The night I saw her praying flew to the front of my mind, but to my surprise she asked about something else.

"What happened with that whole movie thing?"

I laughed. "Well, I ended up in Baton Rouge for a while, and apparently they make a lot of movies there. One night, I was out wandering around and I ended up in this park that was jam packed with people. I thought it was some huge concert, but it turned out they were filming a movie."

"No kidding?"

"Yeah, I guess. I mean, I saw cameras moving around everywhere. There was this big tower in the middle of the park and a cable came from the top all the way down to the stage. Every few minutes the camera would come down the cable and zoom in close to the stage and then back away again."

"What movie was it?"

"I don't remember. Some musical. There were people dancing and singing all over the place."

Izzy gawked at me.

"Yeah, and I ended up meeting this really cool family from Texas, and when the movie stuff was over, they invited me back to the bayou for a crawfish boil."

"Shut up! You've got to be kidding me," Izzy said.

"I'm not. I promise you. There's nothing quite like riding around with a carload of people you hardly know, listening to them tell stories about people who hunt alligators. We stopped at a drive-through daiquiri stand. Oh, and by the time I left they were calling me Uncle Brody, and apparently I can come back to visit whenever."

Izzy looked flabbergasted.

"Sorry if I'm rambling." When I smiled at her again,

Izzy's pale complexion picked up a rosy tint from behind her cup, and I was overcome by a strong desire to kiss her. Then for some unknown reason I actually decided to risk it. When she set the cup down on the coffee table, I leaned in and kissed her cheek. Nothing so pleasant had ever touched my lips, and the tint on her skin became a flush of color. I hoped the small gesture wouldn't be too much.

"Brody…" Her tone was hard for me to discern, and when she continued staring at her cup I worried that I'd ruined everything.

"I'm sorry," I said. "I shouldn't have…"

Ever so slightly, Izzy's head moved from side to side and then her hand was on my arm as she leaned in closer. "You missed," she whispered.

I thought my heart was going to explode when our lips touched. They were so warm and soft, not to mention they tasted like chocolate. But just as quickly as it happened, we pulled apart, silent and surprised.

"Oh my," she mumbled.

"Wow," I muttered.

"Brody?"

"I'm sorry, Izzy. I'll leave if you want me to."

"What? No. I don't want you to leave. Why would I want you to leave?"

"I don't know. Are you sure? Because I don't want to have ruined something." I was stammering now. "It's just you've been so great and I feel like we've been having a good time. Maybe I completely misjudged things. I don't want to be pushy about anything." Hopefully, Izzy found my awkward nervousness cute.

"You're not being pushy," she said. "Please don't leave."

"I won't."

"Okay. Good."

The silence continued as we took nervous sips from our cups. I glanced at her, wondering if her thoughts were as frantic as mine, but still I said nothing.

"Would you care if I stayed down here with you again?" she said.

"What? Really?"

"Yeah. We could watch a movie or something."

"That would be awesome," I replied in absolute awe. "I would like that."

"Yeah?"

"Definitely."

Izzy beamed at me and dashed up to her room. When she returned, I knew there was a nervous grin plastered across my face, but she didn't seem to mind. Izzy flopped her legs across my lap and we started watching some science fiction movie that she insisted was epic. It wasn't long before we were drifting off to sleep. As I fought heavy eyelids, I tried once again to interpret the intense feelings that were brewing inside me.

Our clients for the day met us at the shop early on Saturday morning, puffy-eyed, exhausted, but excited to fish. I offered to sit in the back of the vehicle we were taking, but the guests both declined the front seat since they wanted to keep sleeping. Apparently it had been a late night drive for them from Sacramento, so I strapped into the passenger seat, and when everyone was situated we hit the road.

From the corner of my eye, I noticed Henry glancing at me every few seconds. I figured without the distraction of the shop he more than likely didn't know what to talk about, so I stared out the window watching the sites go by.

"So," Henry said. "What brought you to Eugene?"

"A truck." It seemed funny to me, but I didn't want to be a smartass either. "Sorry. I was just trying to get to the west coast

I guess."

"Do you like it so far? I mean, I know a lot of folks aim for southern California, but you came here…"

"Yeah, I like it—reminds me of where I grew up sort of." As we passed through a stretch of fog, my mind drifted to the old, cobblestone streets of Portland, Maine. I could almost hear the honks of boats and tugs in the harbors as they came off another lobster run. Thinking about the ocean made me think about my favorite lighthouse and the field of black-eyed susans that lined the nearby hiking trail. They were memories of an entirely different life.

I shook my head and fiddled with the door handle. Then I decided to ask a question that had been nagging at me for the last week. "Why do you like fly fishing?"

"A lot of reasons I guess," Henry replied. "Why do you ask?"

"Well, Izzy says she likes it because it's elegant and beautiful, and I'm still not quite sure if that makes sense to me. I mean it's cool and all, but it seems complicated and difficult. No offense."

"None taken. That's probably the reason a lot of folks tend to shy away from fly fishing, but I suppose I like it for the same reasons as Izzy."

"There must be other reasons though."

"Well, it's relaxing. I love being outside. I get to meet all sorts of people and I really enjoy tying."

"Why?"

"Because it's my hobby. Do you like to draw or anything?"

"I don't know. I guess, yeah—but I don't get to that often." In truth, I loved to draw. The last two years of traveling had been laced with many camera-worthy moments, but without the money to purchase a camera, I had to find other means of preserving the captivating memories. In my bag, I kept a pad of paper and a few pens and pencils.

"Well I can't draw, but tying for me is just fun," Henry said. "Sometimes in the winter, I'll tie for hours, trying to mimic nature while daydreaming about all the fish I'm going to catch in the spring. Depending on how into fly fishing or tying you get, you'll come to understand that trout can be very picky. So when you catch a fish with a fly that you've tied, it's a very rewarding feeling."

"How picky?" I asked.

"Well, I've gone out with folks who I know are exceptional at fly fishing, and no matter how good a fly they have on their line, if it doesn't look enough like what's hatching on the water at that time, the fish will ignore it completely."

"That sounds frustrating," I said.

"Terribly. But that's why they call it fishing and not catching."

That made me laugh. "So, where all do you guide then?"

"Well, the shop offers guided trips on four of the big rivers: the McKenzie, the Willamette, the Deschutes, and the Umpqua. But we also guide on a handful of other rivers. You look a little surprised."

I sucked in a breath and closed my eyes. "What? No. I'm just…I have no idea what I'm getting myself into."

Henry stifled a chuckle so he didn't wake the clients. "Well, hopefully today you can figure out if you like it or not. I hope you do."

Me too, Henry. He took another sip of his coffee and I returned to fiddling with the door handle.

"You know, Brody. I've fished all over the world. If you end up liking this and stick around, maybe we can go somewhere."

"Oh yeah?" I turned to Henry in disbelief. "Like where? Canada?"

"Yeah. There's lots of good trout fishing there, and we could fish for northern pike and muskie."

I stared blankly at Henry, not knowing what either of those fish were.

"You have no idea what I'm talking about do you?"

"No, sorry." I started fidgeting with the door handle again. "Henry, when I said I haven't fished much, I mean I haven't fished at all."

"Oh." Henry sucked in a breath. "Well, that's all right."

He glanced at me and I saw the tiniest hint of sadness in his expression. *I wonder if Henry thinks I'm pathetic.* I waited for him to say something, but after a moment he returned his attention to the road in front of us.

"Henry?" I said.

"Yeah. Sorry. Northerns and muskie are two species of really big freshwater fish, like freshwater barracuda kind of. They're a ton of fun to catch. Really aggressive, lots of teeth."

"Sounds kinda crazy."

Henry laughed. "Well if you get into this, maybe we can go sometime."

"Yeah, maybe." I didn't really know what to say to that. After years of stumbling around the country, it was as if I'd suddenly hit a gold mine of opportunities. "Sounds like you're pretty dedicated."

"Yeah, I guess. I just…love fly fishing," Henry replied.

"Which place is your favorite then?"

"Hmm, that's a tough one. I don't know if I could pick one because they all have their perks. I suppose here and Yellowstone would be my favorites though."

"How come?"

"I used to fish here with my dad when he was still alive. Izzy and I went to Yellowstone a couple times, too."

"So you don't have any kids then?"

"Nope." As he took another sip of coffee that one word hung in the air like a storm cloud. I figured the conversation was over so I returned to the window, but then Henry continued. "Her dad's been serving her entire life, so it's cool getting to do that sort of stuff with her."

"I bet she really appreciates that."

"I hope so. Least of all I get to be the favorite uncle. But anyway…are you having fun at the shop?"

"Yeah, it's great. Thank you again by the way."

"You're welcome. Everyone seems to like you, too."

"That's good. I hope so." I glanced at Henry as more potential conversations flowed through my head. *Please don't ask about Izzy. Please.*

"I think one of the other employees might really enjoy you being around," Henry teased.

I sucked in a breath. *You had to bring up Izzy.* It was the one conversation that I wanted to avoid.

"Would it be fair to say that you fancy my niece?" Henry asked.

"Yeah, she's great." I peeked at Henry again. "Probably saved my life. Pneumonia is nasty business."

"Yeah it is," Henry said. "But you know what I mean by *fancy,* right?"

"Of course. When I say she's *great*, I mean that she's the most beautiful lady I've ever seen. She's kind and funny. She smells good and her smile is like a beautiful sunrise. I bet there will be a good sunrise out here today." Henry's jaw dropped and he nearly drove off the road while gaping at me. I clutched anything I could grab ahold of, but our clients kept sleeping.

"Careful there, Henry."

"What? Are you serious? Are you going to tell her this?" Henry stammered. I shrugged but continued holding the handle above the window.

"I'm not sure. Are you gonna tell her I said that?"

"I'm not sure."

"Well, I'm not really sure what's going on and I think there might be some other fellow. Besides, I'm just the random guy from back east she found sleeping on the porch, remember?"

"I don't think that matters to her, Brody."

"Henry, are you trying to set me up with Izzy?"

He scratched nervously at his beard. "I, uh, I don't know. Just don't sell yourself short. So far, you seem like a great guy."

"Thanks." It wasn't much longer before we pulled into a park and the clients came out of their stupor like two athletes ready to run a marathon. I'd never seen people so excited to do something, and their exuberance was definitely rubbing off on me. The closer we got to the river, the more I wanted to see fly fishing at its full potential. While the clients put their gear on, I stood a short distance from the truck, gazing at the wilderness around us.

It was as if someone had flipped a switch on the seasons. Only a couple days into September and the weather had become cooler and more turbid. Drops of rain from the night before clung to the tree branches and grasses, sparkling in the early morning sunlight like miniature diamonds. The air was sweeter than I'd ever smelled it. Birds were chirping as they flitted about the branches, and occasionally the breeze would whistle through the needles of nearby evergreens. Other than that, there was nothing—just a calm silence.

I pulled Henry aside. "I really appreciate you bringing me along and all, but would you mind helping me to not make an ass of myself? I think this could be really fun, and I would hate for you to fire me too."

Henry patted my shoulder in a reassuring manner. "I'm not going to fire you, Brody. Just…be patient and careful. You'll do fine. Enjoy the sights."

So that's what I did. I enjoyed the pristine views along the hiking trail. I soaked up the view of the river snaking through the canyons and valleys while Henry taught our clients how to fly fish. I took notes of the casting techniques as well as Henry's knowledge of the river. He often suggested certain spots in the river where the fish hold up: current seams, fallen rocks, and behind boulders.

When lunch came around, I took Henry completely by surprise when I got a fire going on the riverbank. Our kettle was hanging from the makeshift spit and I was stirring the contents with a long, metal spoon.

"What's this?" Henry asked.

"Lunch for you and those two guys," I said. "I didn't want you to think I wasn't doing enough, so I figured…"

Henry clapped me on the back and started laughing. "That smells awesome. Just do your thing. Let me know when it's ready," he said.

"Hoooo! Henry! I've got a big one!" yelled one of the fishermen.

"Be right back, Brody!" Henry dashed off, grabbing his net along the way. I stopped stirring and watched one of our clients lean back with his rod. It bent so much that I was sure it would snap like a twig, but it held, and then a huge silver fish erupted from the river. Its body contorted in the air, sending water drops flying as it tried to free itself from the hook. When it hit the water again the reel screamed, and I watched the neon orange fly line zoom away into the river as the fish tried once again to escape.

Each time the man got the fish close to shore, it would unleash another burst of energy and dart back into the current. The fight lasted several minutes, but finally the fisherman was victorious. Henry assisted in netting the fish, and the client posed for several well-earned pictures. Afterwards Henry called out to me as he lifted one of the client's smaller catches from the cooler. "Heather says you're good in the kitchen. Is there any chance you know how to cook fish too?"

"You have any lemon and butter?" I replied.

"I'll check the other cooler." Henry returned a few minutes later with an armload of supplies.

"Do you always cook this much on trips?" I asked.

"Only on the full-day trips, and even then the menu varies a little depending on what the clients are in the mood for. Some people want to fish more, so we just pack something simple. I've had people ask for nothing but chips and ham and cheese sandwiches. These two, on the other hand, were hoping to have fresh fish, so I packed accordingly."

"Makes sense," I said. Henry taught me how to properly clean a fish. When the fillets were ready, I placed each one on a sheet of tin foil and began seasoning them.

"You know, up in Alaska, it's not uncommon to fish with grizzlies nearby," Henry said. "Fun fact."

I stopped slicing onions and gawked at him. "Who are you people? That doesn't freak you out?"

Henry chuckled. "Well, of course it's a little unnerving, and you definitely have to be careful, but there's so many fish up there that as long as you give the bears their space you should be okay."

"Well. I don't know if I could do that. That seems a little extreme." I was about to continue cutting onions when I noticed Henry had raised an eyebrow at me. "What?"

"Nothing."

"Tell me, Henry."

"Well, what if Izzy was going? We were talking about going up there next summer."

There was nothing I could do to stop my cheeks from reddening, and Henry laughed again while clapping me on the shoulder. "That's really funny," I said.

"Are you going to answer?" he asked.

"I would love to go."

"Good, because fly fishing in Alaska is amazing. So what are you thinking, Master Chef?"

"I had an idea I guess. Should I run it by them?"

Henry shook his head. "Nah. Don't bother. These two are just happy to be on the river and out of the office. They'll eat whatever you put in front of them as long as there's fresh fish."

I laughed and began dicing several of the potatoes. It was

a chilly day, so we ate lunch while sitting around the fire. There was fruit, salad, a buttery potato stew made over the fire, and lightly seasoned trout wrapped in tinfoil and baked in the coals.

Along with scarfing down their meals, our clients spent a good portion of lunch rehashing their best catches of the morning. Henry added details where necessary, but eventually the questions were directed at him.

"Henry, you seem pretty serious about your fishing. Have you ever traveled out to the Midwest or out east to do any fishing?" I hadn't been paying much attention since I was trying to pace myself with the hearty food, but the client's question piqued my interest since I was very curious about Henry.

"Oh yeah. All over the place. I was telling Brody this morning while you guys were sleeping about some of the trips I made out to Michigan, Wisconsin, and Canada."

Up until this point, I'd thought of Henry as a rather quiet person. Other than the ride up to the river, we'd only shared a few brief conversations at the shop. Beyond that, Henry didn't say too much. After several questions from the clients though, Henry opened up and began elaborating on a trip he and his father had taken in Michigan and Wisconsin. We sat in awe as he talked about catching salmon and steelhead beneath a historic steel dam, rivers and creeks in the Driftless Area that were teaming with brown trout, and the encounter he had with loons and bald eagles while catching trophy-sized brook trout on a remote lake in the Upper Peninsula.

"Get outta here!" yelled one of the clients as Henry finished the story, but I knew he wasn't fibbing. Henry had no reason to make up a story like that.

"I'm not kidding you," Henry said.

"You going to go back?" asked the other.

Henry shrugged. "Maybe sometime."

When Henry's deep brown eyes met mine, I looked down at my plate. I had no idea how long I'd be in Eugene, but it sure would have been cool to see that, especially with someone who clearly appreciated such things like Henry did. Then I felt another nudge on my arm.

"You outdid yourself, Mr. Brody," said one of the fishermen. "That was delicious. I might just be too full to keep fishing."

"Fat chance of that," said the other, slapping his buddy hard on the stomach. Laughter erupted around the campfire. After a while, the two gentlemen pushed themselves out of their chairs and resumed fishing while we cleaned up. When that was finished, I messed around tossing a line in the river, but the current made the process of casting even harder.

When I looked at the other fisherman I saw Henry watching me from a distance and quickly turned back to the river. *He's probably going to send me packing.* After a few minutes though, Henry came to stand next to me in the river.

"I need more practice," I said.

"That's all right. Don't worry," Henry said. "You'll get the hang of it."

"How was it, Brody?" Izzy said, punching my arm playfully. "First guys fishing trip."

"I hurt."

"A little more than you're used to, huh?"

"Just a little. Sitting for a couple hours after walking and wading on uneven terrain all day made me insanely stiff."

"You're an old man now."

"Ha, ha." I groaned as we sat down on the couch. Izzy just kept laughing.

"Do you still think fly fishing is lame?" she asked.

"I never said it was lame, Izzy."

"No, you said it's *complicated.*"

I loved when she tried to imitate my voice. "Well I still think it's complicated. I tried fishing after lunch, but it was hard on moving water. Our clients caught some big fish though, and I'll admit that it looked pretty fun."

"I'll get you to come around. You'll see. We'll have to go sometime."

"You mean other than the park?" I still wasn't used to the fact that Izzy seemed genuinely interested, and I didn't want to misinterpret anything she said.

"Yeah. You and I go and fish and cook out—hang out and have fun," she said.

"That would be cool." I hoped my reply wasn't too eager.

"Thanks again for practicing with me by the way. This past week has been really incredible."

"No problem. It's fun. You teach me math and I'll teach you how to fish." Izzy leaned forward, flicking the zipper on her backpack. "Actually, I didn't mean to sound presumptuous just now, but would you mind helping me with my math homework again tonight?" Her green irises carried a hopeful glimmer that I couldn't have ignored even if I wanted to.

"I would love to."

"Awesome."

It was the icing on the cake, being able to spend the evening with Izzy after a long day on the river, watching her blow wisps of hair from her face as she did her homework. I grinned to myself as a fantastic plan took shape in my mind.

"When's your birthday?" I asked.

"Next month, October fifteenth. Why do you ask?"

"I was just wondering." I had no idea if I'd still be here in a month, but the thought of actually getting to celebrate someone's birthday was kind of nice.

"Brody, you don't have to get me anything," she said.

"Pshh. I couldn't if I wanted to. Vagabonding is an expensive lifestyle." Her laughter filled the living room and when she leaned into me affectionately I wanted desperately to kiss her again, but we didn't. Instead I got lost in her charismatic smile, wondering if it was even possible for us to have a relationship.

"I should probably finish this homework," she finally said.

"Yeah, probably."

"You could make me hot chocolate on my birthday though."

"Done." I already knew what I was going to get her and it was going to be something much better than a cup of cocoa.

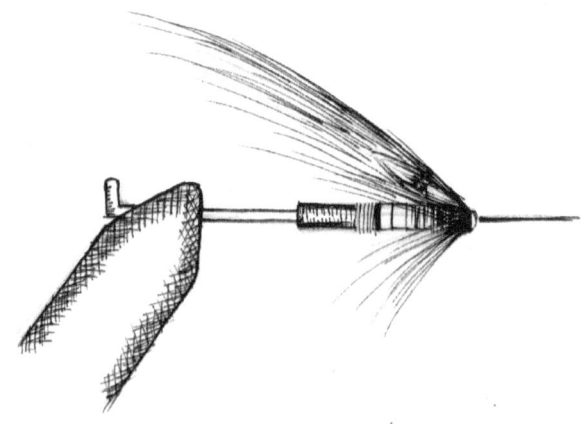

I had found in my travels that no matter what the job, there was always a certain amount of downtime that required little to no work. One of the best parts of working at the fly shop was that downtime wasn't an excuse to sit bored in the corner, twiddling my thumbs. On the contrary, I got to practice tying or read the fly fishing books the store kept in stock. This afternoon was especially informative. Henry was introducing me to tying tube flies and fishing with a spey rod.

"Izzy doesn't like tube flies you know." Henry leaned back on his stool and adjusted his cap. "We've had a few discussions about how she doesn't think they're authentic enough."

I chuckled. "That's okay though, right?"

"Yeah. Of course. Some tyers stay away from synthetics completely. What do you think about them?"

I sat back on my stool and stared at some of the tube flies I'd made with Henry's help. They were special in their own way, bigger and more elaborate than any of the flies I'd tied with Izzy thus far. Henry explained to me that they were quite versatile since you had the ability to switch hooks rather than the entire fly, so I could see the merit in using a tube fly over a traditional.

"I'm not quite sure yet. I like them, but I could see Izzy's point."

Henry broke out laughing. "Smart move," he said. "Stay on her good side." Henry punched me in the shoulder and we both laughed even harder. I hoped it was a sign of our growing friendship. I could see Henry being the brother, uncle, and father that I never got to have. It was an awesome thought, but since I was still unsure of where I truly stood in Henry's eyes, I decided to change the subject to save myself from any further embarrassment.

"What are those?" I asked.

"Oh, the spey rods? Those are another type of rod used for fly fishing. They're built a little differently—usually longer—and you use two hands when you fish with them."

"So the casting style is different."

"Correct," Henry said, and a smile crossed his face. "That reminds me—" Just as he began what was sure to be a promising story, I noticed someone coming to the shop door, and within seconds Molly was skittering across the wooden floor. When Izzy appeared she immediately dropped to her knees to pet Molly.

"Hi, baby," she cooed. Watching her do something as simple as petting a dog made my head swim. Molly trotted off to her bed and Izzy joined us by the rack of fishing poles. "What's up, guys?"

"Your uncle was about to tell me some story."

"Oh! The one about the guy running down the river?"

Henry nodded and my eyes darted between them, eager to hear more.

"Ah, it's a classic," Izzy said. "Keep going, Henry."

Once again, Henry began the tale of the unlucky client, which began when the client's rod separated with the fish still attached. In an act of desperation and possibly insanity, he dove from the drift boat and swam to shore, where he then proceeded to chase the fish down river.

I lost it when Henry began waddling frantically around the store, imitating the client trying to run with waders full of water. Apparently the client managed to retrieve the top half of his pole before tripping on a rock and falling back into the river. His line broke not long after.

By this point, Izzy and I were nearly in tears and Henry was sprawled out on the shop floor, panting after finishing the reenactment.

"Can I steal Brody away, Uncle Henry?" Izzy wheezed.

"Yeah, sure. Wait, what time is it?" he asked, standing up again.

"It's almost five," I said.

"Really? Already?" Henry glanced at the watch on his wrist. I was surprised too. The more Henry and I talked and worked together, the faster time seemed to fly by. Talking to Henry was what I imagined it would be like to have a really good friend. He was patient with me and never pried.

"Wow, yeah. Get out of here, you two," he said. For some reason, Izzy was beaming at me and I was getting warm while I tried not to stare.

"You sure you don't need anything else?" I asked.

Henry clapped me on the shoulder. "I'm all set, I think. Thanks for your help today."

"No problem," I said.

Henry turned to Izzy. "Actually, before you go—did you have a chance to tie any of those flies I needed?"

"Yep." Izzy opened a flap on her bag, producing several bags of flies. "Brody and I tied a bunch this week."

"Great!" Henry said, waving the bags. "You two are my saviors. The rainbows have been nailing these lately." We waved goodbye and headed for the door.

"So, what's up?" I asked. Izzy was clearly excited about something, but she wasn't saying much as we drove somewhere that wasn't back to her parents'.

"I have something to take care of tonight, and I wanted to show you something that I think you might find pretty cool since you seem to be liking your new job so much."

"Alright," I said. We didn't drive long before Izzy turned into the parking lot of a high school.

"Is this your school?" I asked. She replied with a nod and hopped from the car. "I never thought I'd be in a school again."

"Don't worry, Brody. There's no exams or anything."

I managed a smile, but deep down that was the last thing I was worried about. Even after being gone two years, our walk down the empty hallways was like a trip back in time. The silence weaseled into my brain, digging up memories that I didn't want to recall.

One in particular came about while Izzy paused at her locker for more of her homework. It was like a waking dream. The sea of students dissipated to their classrooms and I was scrambling to get my things. I could still hear the hollow clang as the jocks pushed me into my locker, taunting me and stealing my lunch day after day.

"You all right?" When Izzy wrapped an arm around mine, the awful memories faded away.

"Yeah. You ready to go?" I asked.

"Not quite." Izzy showed me a few other parts of the school before finishing the tour at the library. She guided me to a section dedicated solely to fly fishing. "There's a lot of fly fishing history here in Oregon. I thought maybe you'd like to see this. The library here has a bunch of books on famous tyers, famous rivers, drift boat designers...all sorts of stuff."

I couldn't stop grinning as I thumbed through a few books we removed from the shelves.

"I remembered you said you worked in a library for a bit," she whispered.

"Yeah…Izzy, this rocks. Thanks for bringing me here. You look very pretty by the way."

"Thanks." Before I could reach up to grab another book, Izzy took hold of my arm and led me to the back of the library. Soon we were we surrounded by floor-to-ceiling bookshelves.

"Look at this," Izzy said, peeling open a thin book and handing it to me.

"A yearbook?"

"Yeah, my freshman year." I followed her finger across the page and grinned when she stopped at her picture. Although Izzy appeared slightly younger in the picture, the only major difference that I could see was her hair. Unlike the loose, wavy hair she had currently, Izzy was nearly unrecognizable behind a bush of permed hair.

"What do you think?" Izzy asked. "Some kids used to call me Frizzy Izzy."

"No kidding." I tried to hold back a gleeful chuckle. She nodded, and several times I glanced between her and the picture. *What do I think, Izzy? I think that you're beautiful and I'm too chicken to say much else.*

"You are so cute," I said. She bit her lip, closed the book, and returned it to its place on the shelf. I started to get nervous when she didn't say anything. *Maybe I should have said something else.* "Should we look at another?" I was overcome by a sudden urge to read through all the yearbooks.

Izzy, however, was still staring at the bookshelf, apparently lost in thought. "We could," she whispered. "Or we could try something else." She placed a hand on my stomach and pushed gently, causing me to bump into a bookshelf.

"Izzy…"

"Have you ever kissed someone in the library?" My head moved sideways ever so slightly. "Me either…"

When our lips touched, the electricity that zipped between us left my heart palpitating, but I didn't care. Izzy leaned in more and I let my hands come to rest on her hips. When she slid her hands around my neck, I hugged her even closer and she giggled again.

Sadly, our thirty seconds of fun was rudely interrupted by the arrival of very squeaky wheels. At the sound of the disrupting groan we found a grumpy looking janitor leaning against his cart, staring at us. "The library is closed for the evening, you two. Best get a move on."

We both let out an uneasy laugh and left the library as fast as we could. I didn't bother to ask any questions when we didn't head right for her car. The taste of our kiss was still lingering on my lips as we made our way across the campus toward the high mast lights that surrounded the football stadium.

I could hear the cheers of rowdy fans, and I noticed more and more people filing in toward the gate. Soon we fell into step with the crowd. The thrall of people made me uncomfortable, but with Izzy at my side it didn't bother me so much. After getting tickets, she led us up to the candy shack and bought me a cup of cocoa.

"I know it's probably not as good as what you make, but I

thought it would keep us warm," Izzy said.

"You're telling me you're chilly after that?"

"Hush, Brody." She swatted at me, but nothing could stop the dimples from appearing in her cheeks as her smile grew wider still. "Would you mind waiting right here?"

I withheld a sigh and swatted the ball of yarn atop her knit cap. Another smile danced across her face. I wished I could just go with her, but I wasn't about to let her know how nervous I was. "Yes, right here."

"I'll be back in a few," she said. With a quick sip from the cup and a reassuring smile, Isabel disappeared into the crowd. I pulled my jacket tighter and took a sip of the cocoa. Then I started searching the crowd, wondering where she'd run off to.

We just shared another random kiss in the library. She's not going to see some other dude, right? I let my eyes wander across the field. Fans were milling about in the bleachers; some were standing, others were sitting, scarfing down hot dogs covered with mustard and onions, and everyone seemed like they were talking. The constant buzz of speech made it hard for me to think, but just as I scanned the players who were lining up along the sidelines, I spotted Izzy striding toward the announcer's booth. Then a voice came over the stadium's loudspeaker.

"Welcome everyone to another Friday night football match. If everyone could please stand and remove their caps, it's time for the singing of our national anthem, and this evening it will be sung by our very own senior, Isabel Cooper."

I nearly dropped the cup of cocoa on the ground. "What

in the world?" I mumbled. All throughout the stadium, voices diminished until conversation ceased all together. The stadium was absolutely silent. Izzy took the microphone that was handed to her and turned to face the flagpole a short distance away. Then she started singing. In a short time, I had come to adore the way Izzy talked, the way she smiled, the way she was in general. Hearing her sing, however, sent my feelings for her to an entirely new level. Her notes echoed the beauty and perfection of the anthem. They were perfect, just like Izzy.

When the final note came, everyone clapped, but I cheered like Eugene High had just scored a touchdown. I couldn't remember a time when I'd actually cheered for something, and I stopped only when my exuberance drew some strange looks from the other fans. Izzy reappeared a couple minutes later, trying to maintain her inconspicuous expression, so I just handed her the cup of cocoa.

"Thanks." Izzy bit her lip and stared at me with her sage green eyes. "Are you going to say anything?"

"Honestly, I don't know what to say, Isabel. A kiss in the library and then you sneak off to go sing the anthem. That was amazing," I said, and her cheeks reddened even more.

"Did I hear you cheering?"

Before I could answer, another fan gave me away. "Yeah. That was him. You would have thought we scored already." We both laughed, and Izzy guided me toward the fence behind the bleachers.

"That's what you had to do?" I exclaimed.

"Yeah, I sing for a lot of the home games."

"That was…beautiful."

"Thanks. So, did you want to stay or…"

"It's up to you. What do you want to do?"

"I want to go back home and tie flies and have real hot cocoa," she said. Just for an instant I was transported back to a memory of my father yelling and screaming at me. I remembered cowering in the corner of my bedroom, wondering if my life would ever get better—if there would ever be something or someone who could replace the meager moments of happiness that my father stripped from me on a daily basis. The touch of her hand on my forearm brought me back to the present.

Fans cheered as Eugene High scored their first touchdown, but neither of us paid any attention. I continued to stare at Izzy, utterly speechless and wondering if I'd found that person to make me happy. I finally smiled and nodded and we left the stadium. When the sound of the game was only a dull roar, I leaned into her again.

"You know, I was thinking we could try making *tube* flies tonight."

Just like the day we met, Izzy stopped in her tracks and the expression on her face was priceless. Her eyes grew wide and her mouth shrunk to an adorably thin smirk. "What did you say, Brody?"

"Huh?" I said playfully.

She swatted at me, but I backed away. "My uncle told you to say that, didn't he?"

I laughed and started running across the parking lot toward her car. Izzy chased after me.

"He did, didn't he, Brody? I never told you about them!" She caught up to me and jumped on my back. Her hair brushed against my cheeks as she leaned forward, clasping her arms around my neck. I caught her legs and we both kept laughing as I spun us around in circles. For the first time in a long time, I felt like I belonged somewhere.

The days were starting to blur together as I became more and more accustomed to this new life in Eugene. Every day it seemed like I was meeting someone new—whether it was at the fly shop, the grocery store, or the library—and they were all friendly. Just before closing, many of the regulars came in off the rivers to make small talk with Henry or whoever was covering the counter. They would display photos of their best catches and share their stories of the day.

More and more I also noticed that I was truly enjoying life instead of dreading the lonely existence I'd been living before coming to Eugene. I mean sure, traveling was fun and all, but when you didn't have a place to call home or someone to spend time with, it made enjoying things much more difficult. Much of the enjoyment that I was experiencing now came from my time spent with Izzy and her family, but there were still moments when I sought out solitude.

Not long after starting my job at the fly shop, Henry gave me my own key to the shop. He said I was more than welcome to work a few extra hours cleaning up and packaging orders, so I used this to my advantage, tying flies in the back room once the shop closed in the afternoons.

One night, much like the night I arrived in Eugene, a cold rain was drumming down on the roof, but this time I was safe and dry in the shop. I pinched a fresh hook in the vice, careful not to catch my finger on the sharp point, and began tying another fly. Strewn across the counter were several reference books like *Charlie's Fly Box*, *The Complete Book of Fly Tying*, and *The Orvis Guide to the Essential American Flies*. Every few minutes I would flip to a different page in one to find a new pattern to try, and so far that night, I had tied ten new patterns. After giving the latest fly a dab of head cement, I stuck it in the box with the others. *Almost there.*

When the track on the CD player changed, I spun slowly on the stool while taking sips from a glass of water. Izzy had been kind enough to compile several CDs of hit music from the last two years, and I was listening to them on a radio that Henry kept in the back room. With a smile, I set the cup aside and returned to the vice. My thoughts began to drift like a fly on the current.

It's difficult to describe the emotional state I was in for most of those two years. Sure, there had been some bright moments: visiting the Bayou, working with the greens keeper, and riding around with Big Sammy. But those had only been short periods of time and hardly permanent. In the end, the result was always the same. I ended up alone, groping for any type of reassurance I could find.

It was times like these when I faced some of my toughest moments. I receded to some secluded place, alone with my thoughts. They would fester and spread, leaving me feeling powerless and without purpose. My father yelled at me in my dreams, and the memories taunted me in my waking hours.

Not even my precious paper and pen were enough to deter these thoughts. All the drawings that I'd worked so hard to make seemed worthless. I considered using them as fuel for a fire, and when that fire burned out, I'd let my fire burn out too. But I always woke up the next morning with the tiniest inkling of hope, and somehow that was enough to keep me going.

Despite knowing I shouldn't base my happiness on others, I was aggravated by couples who could be affectionate with one another, or worse yet, people who I knew were in relationships and let their work life interfere with their personal ones. I hated seeing people taking each other for granted. I promised myself time and time again that if I was ever lucky enough to find someone, I would never do that to them. I still wasn't quite sure where I stood with Izzy. Our random kisses were constantly floating around my brain, and yet I distinctly remembered glimpsing a guy's name on her phone.

Regardless, I certainly wasn't going to take her for

granted. I'd found solace in Eugene and hopefully it would last. The fly shop was a special place and the people that worked there seemed to appreciate my help, and for that I was truly grateful.

When the last fly was finished, I tucked the tackle box away in its hidden spot and closed up the shop. The rain was still falling when I left, but I didn't mind. I actually had a raincoat now, and that made the walk back to Izzy's rather pleasant. As the rain pounded down around me, I found myself thinking about the rainy days growing up. Nearly all of them were awful because my father had always gotten the most tuned up on those days. I knew that if I allowed myself to fall into those memories completely, I would be able to feel my father's drunken fury as if it were happening all over again—the kicks, shoves, slaps—everything.

But I didn't. I pushed those memories away in favor of happier ones, like the day Izzy and I met, or our most recent kiss in the library. I could have sworn the rain itself even picked up a more harmonious sound as it fell to the earth. Then the sound of a car jarred me from my daydreams. Cars passing in the night always made me nervous since cops often kept a strict lookout for miscreants. Even though I had nothing to hide, I had no desire to get picked up for appearing suspicious. When the car started to slow down, my body became tense like an Olympic sprinter. I was ready to run, but the voice that followed was a welcome one.

"Hey! Is that you, Brody?"

I pushed back my hood and gladly walked over to the driver's side of Izzy's Jeep.

"Yep. It's me."

She grinned and tugged playfully on the zipper of my jacket. "What are you doing out here? Mom stopped home before class and said you weren't there, and I checked the shop but you weren't there either."

"You must have just missed me. I was hanging out down there, doing some cleanup work for Henry. How was your ACT study group?"

"It was fine—kind of dull. Is everything all right?"

Instead of answering her, I nodded and stood there like an idiot getting rained on.

"Are you sure? I mean, I don't want to disturb you if you're on a moody jaunt or something," she said.

"You're a goof. I'm good. Really."

"Well get in! Let's go home."

I dashed around the front of the car and got inside.

"We should really get you a phone. Then you can call me for a ride or whatever."

"It's not a big deal," I said. "I don't mind."

"Well I do," Izzy said. "I don't want you to get sick or something." Her compassion seemed to know no bounds, and as I clicked the seatbelt into place I silently wished that I had courage enough to ask what was going on between us.

"You're really something," I said instead. When we got back to her mother's house, it didn't take either of us long to change into comfy, warm clothes and take our respective seats on the couch.

"Can I ask you something, Brody?" Her homework was spread out on the coffee table, but she hadn't touched it since retrieving it from her backpack.

"You always do that, you know."

"What?" she said.

"You always ask me if you can ask me a question. I think it's funny."

"Well, I just don't want to pry."

"You're not prying. If you haven't noticed, Izzy, I really like talking to you, so just ask."

"Okay. Why have you been trying to do so much around here? Sometimes I feel like you're putting a ton of pressure on yourself."

My teeth clicked together as I tried to come up with something to say. I wasn't sure how honest I could be. "With everything that's happened to me, I've had a hard time feeling like I'm good enough to do much of anything. I want to feel useful. I want to feel like I'm doing something meaningful."

"Well I think you're very useful, Mr. Math Tutor," she said with a grin.

"Thanks."

"Seriously! Okay, how about Mr. Chef? All the cooking that you do around here. I know my Mom appreciates that and so does Uncle Henry on the trips."

"You're being very kind."

"Well, I think you're great," she said. "Really great." Her voice was quiet now; only loud enough that I could hear.

"I think you're great, too," I replied. Her hand brushed against mine and then slid down to my elbow. We leaned in closer, and I briefly imagined the hopelessly romantic couple on some television show.

"I hope so," she whispered. "Because my momma's right. I'm pretty fond of you. I keep wanting to kiss you, especially after the library…"

My heart was starting to race. We were so close now. I slid my arm around her back and she scooted closer, but I could see the hesitation in her eyes. I felt it too. I wanted desperately to give in, but part of me still wondered for some reason if this would be nothing more than a fling. She was amazing and she could have anyone she wanted. Why me?

I also had no idea what I was doing, but I loved feeling her nervous breaths against my face. She put a hand against my cheek and without hesitation, I gently kissed her palm.

"Yeah," I whispered. "I've been a little nervous to bring anything up…"

"Me too." A playful giggle escaped her as I ran my hand along her leg. Our foreheads met as she leaned in closer.

"I think you're really beautiful, Isabel." The longing was becoming unbearable. Her perfume was like a drug sending my heart and brain into a frenzy.

"I think you're really cute, Brody…"

Whatever else she planned to say fell away when we

closed the gap. I couldn't believe how good it felt to kiss her again, and before I knew what was happening I was laying on the couch with Izzy on top of me. She slid her arms around my neck and I could feel her heart beating against my chest. When her shirt slid up exposing the small of her back, I let my fingers graze past, which made her giggle and kiss me even harder.

Then we both heard the discernible sound of the front door opening. With one last beautiful embrace, we separated and picked up our school work and book respectively just before her mother walked into the living room.

"How's it going, you two?" Heather asked.

"Good," we said in unison.

Heather yawned and lifted up the paper bag in her hand. "Not sure if you guys ate already, but I brought home dinner."

"Great," I said. "Thanks."

"Yeah. Awesome. I'm starving," Izzy replied.

Heather gave us a sleepy nod and expelled another huge yawn as she walked away. I was just about to give Izzy another kiss when her mother reappeared.

"How was your ACT group tonight, Izzy?"

"It was great. I mean, kind of boring, but every bit helps, you know?"

I grinned wildly at my book, trying not to laugh.

"Good," said her mother. "How was work today, Brody?"

"Huh? Um, it was great. I love my job."

Izzy snorted into her hand, but Heather must have been too tired to notice, because after yet another yawn she disappeared. We waited with baited breath, and soon Heather's footsteps could be heard going upstairs. Izzy turned to me, her eyes aglow with anticipation.

"My goodness, Brody, that was amazing," she laughed. "Are you all right?"

"What? Yeah. I just don't know what to say."

"So don't say anything." Izzy leaned in closer, letting her nose brush against mine. "Don't stop…"

I sank into the couch wondering if my life had truly taken a turn for the better.

For many teens, a Friday night in high school might mean hanging out with friends, going to the movies or perhaps the local football game. As I spent more time with Izzy, I realized this wasn't the case for her at all. Although she sang for some of the home games, Izzy was sort of a homebody, and for the last several years many of her Friday nights consisted of going to the pond to fly fish by herself. If she wasn't fishing, Izzy would hang out at home, spending time with Heather and tying flies for the shop. But since my arrival that simple routine had changed slightly.

In an effort to help me catch up on everything I'd missed while being a nomad, we spent many hours watching movies, which Izzy seemed to love because there was absolutely no way I could contain the childhood innocence that appeared when we watched any of the new action or superhero movies. It was even more pronounced when she took me to the theater for the first time. I stared in starry-eyed surprise at the giant screen while we whispered jokes and ate popcorn.

Some nights I would teach Izzy how to cook, and if Heather wasn't at class, she gladly played the role of the guinea pig. On other occasions Izzy and I would go out for dinner. It was strange for me, since normally I didn't have money enough to buy anything more than a grilled ham and cheese, but after several random nights of visiting the diner or a local fast food joint, there was a playful magic associated with each dinner date.

Most evenings would end with us tying for a couple hours. As I became more confident on the vice, we usually raced to complete a certain number of popular patterns that the shop needed most. One evening, Heather was attending class, so Izzy and I had gone out for dinner. We were lingering outside the diner talking, laughing about the slip 'n' slide that the greens keeper had made, when her phone rang.

I loved watching Izzy talk on the phone. Her expressions changed constantly, and then she would laugh and pause with a quizzical look on her face. Her hair would dance playfully when she tipped her head from side to side, and depending on where we were, Izzy would trace things with her fingers. But as this particular call came to a close, Izzy's expressions grew increasingly sour.

"Who was that?" I asked.

"My friend Taylor. She said there's some party downtown

by one of the universities."

All of a sudden, my stomach was rolling about like a boat on stormy waters. "Did you want to go?" I asked.

"I don't know. Something to do I guess."

"If you want to." I could have sworn there was a brief moment of hesitation on her face, but it disappeared in the blink of an eye. *Maybe she doesn't want to go either.*

"Do you really want to go?" Izzy asked.

An uneasy grin crossed my face. I hated lying. *Nope. I want to go back to your mom's and tie flies and stay up late talking with you.* "Do you?" I replied. We both laughed.

"Maybe it would be kind of fun." But there was no excitement in her words, no sense of adventure. Somehow I think we both knew it would be a drag, and yet neither one was confident enough to admit it.

"Yeah. Maybe," I said.

"So we'll go?"

I saw it this time. The way her eyes glanced at the ground before coming back to me. I knew part of her wished I would say no. But I wasn't completely certain. The only thing I was certain of was that I was a chicken. I didn't want her to think I wasn't adventurous.

"Sure."

After driving across town, Izzy parked the car a block or so away from the party, and even then we could hear the loud music blaring into the night. Izzy and I shared an apprehensive glance and started walking. My nerves were on edge, and I had to force myself not to count the sidewalk lines. I considered reaching for her hand, but I didn't do that either.

Several individuals were hanging around the porch having a smoke as we made our way up the steps of the party house, and I could feel the heavy bass notes booming in my chest. Once again I wished we could turn back the way we came.

But instead, we walked through the door and lingered in the entryway, waiting for Taylor. My head was swiveling every which way as I tried to get my bearings in the sea of people. One of the first things that caught my eyes was a couple in the living room. The lady was kneeling on top of some guy sitting in a dingy recliner. As she kissed his neck, his hands fondled every part of her body they could reach. When I looked back at Izzy, she was also staring at the pair on the recliner, looking equally disgusted.

"What's wrong? Do you know them or something?" I asked.

At first Izzy didn't say anything, but when her words finally came, they were barely audible over the loud music. "That's Derek."

The woman flashed Derek a seductive smile and reached for his hand when she stood up. Before disappearing into the crowd, Derek gave the woman's butt a squeeze, which she seemed to enjoy. I cringed slightly, wondering how that made Izzy feel. Then I felt her hand on my arm. She gave me a quick smile, which I tried to return, but all I managed was an awkward shrug.

It was difficult to maintain the same level of composure that she had. There were so many people cramped in the small space of the frat house, and I didn't care for it. Many of the girls were clutching red party cups and dancing to the music that thumped from unseen speakers like a heartbeat throughout the house. I noticed that some of them barely had any clothes on, and many of them were being eyed up by the sultry, jockey types who lingered around the edges of the rooms. The house reeked of sweat, weed, and alcohol that was getting pressed into the floors as it splashed out of people's cups.

"Hey!" We both turned to see a girl with reddish hair and freckles come up to greet us. "Wild party, huh?"

"Yeah," Izzy said. "I didn't know you were into this sort of thing."

"What? Yeah! I mean, once in a while," she said. "Getting ready for the college experience, you know?"

"Sure." Izzy was looking more thrilled by the second. I couldn't blame her. While Taylor swayed to the music, Izzy and I watched a group of guys trying to support a buddy who was clearly too drunk to walk any more. He finally puked in the container of a very depressed-looking house plant, and the rest of the group roared with laughter.

"So, who's this?" Taylor asked.

"This is my friend Brody." Izzy frowned slightly as a new, even louder song began blasting through the house. "This is Taylor."

"Nice to meet you," I replied.

"You too. You guys want something to drink?" Taylor asked.

"I just want a water," Izzy said.

"Me too," I said.

"Aw, come on," Taylor said. "You guys are gonna hang out for a while, right?"

"Yeah, maybe," Izzy said, and apparently that was enough for her buzzed friend. We made our way down one of the hallways toward the kitchen, and in one of the rooms along the hallway I caught a glimpse of a few girls and guys sectioning out lines of white powder with playing cards. It made me shudder.

I was no stranger to drugs, but I wondered if Izzy had ever seen this before. If she had, she gave no indication. I shuddered again when I saw the kitchen. It was a mess of blenders, margarita mix and liquor bottles, beer cans, and pizza boxes. I could feel something unsettling brewing in my stomach, but I tried not to pay attention to it. Taylor yanked open the fridge door and grabbed a bottle of water for each of us.

"So!" Taylor said. "How did you two meet anyway?"

"What?" I asked. Izzy smiled and watched her friend repeat the question. "I work for her uncle."

"Oh, at the shop. Very cool!" Taylor said. "So you're a fly fishing junkie like Izzy, too?" Whether she meant it to be insulting or not, it bothered me. A quick glance at Izzy let me know that the comment had stung her as well.

"I love it," I said. "It's the best thing I've ever done."

"Cool, cool," Taylor replied, before burying her face in the cup. Then her eyes dilated as if she was struck with the ultimate epiphany. "Can I talk to you for a second, Izzy?"

"What? Yeah, sure," Izzy said.

"In private," Taylor added.

Izzy glanced at me and rolled her eyes. Somehow I knew exactly what she was thinking. *Good luck finding any privacy here, Taylor.*

"Oh, um…yeah," she said. "Do you care, Brody? I just gotta chat with her for a sec."

"No, go ahead," I said. "I'll be fine." In truth, I was terrified. This was growing increasingly uncomfortable, and no sooner had Izzy wandered off than I felt someone nudge my shoulder. I turned to find a girl in a tight black dress staring at me. The high heels she had brought her up to my eye level, but the icy blue eyes hiding behind her sleek blonde hair couldn't seem to focus on anything.

"Hey." Her voice was whiny and irritating and she stepped closer to me, trying to press her chest against me.

I don't know who you are, and I know that some of the guys here would probably be all over you, but not me.

"Hi." I promptly stepped back because the smell of cigarettes and stale perfume hovering around her was making my eyes water.

"Isn't this party nuts?" she said.

"Oh yeah, a real rager," I replied. "It's legendary." My sarcasm was lost on her.

"Totally, right?" She started laughing after taking a sip from her cup. "Have you seen all the bubbles?" she asked.

"Excuse me?"

"Check this out, dude." Her hand grazed my arm again as she leaned forward, offering me her cup. It was full of foamy beer, fresh from the keg.

"Look at all the bubbles," I said.

"Right? There's so many. I love bubbles." She took another gulp and I stared helplessly at the ceiling.

Dear God, please let Izzy come back. I glanced around but there was still no sign of her. Bubble girl nudged my arm again.

"What's your favorite kind of bubbles?"

I stared at her, utterly speechless and wanting to burst out laughing. "Um…dish soap bubbles, I guess."

"Oh, those are great. They make good bubbles, but I think I like these bubbles better. I can drink these bubbles." The girl took another swig from the cup.

I looked around again, desperate for Izzy to return, and then finally she was back. I beamed when she got up on her tiptoes to whisper in my ear. "You ready to get out of here?"

"Yes, please," I said. "Nice talking to ya." Bubble girl raised her nose in disgust at being rejected, but within seconds she was yanked away by another frat guy. Izzy and I threaded our way through the maze of people, only to be waylaid just short of the front door. A guy stepped out in front of Izzy, and foamy beer sloshed over the side of his cup. I watched in disgust as it ran down his arm and began dripping onto his shoe.

Apparently he was already too drunk to notice.

Chills ran down my spine as I thought of my father stumbling around the house, spilling liquor from his glass as he cursed at me. The frat guy's voice brought me back to the moment along with a bubbling sense of anger.

"Is this guy bothering you, sweet thing? Wouldn't you rather stay here with me tonight?" he asked. "I've got a great room upstairs."

"No, dude. I'm fine. We're leaving," Izzy said. His eyes flashed to me as if telling me to get lost. He was taller than me, but not by much, his chest a little broader than mine. That much was evident from the dorky, tight clothes he was wearing, but I just kept staring at his stupid, drunken sneer.

"I don't think so," he said. "I think we should dance and have a little fun. Derek said you probably won't call back, but that's fine. One night is good enough for me." When the frat guy made a motion to grab Izzy, she stepped back and shook her head. Her eyes were alive with anger.

"I said I'm good. Would you mind moving out of the way?"

"Come on, baby…" The frat guy tried to step between us and my nerves flared into something I'd never felt before. My hands flew to the guy's chest, and with little effort I sent him into a nearby wall with a resounding thud that cracked the drywall.

"She said *we're leaving*. We're leaving."

The guy's macho demeanor faded instantly as the remnants of the cup ran down his face, soaking his shirt.

"Yeah. Alright man. Whatever," he said. "I don't want Derek's leftovers anyway."

The sound of the party disappeared as adrenaline and anger surged. I lunged forward, ready to bury my fist in his mouth, but at the last second Izzy caught my arm.

"Let's go, Brody. It's not worth it."

I could barely hear her over the heartbeat drumming in my ears, but I felt her tug on my arm again. "It's not worth it, Brody. Come on."

The world was a blur of whispers and startled expressions as Izzy pulled me out to the porch and led me down the steps. While we hurried down the sidewalk I took several deep breaths, and gradually my pounding heart subsided. Izzy eventually let go of my arm, but continued shooting me nervous glances. When her car came into sight her pace slowed, and then she stopped completely.

"What was that, Brody?"

"I could ask you the same thing, Izzy."

"What's that supposed to mean?"

"You know exactly what I mean: 'Derek's leftovers.'"

"Please tell me you're not going to take something that drunk dumbass said seriously."

I shrugged.

"You're unbelievable." Izzy started for her car again.

"Well come on, Izzy. We just met not too long ago. How am I supposed to know?"

Izzy stopped on a dime. Before I could say another word, she was back in front of me, jabbing a finger against my chest. "If you hadn't noticed, Brody, Derek was getting dry humped by his new play toy in the middle of that living room. I found out all about the bullshit games he played. That's why I never did anything with him. He probably told his stupid-ass roommates how he broke my heart, when I was the one that told him adios! So if you want to know something, ask me!"

The silence that followed cut through me like a knife. "I'm sorry, Izzy." I tried to nudge her shoulder and keep walking again, but she jabbed me in the chest again.

"No way, Brody. We're not done yet. You still have to answer my question."

I shrugged again. "Don't worry about it. It doesn't matter."

"It matters to me! You looked like you were ready to blow that guy away."

"Well, I'm sorry if I scared you," I said.

"I'm not scared. I just want some answers. Is this what you meant by the fights in school? Did you just wallop on kids? Because if you were a bully—"

"I wasn't a bully, Izzy." I stared down at my feet, taking a deep breath to steady my nerves. Then she lifted my chin up with a finger.

"You got picked on then?"

I nodded. "All the time."

"Are you lying to me? Because that was wicked intense."

I gritted my teeth. "No, I'm not lying, and like I said—I'm sorry. I didn't mean to get so worked up."

"Everybody gets angry, Brody, but that was more. That was something else."

"I just don't like that kind of stuff. Drunk guys piss me off. You've been so nice to me, and I wasn't going to let him be an ass about anything." My heart was starting to pound in my ears again. Izzy stared back at me with worry and indecision in her eyes. When I still didn't say anything, she turned for her car, leaving me standing like an idiot on the sidewalk. Then the passenger window rolled down.

"Are you coming?"

"I can walk back."

"Brody, we're on the other side of town," she said, but I only shrugged. "Don't be dumb. Just get in."

The engine rumbled to life and I stood there on the side-walk, unable to shake the feeling that I'd ruined everything. It made me want to run. But at the same time, I couldn't help but notice how frazzled she was. The last thing I wanted to do was abandon her, so I climbed in. I was hoping for some conversational epiphany to manifest itself, but each block that passed was more quiet than the last.

Izzy left the radio on, but only on a low murmur, like a mosquito buzzing in my ear. She was definitely upset. Although her focus was on the road, her hands never stayed in the same place for long—steering wheel, lap, door latch. She even rolled down the window and let her arm dangle in the breeze for a while. I wanted desperately to take her hand, but instead I let my forehead thud against the window where it stayed the remainder of the drive.

My hopes of talking when we got back to her mother's were also thwarted. As soon as we walked in the door, Izzy hurried off without a word, leaving me standing dumbfounded in the entryway. I listened to her fading footsteps and the eventual closing of her bedroom door. With a sigh I headed for the bathroom, and then the living room, where I stared dismally at the ceiling.

I don't want Derek's leftovers anyway. The words replayed in my head over and over. Just hearing him mention Derek made my blood pressure surge. When I closed my eyes, all I could see was that pitiful expression locked onto Izzy like she was a piece of meat. I rolled over again, trying to rid myself of those images, but nothing seemed to help. When I finally decided sleep wasn't going to happen, I went to the closet where Izzy kept her tying supplies. I spent the rest of the night at the kitchen table, drinking tea and tying whatever came to mind.

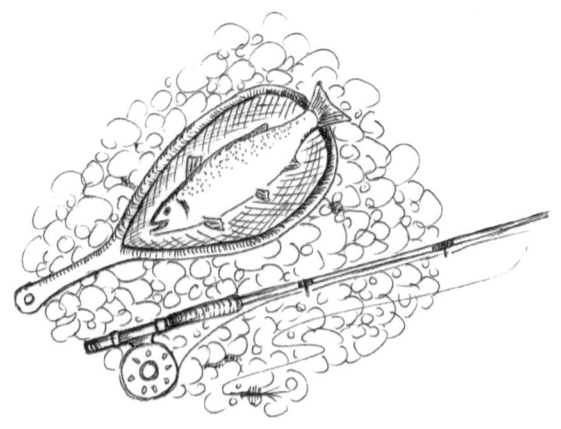

A few hours later, someone nudged my shoulder.

"Wake up, Brody."

When my eyes fluttered open, the kitchen was dark, but I could just make out the huge pile of flies I'd tied beside my empty cup. Then I noticed Izzy standing beside me.

"Did you tie all night?" she whispered.

"I guess. I couldn't sleep."

"Probably my fault."

"You're not the one that pushed someone into a wall. You're fine, Izzy."

"Yeah, well, we'll talk about that later. Can you be ready to go in twenty minutes?"

I replied with a sleepy groan.

"Is that a yes then? Or do you need more beauty sleep?"

161

"Beauty sleep?" I repeated. Her quiet laughter filled the kitchen. Then to my surprise, she ran a hand through my hair before leaving to get ready. I slouched back against the table enjoying the smell of her perfume that lingered in the air. I got up to get dressed, and when I returned Izzy was just dashing from the kitchen again.

"Here's a bowl of oatmeal," she said. "Wait here. I'm gonna go say bye to Mom and then we can go." I'd barely managed a bite of breakfast before she was hurrying back into the kitchen.

"Where are we going?" I asked.

"You'll see. Can I have a bite?"

I lifted the spoon to her mouth after she slid into her hoodie, and then we were off. At first there was only the sound of music and the clinking of dishes as I finished the bowl of oatmeal in the passenger seat. No matter how good breakfast was though, there was a question nagging at me that food couldn't deter.

"Are you still mad at me?"

"Mad at you?" Izzy glanced at me. "I wasn't mad at you, Brody. I was just startled. Last night was ridiculous. I didn't really want to go to that party."

"Me either."

"I'm sorry. Taylor said it would be fun. I didn't know she was into that kind of stuff."

"Don't be. I don't care. I didn't want you to think I was lame or something if I didn't want to go."

"Seriously? Because I didn't want you to think I wasn't adventurous or whatever," she replied.

"But you're the most adventurous person I know. You like to go out hiking and fishing and everything. Going to a frat party isn't adventurous. It just seems kind of pathetic to me."

"So, you wouldn't have done anything with that girl then?" she asked.

"Are you kidding me? No way! Talking to her was like talking to an intoxicated baby. She was fascinated by the bubbles in her cup. That's what she kept laughing at the entire time you were gone. I hardly said anything."

Izzy giggled. "Well, just for the record, that was pretty cool what you did there—getting that guy to buzz off." She reached over and ruffled my hair. "Sorry about stressing you out last night."

"It's fine. Gave me an excuse to practice tying." I fingered the door latch as another question came to mind. "So how long did it take to convince your mom to let us go out on a real trip?"

"It took a little while. You've sort of been going through a probation period," Izzy laughed.

"Ah, good ole probation." I stared out the window at nothing in particular since the sun had yet to rise.

"I'm sorry," she blurted out. "I didn't mean to offend you—"

"No, no. You're fine," I said. "It's like that in every home I've been in. You know, because the foster parents have to see if I'm a good fit—if the checks will be worth it type of thing. This is the first time I've actually really enjoyed being somewhere. Glad to know I made it through."

"The checks?"

I turned away from the window and stared at her. "Foster parents get paid by the State to take care of foster kids. Some do it because they love to help kids. Others see it as a lucrative business opportunity, and usually that means the kids get the short end of the stick."

"That's terrible," Izzy said.

"Yep, it's pretty sad."

"Brody, I hope you know that my mom really likes having you around. She wouldn't do this for any sort of money."

I turned to Izzy, hoping deep down that were true. She had the one thing in life that I wished for every day. As signs and street lamps passed by, I tried to imagine what it would be like if my mom and I could have spent time together traveling.

"I'm serious, Brody, and I like having you around too."

"So I can help you with your homework." That earned me a punch in the shoulder. When our laughter subsided, I decided to risk another question. "Are you embarrassed by me?"

"What?" Izzy asked. "Why would I be embarrassed by you?"

"I don't know. I mean, since we started hanging out I haven't really seen you with any of your friends. I know I met Taylor yesterday, but I was just kind of wondering if maybe…you were embarrassed by me or something." When she didn't say anything right away, I turned back to the window. "It wouldn't offend me if you are. I mean, I'm not exactly like—"

"Brody," she said. "Look at me."

"No. You're driving," I said, and we both laughed.

"Good point. Brody, I'm not embarrassed or ashamed of you at all. I really like hanging out with you. I just don't have that many friends."

"What do you mean? Why not? You're great! You fish and you sing!"

Izzy shrugged. "I don't know. It's just been hard with my dad being gone all the time and my mom being back in school. My sister is way older than me, too. I just got used to being alone, I guess. I like spending time at home because then I can see Mom more, and I like helping Uncle Henry out with shop stuff. I don't know. I guess to me, it just seems like family is something a lot of people take for granted."

"Is that why you helped me?"

"Partially. I mean, yeah. Clearly something was wrong and I wanted to help. Does it bother you that I don't have many friends?"

"Not really; just means I get to spend more time with you."

Izzy's lips curved into a smile as she turned up the radio.

"Until you need a break from me because my humming gets too annoying for you," I added.

She faked an exasperated sigh, but did nothing to hide another grin. "Or until I get impossibly needy for you, Brody, and you run away to Portland." She shoved my shoulder again.

I was grateful for her sense of humor and for her taste in music. My worries about the night before finally were gone and I drifted into a daze, staring out the window again, enjoying the catchy beats and melodies.

As we followed the highway into the mountains, rays of early morning sunlight broke through the swirling mass of clouds, illuminating fields and forests alongside the road. The lively green hues made me think of Izzy's eyes, which I loved. The vibrant scenery along the rivers only seemed to get better, and I couldn't help but take pictures with my guide camera.

Izzy slowed the car and turned off the highway onto a gravel road, and not long after that we came to a stop. I sat back in my seat, wondering what the day might bring.

"What do you think?" she asked.

"It seems even better than usual."

"How come?"

"I don't know. Maybe because...the air is just a little sweeter and crisper on this beautiful September day."

Izzy rolled her eyes and got out of the car. "Uhuh," she said.

I smirked and followed her to the trunk. "Or maybe, Izzy, it's because...when the sun finally rises it's going to shine down brightly upon us."

"Oh my goodness. Get out of here." Izzy gave me a shove while I was trying to put on my waders. It was just enough to knock me off balance, and I collapsed into a fresh mud puddle. I stared up at her in dismay as she cupped a hand over her face, trying not to laugh.

"Oh, Brody, I'm sorry."

I pretended not to hear her. "Or maybe it's because I'm up in the mountains with this girl I like, and not even a muddy butt can disappoint me."

Her laughter filled the morning air as she helped me up. Once our gear was situated, we wandered down the trail from the parking area, welcoming the sounds of branches and leaves crunching under our boots. Soon the familiar sound of rushing water met our ears.

"This moves a little faster than the pond," she said.

"I know. I've been having a hard time figuring this out." So far, I'd been out a half dozen times with Henry and had yet to catch a fish.

"I'll show you," Izzy said. She suggested we hike to a spot where the river was calmer, and I made no objections to this. We followed the winding trail, dodging scraggly brush and low hanging branches. After skirting around a set of rough rapids, the river opened up significantly. It was perfect.

While Izzy retrieved a box of flies from her pack, I gawked at the river from behind the lens of my camera. Wading would be easier because the edges of the river had slowed to a gentle drift, but the main part of the river was still moving at a good pace.

"How do fish even see these when the water is moving this fast?" I asked.

Izzy shrugged as she tied a fly to her line. "It's what they do. Here. Which one would you like?"

I stared at the assortment of flies and picked out a thick, olive-colored wooly bugger. Izzy watched patiently as I fiddled with the leader.

"You've been practicing that knot I showed you," she said.

"Yeah," I replied, giving the leader a final tug. The knot held. I grinned proudly and we stepped into the river.

"Okay. So the first thing, I'm sure Henry already told you, but don't rush. Just be patient and watch your footing. There can be all sorts of funny drop-offs and surprise currents. I don't want to see you washed down river," Izzy said.

"Me either."

"Let's fish then," she said. With her demonstrations and patient instruction, I finally began picking up the subtleties of mending my cast on moving water.

"How long did it take you to get good at this?" I asked.

"Probably a few trips was enough to get a general idea, but I'm still learning stuff because the conditions are always changing and each river is different. A lot of the rivers out here are really wide, but when you go out east where you're from, a lot of the rivers are narrow and brushy, so you have to change up your strategy a little bit—use a smaller pole, stuff like that. I used to come here a lot when Henry had more free time. The shop has really picked up in the last few years though, so we haven't had as much time to get out. You're doing good though."

"Thanks," I replied, but after a few minutes of nothing

exciting happening I began to feel discouraged. Bluegill were opportunistic feeders that hit flies almost relentlessly, but trout were much more selective, and it was a lot of work paying attention to my casting as well as my footing. On top of that, I found myself glancing at Izzy since she was by far the best distraction. Her casting was beautiful and elegant, just as she had said to me the day we met. Then her pole bent sharply.

"Whooo, Brody!" she called out. "Could you grab the net?" I grinned and reeled in my line. After retrieving the net from shore, I waded down to her and listened to the line whistle off the reel. Every few seconds she would slow the reel down with her palm and pull back on the rod in an effort to slow down the fish, but it was no use. The end of the pole continued to bob this way and that as the fish tried to get away.

"Did you see it yet?" I asked.

"Not yet. But I bet it will jump—" The words had barely left her mouth when a chrome fish burst from the river.

"Oh my goodness," she breathed.

"What?"

"It's a big one," Izzy said. I watched as she slowly worked the pole, making sure to keep the line taut against the fish. Finally it was too worn out to continue, and she reeled the steelhead into the shallows. I slid the net around the magnificent specimen. Its back was smoky gray and covered with black dots, while its belly was a combination of silver and white. These two colors were separated by a faint strip of pink running the length of its body.

"Can you hold it there? I'm going to grab my camera," Izzy said.

"Definitely." A moment later, she set the camera strap around my neck and then carefully lifted the fish from the net.

"Wow," I gasped.

"What?"

"Nothing. Just keep smiling." I did my best to hold the camera steady while my legs wobbled underneath me. Her wavy hair was blowing all over the place and her green eyes sparkled like emeralds. I clicked the button a few times. "Alright you're good."

Izzy nodded and gently set the fish back in the river. Very slowly, she moved it back and forth, letting the water flow over the gills. Then she let go, and with a powerful stroke of its tail the fish disappeared into the current.

"Why did you make that face when you were taking the picture?" she asked.

I shrugged and handed back the camera. The truth was, I had no idea what to say. All the excitement and adrenaline had left me speechless, but when Izzy snapped a few pictures of me, the silence was broken with jovial laughter. She leaned into me and snapped a couple more of us together. If ever there was a romantic moment, it had to be this one. I wanted so badly to spill my guts and kiss her, but instead I trudged back to shore and picked my rod off the bank.

"Hey!"

I turned to see Izzy staring at me. "Are you really not going to say anything?" she asked.

Somewhere in my head, my brain tried to punch me. *Stop being a wuss, Brody.* "You're absolutely stunning."

All I could hear was the river, so I wasn't sure if she heard me, but several times her mouth opened and closed as if she wanted to say something. In the end, she just smiled and sent out another cast.

As I waded out into the river again, it finally began to dawn on me why Izzy and Henry and everyone else enjoyed fly fishing so much. It wasn't just about catching some prize-winning steelhead or muskie. It was about appreciating life and nature. Being out on the river was like hitting the reset button. Standing there knee deep in the crystal blue water, casting my line, it felt like my life was finally starting to mean something.

A sudden sharp yank brought me back to reality, and I hastily tugged on the line and pole. There was definitely something, and then another fish burst from the river.

"Izzy!" But my whoop of joy was premature. The fish's body torqued and twisted in the air and then the line went slack. I watched the fish fall with a splash back into the current.

"It spit the hook!" Izzy exclaimed. "Do you still have your fly?"

"Yeah!"

"Cast out again. Don't let it get away!"

I whipped the line back and forth, thinking about her reassuring smile. The fly hit the water and disappeared into the current. When the next bite came I was ready, and the hook set was perfect. Just like Izzy's had done, my reel screamed as the fish fought to get anywhere free of the line, and suddenly I felt like the one holding on for dear life.

"Be patient, Brody." Izzy's voice was calm but excited as she waded up next to me. It was nothing like the bluegills back in the pond. Fighting little panfish was comparable to pulling a paper plate through the water. Steelhead, on the other hand, tugged continuously, threatening at any moment to snap the line if the angler wasn't paying attention. The anticipation was insane, and I could feel my heart pounding in my fingertips. I tried to play the fish as carefully as possible, and after several minutes I was able to guide the fish into shore. The twenty-four inch specimen glistened in the shallows, and I stared in disbelief at what I'd just accomplished.

"You did it, Brody!"

"Holy crap, Izzy. They're so strong." It was hard to talk between my exhilarated breaths.

"I told you, Brody! Pick it up. Let me get your picture!" She lifted the camera and snapped several pictures of me holding my first ever steelhead. Once the fish was back in the river, she hugged me as hard as our bulky fishing clothing would allow. Nobody had ever hugged me the way she did. When we separated, it started to rain.

It was pleasant at first—a soft rain that carried the smell of fall. But after a few minutes it came down harder, so we retreated to the bank to have lunch. Izzy retrieved a tarp from her pack and made a makeshift lean-to while I got a fire going before the wood around us got too wet.

"Do you have another funny story?" Izzy asked.

I shrugged while watching the flames catch on the sparse bits of dry grass and pine needles. "I don't know. Maybe."

"Come on. Something random like the movie story," she said. "I need a good laugh."

"Alright, how about disturbingly uncomfortable funny?"

Izzy's bangs bounced up and down as she nodded excitedly.

"Okay. Well, I was in New Orleans for a while, and it seemed like they were always having some sort of parade or festival, which meant I saw a lot of weird stuff."

"Tell me!"

"I picked up a few shifts at this divey bar, and after I got off one night I started wandering around, looking for a place to crash."

"Doesn't that freak you out?"

"I got used to it," I said with another shrug. "Anyway, I was walking down the street and I needed to go to the bathroom. There's bars everywhere, so I decided to go to the next one I saw."

Izzy was already grinning from ear to ear.

"I started walking up the steps of this bar, and I saw a woman outside talking on her cell phone. No big deal right—except all I could hear was a dude's voice."

Her laughter was instantaneous. "Brody, are you going to say what I think you're going to say?"

"Yeah, and by that point I had already committed, you know? So, I went through the door and made for the bathrooms. But the bathrooms were…"

"What? Did you have a run-in with another drag queen?" she asked. I shook my head as more of the bizarre memories resurfaced.

"No, but the sign that should have said *Ladies* said *Others* instead, and the artwork in the guys' bathroom was so disturbing. Imagine trying to take a leak while staring at a row of dudes bent over, taking their pants off."

Izzy laughed so hard that she slid off the log we were sitting on. "Oh my goodness, Brody."

"Are you okay?" I asked, helping her back up.

"Yeah. I'm good. Was there any other artwork?"

"Yeah, but you don't want to know."

"Yes I do."

I shook my head. "No you don't."

"It's that bad, huh?"

"Yes. Sometimes it haunts my dreams."

Tears were starting to run down her face from laughing so hard. "Can you please give me a little hint?"

I sucked in a breath and stared at the tarp above my head. "It was very…phallic."

Izzy slid from the log again, but stayed put in the dirt, trying to wipe her eyes clean. "Will you ever tell me?"

"Maybe someday." I took her outstretched hand and pulled her up once again. Then I prodded the sticks in the fire. A welcome warmth danced across our bodies as the flames grew higher. She scooted closer to me.

"Did you listen to them sing?"

"I may have stayed for a song or two."

"Did you sing along?"

"Excuse me?" My head moved from side to side, but my lips curled into an awkward smile.

"You did, didn't you, Brody?"

"Maybe."

Izzy shrieked in delight. "You sang with drag queens?"

I could only guess how red my cheeks were when I finally nodded.

"Would you ever sing with me?" Izzy asked.

"Seriously? You sing like an angel. I'd be like nails on a chalkboard next to you."

"No, no, no. I bet you have a lovely voice, Brody. You probably got fantastic lessons from the drag queens."

I pushed her playfully. "You know it…maybe I will hum along with you sometime."

Izzy beamed at me, and then to my surprise she produced several containers of food from her bag. "What? Did you think I was going to make you fend for yourself out in the wild?"

"I don't know," I said. "We could have had fish I suppose."

"Just flatten out a spot on those coals, okay?"

I obliged, and a few minutes later she plopped a cast iron pan onto the fire and started heating up some meat and beans.

"That right there is a meal fit for cowboys, Izzy. I feel like we're on the frontier."

"I know, right? And definitely delicious," she said. "I've been practicing more since you started teaching me."

"Great. I can't wait." From our spot on the bank I watched the hazy, fragrant smoke drift out over the river. Even with the falling rain, part of me wanted to keep fishing because I love being in the river, but then I was possessed by the strongest urge to put my arm around Izzy. Before I could take the chance though, she asked another question.

"Brody, I was wondering something."

"What's that?"

"Well, we've been hanging out a lot, and I think of questions to ask you. A lot of questions actually, but then I worry about offending you and I don't ask them."

"Isabel, you can ask me anything."

"Well... What was last night about? What really happened to you anyway? I mean, can I ask you that? Does that count as 'anything'?"

I sighed and prodded the coals with a stick. "Do you really care? Not many people really care about depressing shit."

"Do you think I'd be spending this time with you if I didn't care?" The look in her eyes was so intense that I had to look away. It was clear to me that she wouldn't be deterred by anything. I loved that about her, but it also made me nervous because she was breaking through every wall that I'd put in place to protect myself against my emotions and memories. When I looked at her again, Izzy's green eyes had yet to move.

"I suppose not," I said.

"So…" She handed me a dish with some carrots and cucumbers.

"Well, I was a foster kid by twelve and on my own by sixteen," I said. "I told you that already."

"A vagabond."

"Yes, thank you. Actually, now it's a fly fishing guide."

Isabel laughed. "Right and tomorrow it will be…a trucker like Big Sammy?"

"Eh, I don't know if I'd like trucking. Plus, I'd need another license. Being a guide for this stuff would be more fun I think."

"You'd have to stick around for a while then."

"Yeah and I'm liking it here more and more. And your uncle helped me get trained and CPR certified—don't want to waste that."

"No, of course not," Izzy said. "So, what else did you do besides truck driving and stage singing?"

"Well you know about me being a farmer, a janitor, and a greens keeper…" We both knew I was stalling, but Izzy didn't seem to mind. She spooned our lunch into bowls while I stared at the steady stream of water dripping off the lean-to roof, wondering if I was really ready to open up to her. After adding a sprinkle of cheese, she handed me the warm bowl.

"Thanks, Izzy." Her hand grazed mine, leaving behind a soothing tingle. It occurred to me then that Izzy made me feel like we were in the eye of the storm. Whenever I was around her, it was calm and peaceful. The cheery smile on her face made me feel warm in a way our fire could not. Her radiant personality made me think of Christmas—full of hope and happiness. Sadly, nothing I was about to tell her was happy.

"I never met my mother, Izzy. She passed away giving birth to me."

The smile on her face vanished. "Brody. I'm so sorry."

"That's not even the worst part, Isabel." A funny noise escaped me.

"Brody…"

"My dad raised me for a while, but my mom dying really ruined him, and he blamed me for it I think. Stuff was all right for a while, but the older I got the more he drank. I think maybe it had something to do with the fact that I looked more like her or something…" It was getting hard to talk and Izzy was looking at me in this way that just…I didn't know what to think. Her eyes were getting shiny, and part of me wished we could just eat in silence and keep fishing. Thunder rumbled in the distance and then the floodgates opened.

"He was an alcoholic and a drug addict before I even got into middle school. He beat me all the time. The last night he did, the neighbor called the cops and he was arrested. I didn't have anyone else, so I got put into the system. The rest is history and I haven't seen him since."

"Brody…" There were no words and I didn't expect there to be. Her eyes filled with tears and she just kept staring at me. I just sat there feeling the same way I did whenever I thought about my earlier years. Awful. Empty. Frustrated. I was worried that my sob story had fatally wounded the mood, and I stared in dismay at the bowl in my hands, no longer hungry. More thunder rumbled above us as we sat in silence on the log.

"So that day you were super worried about my mom thinking you were a drug addict…"

"Yeah. It kind of hit close to home, and your mom seems pretty awesome as far as moms go. Seeing as how I don't have one, I would love for her to like me."

"She does like you, Brody."

"I hope so. I'm sorry. I didn't mean to ruin the fun vibes or romantic vibes or whatever is going on."

In a flash, Izzy's hand was on my face, but it wasn't heavy handed like a slap from my inebriated father. It was a smooth, kind hand turning my face to hers. Then her forehead was against mine and I could feel her breath on my face. "Romantic vibes?" she repeated.

"Yeah, I don't know. This seems nice. You brought carrots and cucumbers and you're so nice. I mean you're great…"

Then we were kissing. She ran her fingers through my hair, grazing my cheeks along the way. Tingles shot down my spine, spreading through my body like wildfire. I held her close because I never wanted to forget the soft tenderness of her lips.

When she pulled away, we both giggled and the rain pounded down around us, but our lean-to held. Then something dawned on me and I gaped at her, no longer afraid to ask the question.

"Isabel, what was the deal with that Derek guy? I mean, I know he called you…"

She just laughed and shook her head.

"That first night you were at my house, I told him we were done. I mean, he was going to college and we weren't really a thing anyway, but I still told him that I didn't want anything."

"What happened?"

"You happened."

"Oh. Alright then," I said. "That's great."

"Yeah? So, you're interested then?"

"Interested. Yep."

We scooted closer together on the log and waited for the storm to run its course.

By the time we finished lunch the rain had passed, and we returned to the river to enjoy what Izzy called an absolute miracle. The fish were biting anything we put in front of them—streamers, buggers, nymphs. It didn't matter what was on the end of our leaders, and by the end of the afternoon I'd reeled in so many fish that my arms were sore.

"This was incredible. Thank you for bringing me."

"I'm glad you had fun. Did your waders and everything work okay? You didn't get a blister or anything, did you?" she asked.

"No, no. They worked great; wore my extra socks."

"You and your socks." Izzy giggled and ruffled my hair. We were taking turns packing items into the trunk of her Jeep when our trip decided to unveil one last surprise. A rustling off in the woods caught our attention.

"Did you hear that, Brody?" It wasn't really dark yet, but it was still overcast and eerily quiet after the storm. It didn't help any that the dense forest around the river became dark only a short distance off the road.

"Yeah, but it's probably just a squirrel or a rabbit. Or could even be a porcupine. I've read they come down about this time to change trees, I think."

"I don't know." Izzy actually seemed sort of nervous. I'd never seen her that way before.

"Maybe it's Bigfoot," I whispered.

"Don't say that, Brody!" she hissed. The rustling came again, louder this time, even over the clatter of trying to fit our rods in the trunk. Izzy cautiously glanced around the side of her car, and I was sure by the strange noise she made that she nearly wet her pants. In a flash her hand was clenched on my forearm.

"Brody, there is a bear in front of my car."

"Very funny, you dork." But sure enough, when I glanced around the back hatch, a burly black bear had wandered out of the woods and was making its way across the road toward the river. "Holy shit. It's a bear."

"What are you doing?" Izzy squeezed my arm again as I crept around the side of the car, trying to get a little closer.

"I want a picture. I've never seen a bear before." At the sound of my voice, the bear stopped, and expelled a series of low grunts. Its hot breath steamed in the evening air and its round ears twitched at every minute sound it heard.

"What do we do now, Brody?" Izzy whispered. "You probably pissed it off."

"Nah, just stay still. We're in its home, and it's probably just passing through."

"Who are you? The next Jack Hanna?"

"Who's Jack Hanna?" I asked while carefully unzipping the camera pack.

Izzy gasped. "You don't know... He's a famous animal guy...but it doesn't matter who he is. We should probably go before Bertha decides we'd be great for dinner."

Just as I was about to answer, the bear pawed at the ground and shook its head, unleashing more grunts.

"Brody..."

"Hang on just a minute..."

Izzy squeezed my arm again. "What if staying still doesn't work, Brody?"

"Then I will try and scare it so you can get in the car." Although every ounce of my being hoped it would not come down to me trying to scare a four-hundred-pound bear.

"Don't be stupid. You get in the car, and I'll try to scare it," Izzy replied.

Our nervous laughter was quickly silenced by more snorts from the bear. Fortunately, it didn't seem too bothered by the chirp of the on button, and in no time at all I had several priceless pictures. After another minute the bear must have decided we weren't anything to worry about. It sent out a final few grunts and continued on its walk.

"Alright. You happy? Let's go."

"No, no, no," I whispered. "Listen."

More rustling was coming from the woods, and to our immense surprise, a pair of cubs tumbled from the brush.

"Aww, look Brody," she whispered. "They're adorable."

"Oh, now they're adorable, huh?"

Izzy prodded my side as I picked up the camera again. The pair of cubs dashed awkwardly across the street, and at one point toppled over one another. I couldn't snap pictures fast enough.

"Brody, I want one."

"Alright. Let me just get my suit of armor and I'll go grab you one."

Izzy laughed again and swatted at me. Once the cubs rejoined their mother on the opposite side of the road, they disappeared. Curiosity got the better of us and we cautiously followed to see where they went. To our delight, the mama bear knelt down and the cubs crawled onto her back. Then all three proceeded to cross a shallower spot in the river we had just been fishing in.

"Can you believe that?" I asked. "We were literally right next to a huge bear."

Her mouth hung open in disbelief. It was an awesome sight—watching the bears make their way across the river. When they reached the far bank, the cubs slid from her back and all three disappeared into the woods once more.

"Ow!" I exclaimed. Izzy wrapped an arm around mine

after pinching me. "What was that for?"

"Just making sure we're not dreaming." She grinned and gave me a quick kiss on the cheek.

Soon we were back on the road and I was staring at the camera screen, listening to the gravel popping and clunking off the fenders.

"I can't wait to hang some of these pictures in the shop," I said.

"Me either. Brody, were you serious about what you said? You'd try and scare that bear so I could get in the car?"

I clicked off the camera and dropped it back in the bag. "Of course I would. I don't want you to get hurt. Seeing you get mauled by a bear isn't exactly high on my priority list."

"Wouldn't you be scared though?" Izzy asked after a nervous laugh escaped her.

"Well, yeah. Probably a little, but I can think of things scarier than that bear." My father came to mind first, but I didn't want to talk about him any more. "I'd be way more afraid of starving or drowning or getting stuck in a cave somewhere."

We crested the top of a hill, and a break in the clouds revealed the setting sun. Gorgeous colors were streaking across the sky as if some celestial being was going crazy with a paint brush.

"Would you mind pulling over for a bit so I can grab a picture?" I asked.

"Sure." After coming to a stop, Izzy joined me outside the car and took the camera so she could get more pictures of us together. Then we just stood there watching the sun sink into the horizon.

"Brody, I've never felt this way about a guy before and it feels pretty awesome. Does that sound stupid? I don't want to sound lame. Do I sound lame?"

"No, you don't sound stupid at all." I reached for her hand. Our fingers intertwined and I gave her hand a gentle squeeze. "I've got something else to tell you."

"Oh, goody. Are you going to tell me the rest of the drag queen story?"

"No, something else," I chuckled.

Izzy leaned in and I brushed her hair back to caress her cheek. The soft kiss that followed left my entire body tingling.

"Izzy, I've never really had anyone to take care of besides myself. I don't ever want anything bad to happen to you, and if you want me to—I would like to keep being there for you. Not that you need taking care of. I just meant…" I stopped talking, suddenly worried it was too much.

Ah, I should have just let her keep driving. I wasn't trying to make any sort of statement or fact. It was just meant to be a kind, loving offer. I hoped she knew I didn't want to be pushy about anything. I'd never had a girlfriend. In fact, I'd never had anything as memorable as my time with Izzy.

"Like my boyfriend?" she asked.

"Yeah. I guess. Yeah."

"I would love it if you were there for me like that. So, just to clarify: you're asking me out?"

"If you don't mind hanging out with a vagabond, then yeah."

Izzy laughed. "You're not a vagabond any more. I can't believe it takes a bear scare for you to ask me out."

"Keeps things exciting."

No matter how confident I was feeling, I still waited for the *but* that I worried would follow the statement I'd made. It never came though. Instead a chilly breeze came up, and Izzy came close for a hug. We stood there until the sky was nothing but a swirl of pinks, oranges, and dark purple clouds.

It wasn't long before Izzy and I were cruising down the streets of Eugene, and the closer we got to home, the more apprehensive I felt. I should have been celebrating the fact that I technically had a girlfriend now, but I couldn't help fidgeting in my seat, imagining how worried Heather was to let Izzy take me somewhere. I was right. Izzy and I were laughing about my horrendous attempt at singing along to some pop song when we walked in the door, and Heather met us almost immediately. She was wearing ratty, worn out clothes for cleaning and her dark hair was more disheveled than usual. Everything about her expression looked tired.

However, when Izzy dropped her pack on the floor and gave her mother a sideways hug, the worry vanished within seconds and her wholesome smile returned once more. I even thought for a second that Heather might cry.

"Hi, Momma!" Izzy exclaimed.

"Hi, yourself. Thanks for the hug. What's so funny?"

"Brody was just singing with me in the car!"

Heather stared wide eyed at me. "You sing?"

"I dabble."

Before Heather could answer, Izzy wrapped an arm around her mother's and led her back to the kitchen. "Brody and I have the craziest story to tell you!"

"Did you guys have fun?" Heather asked. "Did you get any fish?"

"Oh yeah! We had a blast, Momma. Come on, I'll show you pictures."

I made us cinnamon french toast for dinner, and when that was finished Izzy excused herself to clean up for the night. Heather lingered in the kitchen for several minutes while I collected all the dishes. I knew she wanted to say something. There was a hesitation to everything she did, but in the end she retreated to the study. I had a sneaking suspicion she was only pretending to do her homework. When the bathroom door opened and closed upstairs, Heather quickly went up—probably to interrogate Izzy.

I sighed and stopped washing the dishes. The gloves I normally used had ripped, and my hands were starting to get pruny from the hot water. I put them aside and stared around Heather's beautiful kitchen. The dark countertops that surrounded the stainless steel sink were covered with little white specks that resembled stars in the night sky. There was the long, bar-style counter that sectioned off part of the kitchen, creating the perfect dance space for a hopelessly romantic couple making dinner together. Exposed wooden beams running the length of the ceiling gave the kitchen an air of antiquity. Beneath the dark wood cabinets that hung from the walls, various kitchen appliances lined the counter top, and amongst them was a small radio.

I reached over to turn it on, hoping the music would calm my ever-growing nerves. I could only imagine what Heather and Izzy were talking about upstairs. My past was still my past, and not everyone could handle it. People often choose to fear what they don't understand, and since I had yet to open up to Heather, it didn't really surprise me that I made her uncomfortable sometimes.

Then I laughed. The song I sang with Izzy during the car ride home came on the radio. I was just starting to hum along when the music suddenly disappeared. I jumped at the sight of Heather standing by the radio.

"Hi," I said.

"Hi, yourself. Sorry, I didn't mean to shut it all the way off—just meant to turn it down."

"Oh. I'm sorry if it was too loud."

"No, you're fine. I was just wondering if we could talk."

"Yeah, sure." *Here it comes. I knew she was upset about something...*

"Thanks for doing the dishes by the way. I really appreciate it. I've got a lot of studying to do for my class and I didn't get much done today like I had hoped…." She drifted off and I noticed that her knuckles had gone white from clutching the textbook so hard. She also kept taking tiny sips from her glass of wine.

Yep, something is definitely bothering her.

"It's no trouble," I said. "I'm used to doing dishes."

"Yeah. Well, I was wondering—is everything okay, Brody? I mean are you liking it here?"

I took a deep breath. *That is an interesting tactic. Is that some sort of passive aggressive threat?* "Yeah, yeah. It's been great. I don't miss sleeping outside, that's for sure."

"Well, I know you end up sleeping on the couch a lot. We could probably get a room set up for you."

I actually laughed. Heather probably had no idea how happy I was to even have a couch. "You don't have to do that. It's a very comfortable couch. Seriously. You've done more than enough just by giving me a place to stay. Thank you again. It's incredibly kind of you."

"Oh, it's no trouble…"

"No, Mrs. Cooper. I know you were worried about us today—worried about Izzy. I really don't want to be a bother."

Her demeanor changed instantly. "I wasn't worried so much about today as I was about last night. I went to do laundry this morning and your clothes reeked. What happened?"

"I assume you already asked Izzy."

"Yes, and now I'm asking you. And you'd better not lie

to me."

"We went to a party and it was incredibly awkward," I said. "We didn't stay long at all."

"That's what Izzy said."

"Yeah. We stopped to see that friend of hers after we got some dinner at the diner. They talked for a bit and then we left." I thought it best to leave out the part about the drunk frat guy I pushed into a wall.

"That's it?"

"I promise that's it. It's not exactly in my best interest to lie." I knew Heather meant well. She loved her daughter and I had never known a mother's love, but I didn't like people prying either. It was just another indication of distrust, and people had done that to me my entire life. She nodded and thankfully let the conversation go.

From the corner of my eye, I could see that she was still watching the methodical motion of my hands as I rinsed the plates. I glanced down at my forearms when I heard the gentle clunk of the wine glass on the counter. Even in the dim light of the kitchen, I knew she could see what I tried to hide every day.

Her soft footsteps barely made a sound, and soon she was standing beside me. I could almost feel her praying that this moment was just a bad dream. But sadly, it wasn't. There was a reason I always wore kitchen gloves and long sleeve shirts. This was the first time she had seen my forearms exposed. When I moved to set a dish in the drying rack, a nearly four-inch jagged scar was visible, running along my forearm like a bolt of lightning.

The clinking of dishes stopped as I waited for her to say something, but she only continued to stare. Amidst the hair and freckles, my arms were riddled with dark pink depressions and bumps from gashes long since healed. I did my best to ignore them, but they popped out like mole hills in the lawn.

"Your arms," she mumbled.

"Yeah, there's a lot of them." I closed my eyes, trying to keep the awful memories at bay. None of them were worth remembering, yet I couldn't forget them. All I could do was bury them. Gently she took my fingers and turned me to face her. She wouldn't touch them and I couldn't blame her for not wanting to.

"Does Izzy know?" Her voice quavered.

"Kind of," I said. "She hasn't seen these yet though." From the expression on her face, it was clear that all Heather wanted was to return to her glass of wine. Then she did something that took us both by surprise.

It wasn't a long hug, but it wasn't short either, and it was drastically different from the hugs I'd shared with Izzy. Heather's embrace emanated motherly compassion that I'd never felt before. When she gave me a final squeeze and kissed my head, my legs just about gave out. I barely looked at her, but I knew that stupid party was the last thing on her mind now. Afterwards, she retreated to the opposite side of the counter and immediately picked up her book and glass of wine again.

"I won't say anything," Heather said.

"Okay."

"Really. I won't. It's not my place." When I finally looked at her, I knew Heather was trying not to cry. "You can tell her when you're ready."

"Thanks." More emotions swirled and I found myself wondering if I should be thankful or frustrated with Heather. She continued to stare, but I didn't know what to say.

"What was it like?" Heather asked. "Being that alone."

"Cold," I said. "So many cold nights. Like I said, I worked when I could and usually made enough to buy some food and clothes or whatever. But I didn't usually have enough to pay for any kind of housing."

"My God."

"Yeah. There wasn't nearly the certainty that you have here. I didn't know when I would eat sometimes. I spent a lot of time trying to stay dry so that I didn't get sick. I don't exactly have premium insurance to see a doctor."

"Yeah," she said. "And Izzy?"

A breath of air escaped my lips and I shrugged again. "Mrs. Cooper, I would never do anything to hurt your daughter. If you're uncomfortable with me being here because of her, I'll leave. I really don't want to cause any problems."

"Would you want that?" she asked.

"No. I actually really like it here and—"

"You like Izzy," Heather finished.

"Yeah. She's amazing."

"She is, and I know that you've been helping her with

school work and I really appreciate that, too. I may be getting a teaching degree, but me and math are like oil and water."

"It's no problem. I really enjoyed math when I was still in school. It always made sense and it always worked out the way it was supposed to, unlike reality…"

"You know, Brody, it's been a long time since I've seen Izzy this happy, and I've never seen her smile like the way she does around you. I'm very glad that you two found each other."

Heather got off her stool again and I turned back to the sink, listening to her footsteps receding toward the living room.

"Brody, I'm not going to pry. It's none of my business, but I really do hope you decide to stay. I know Izzy would miss you if you left, and I know you haven't been here that long, but for what it's worth I would miss you, too."

"Thanks, Mrs. Cooper." When her footsteps faded away, I returned to washing the dishes and did nothing to stop the tears from rolling down my cheeks.

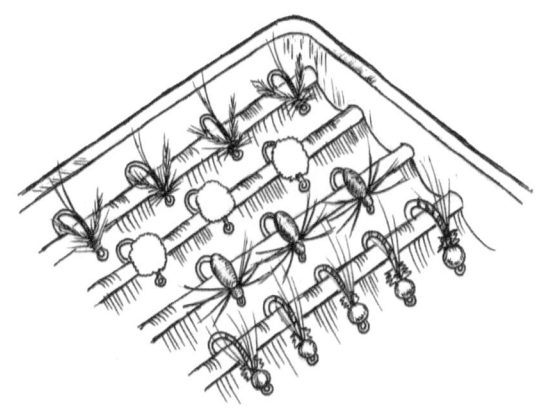

I couldn't believe it had already been over a month since I arrived in Eugene, Oregon. Seven weeks was the longest I'd spent anywhere since turning sixteen. It was another record. But instead of savoring that joyous fact, I was still reeling from my recent confessions to Izzy and Heather. I'd made the assumption that telling them would help, and it had somewhat. But now there was this lingering feeling that I couldn't shake.

A heavy downpour was assaulting the pavement, and I watched from my seat behind the counter. The fly shop was quiet, and Henry was busy in the back doing something. I hadn't bothered to ask what. I just kept staring out the window, watching the rain.

At first I wondered about simple things like how many raindrops were hitting the pavement every second, or how long does it take for one raindrop to fall from the sky. Then I could hear Mrs. Henderson, my old fifth-grade teacher, talking as if she were standing right in front of me. I could see the classroom again and all my classmates. But even back then, I stared out the window at the rain.

I didn't have to picture my father. I knew he was there, even though I tried to block him out of the memories. His heavy footsteps as he came into my room. Someone had upset him at work that day and he took it out on me. The cursing. The slaps. The cracking of his belt…

When a hand came down on my shoulder, it scared me so bad I fell off the stool.

"Hey, are you all right?" Henry asked.

"What?" I tried to collect myself, but my breathing was heavy and I was having a hard time focusing.

"I said your name a couple times, but you weren't answering. I'm sorry I scared you," Henry said.

I shook my head and finally everything returned to normal. "It's fine. No worries. Just a little zoned out. That's all."

Henry's eyes remained glued on me and I knew he wasn't going to buy that answer. "Are you sure you're all right?"

"Yep. I'm good. Just thinking about some stuff." It was embarrassing having Henry see me like this. I stepped around him, eager to be alone.

"Brody—"

"I'm gonna be in the store room if you need anything. The FedEx guy dropped off some stuff, so I'll get that sorted for you."

Thankfully, a customer walked in the door, and I left Henry behind the counter. But instead of unpacking new supplies, I retreated to the back room and started tying flies. There was something very therapeutic about tying. The rest of the world melted away as I tried to make something elegant and beautiful on the vice. Within minutes, I churned out a few elk hair caddis flies and Griffith's gnats. Then Henry reappeared.

"I thought you were going to the store room."

"Yep, sorry. I'll go get that done." I dropped the bobbin and got off the stool, but Henry held his ground in the doorway.

"Sit down, Brody. I want to talk to you."

I sat, and Henry kept staring at me. It made me nervous to be stared at by someone who was always so calm. I wondered if he was going to explode at me, but then he grabbed a stool for himself. He adjusted his hat and scratched at his beard. "It's none of my business, but you are my employee and I want to make sure that everything's okay."

"There's just a lot on my mind, Henry. I can't believe I've been here over a month already."

Henry's shoulder's relaxed some. I wanted to tell him what I told Izzy and Heather, but at the same time I didn't want everyone knowing. The last thing I wanted was for people to start treating me like some sort of fragile egg shell.

"Is that a good thing?" Henry asked.

"I think so. I really like it here."

"Good. I'm glad to hear it. That being said, I hope you

don't think I'm some tyrant of a boss or something. You can talk to me, you know."

"I know. It's just…I've never really had this much time to sit and think since I've had to spend so much time just trying to take care of myself. It's just a little overwhelming sometimes."

"I know exactly what you mean, Brody. If you ever want to talk, just let me know." Henry stood and headed for the door. "Now come on. We're going to the diner. Remember?"

While Henry went to close up, I stared at the bobbin dangling from the vice. So much had changed since coming to Eugene, and I just wished that my past would stop holding me back from enjoying the present. Especially when it was Izzy's birthday.

Not long after Henry and I sat down in the diner, Izzy appeared with her mother. The clever and beautiful girl who had found me on the porch was now eighteen, and I was excited to give her my gift. Several times, I'd heard Heather ask Izzy what she wanted for her birthday, but the reply was always the same.

"I don't know, Momma. Let's just go to dinner." I hadn't known Izzy that long, but it was clear that material objects didn't really matter to her. She just wanted to spend time with her family, and I knew that had to do with the fact her father was gone.

After ordering our meals, Henry and Heather each gave Izzy a gift. Henry's was a fat envelope stuffed with one of those obnoxious birthday cards that sings when you peel it open. It also contained a gift card for tying supplies at the shop.

"Can never have enough supplies, right Uncle Henry?" she said.

"Absolutely not," he replied. "But I'm not going to lie to you, sweetheart. I also have no idea what to get an eighteen-year-old girl, so…"

Izzy laughed and gave him a kiss on the cheek.

"Thank you very much," she said, and moved on to the bag her mother set on the table. Izzy peered at her mother with a cautious eye, but Heather just smiled as she sipped from her drink. Hiding beneath a few sheets of colorful tissue paper were several new shirts.

"I thought maybe if you and Brody go out sometime, you'll have something nice to wear."

"Mom!" Izzy exclaimed. I tried to hide my red cheeks by taking a giant gulp of my own drink. "They're awesome. I love it. Thank you."

"You're welcome, sweetie," she said. "Happy birthday."

Henry nudged me in the ribs. "Where's yours?" he whispered.

When I caught Heather staring at me, I knew she was wondering the same thing. "I got a present for you, Izzy, but it's at your mom's house. I was going to give it to you later," I said.

"That's totally fine," she said. "I hope they didn't pressure you into getting me something."

"Nah. I came up with it all on my own."

Izzy grinned as she folded up her new shirts, and I took a few more nervous sips of my drink. By the end of the meal, no one could manage another bite. Henry disappeared for a moment, and when he returned there was a mysterious grin on his face. Izzy was quick to badger him, but he gave up nothing.

Then, to Izzy's surprise, a pair of waitresses appeared carrying a platter of cake heaped with ice cream and covered with sprinkles. Protruding from the center was a popping sparkler. If that wasn't embarrassing enough for Izzy, we sang "Happy Birthday" to her.

For just an instant, time slowed down. My little episode in the fly shop with Henry was like a fuzzy dream now, and all of a sudden I was happy. It was surreal. Everyone was smiling, especially Izzy. Henry had smeared frosting on her face, and Heather was laughing as she tried to capture the moment on camera. But honestly, there was no camera that would ever do this moment justice.

When everyone was too full to eat another helping of dessert, Henry said his goodbyes in the parking lot and I went home with Heather and Izzy. It was a quiet car ride, and I sat alone in the back seat looking out the window. After walking in the door, Heather gave Izzy one last hug and kiss before heading to bed, leaving Izzy and me to share the last hours of her birthday together.

"So," Izzy began.

"I hope you had a good birthday," I said. "Do you still want me to make a cup of cocoa?"

"That would be awesome, even though I've probably had enough sugar to OD."

I laughed and Izzy disappeared to change into her night clothes. By the time she returned I had a steaming mug of cocoa ready for her, complete with whipped cream.

"Happy birthday, Isabel Cooper."

"Thank you, Brody. Please tell me we're sharing this though."

"You bet, but I have to get one more thing."

"I'll wait for you." Izzy took a seat on a kitchen stool. With a smile I made my way to the closet where I kept my small pile of belongings, and after digging to the very bottom I found the glossy, new tackle box wrapped with a bow.

"You want to close your eyes?" I asked, stepping back into the kitchen.

"They're closed."

My hands were starting to shake. I'd never given anyone a gift before. "Okay. Pardon my little speech, but I just want you to know how thankful I am for you. You changed my life, Isabel Cooper, and I'm so grateful for that. Happy birthday." After kissing her cheek, I picked up her hand and gently set the tackle box on her lap.

Beneath the hard plastic lid was a robust collection of brand new flies. Glinting on a row of hooks were the shiny, colorful beads on flies meant to be midges and pupae. Carefully wrapped hackle feathers formed the wings on a collection of her favorite dry fly patterns. Another row was dedicated to the foam spiders we used at the pond. Other flies included woo-ly buggers, egg flies, caddis flies, grasshoppers, gnats, and a few Royal Coachman flies. Izzy gave me a sassy grin when she found the tube fly I threw in as a joke.

"I know it's probably a little corny, but since you love fly fishing so much, I wanted to do more than get you a card."

"Are you kidding me? This is amazing. You were really paying attention. I mean—you made all of these?"

I nodded. "Yeah, for you."

Izzy slid off the stool and wrapped her arms around my neck. "You're the best," she whispered.

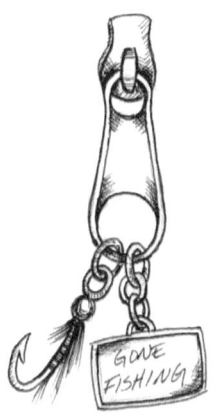

The fall fishing season was really ramping up. Henry, Jack, and Tim were gone nearly every day as people came in from all over to enjoy excursions on the nearby rivers. I spent the better part of each day in the store room putting together online orders. It hadn't really occurred to me just how successful Henry's business was until I started sending packages all over the country. Sometimes it was waders and poles. Other times, like today, it was all fly tying materials.

1 - Daiichi 25ct Size 6 Wet/Nymph Hooks
1 - Krystal Flash – Chartreuse
2 - V-Rib Vinal Rib
1 - 12 pack Ice Dubbing

I loved these kind of orders in particular because they always left me wondering what types of creations these other tyers were coming up with. Just as I finished up, one of the other employees walked in.

"Don't mind me, Brody," Jack said. "Just got to grab a few things before a trip later this morning."

Jack was a little shorter than me, with a thin frame. His aging facial features were covered with gray stubble that was quickly becoming a full beard as the weather got colder. His light brown hair was parted neatly atop his head. When we first met I guessed that he was five years, maybe even ten years older than Henry, but he didn't look it. I attributed that to the hiking and guide work, which kept him in good shape. That morning, however, he resembled my old acquaintance, Big Sammy, after a long night of driving. There were heavy bags under his gray eyes, and every few minutes a hefty yawn escaped him.

"You all right?" I asked. "You look like you're going to keel over."

Jack laughed. "Yeah. I'm really tired, and the coffee hasn't kicked in yet. We got back late last night from a trip. The clients wanted to have one last dinner on the river, which I can't blame them. It was gorgeous last night. Thanks for making up that extra food for us to take. They really enjoyed it."

"Yeah. No problem."

"I think you're becoming quite popular."

I stared at Jack's youthful smile, slightly amazed at the idea I was popular for something.

"So, are you liking it here?" he asked. "What's it been? A couple months?"

"Yeah. It's great," I said. "I'm really thankful to have met Henry and his family."

"I know the feeling," Jack mused as he pawed through a box of tippet spools.

"What do you mean?"

"Ha. I can't imagine you'd be interested in the woes of an old man."

"You're not that old. And besides, I'm curious. Humor me."

Jack pulled himself out of a storage bin and leaned against the shelf. "Well, about fifteen years ago, my marriage fell apart and I decided to fish my way across the country. The only problem was that when I got out here, I didn't have anything left except my dog and my fishing equipment. Even my car was on its last legs by then."

"Alright…"

"Yeah. Anyway, a couple days after I got to town, Henry and I happened to be fishing the same stretch of the Willamette north of the university. We started chatting, and he told me about a fly shop he'd just opened. One thing led to another, and here I am."

"Interesting," I replied.

Jack yawned again and kept poking through boxes while I read through a new order that popped up on the computer screen. Something was nagging at me.

"What's his deal anyway?" I asked.

"Henry's? I was hoping you could tell me."

"Me? I hardly know him."

"Yeah, but you two seem pretty close. I figured maybe he told you something." Jack shrugged. "I don't know, Brody, but I'm pretty sure Henry has had a rough go of it himself."

"In what way?"

"In the fifteen years I've been here, Henry has never been with anyone."

"A lady you mean?"

"Yeah. Ask him about it sometime if you want," Jack said. "Maybe he'll talk to you."

"I doubt it. Like I said, I hardly know him."

Jack shook his head. "He's different with you. I bet he'd tell you."

With a final shrug, Jack left the store room, leaving me to my thoughts. When the online orders were all packaged and ready to ship, I went to ask Henry a question about one of the inventory slips. But when I caught him speaking with a very flirtatious blonde-haired woman at the front counter, my question was put out of my mind.

She was certainly the outdoorsy type with her plaid shirt and unzipped bomber jacket. Beneath her ponytail, a thin scarf hung loosely around her neck, and her navy jeans disappeared into her socks and rugged hiking boots. Where girls normally wore a purse, this woman had a trendy sling pack across her back. When I looked closer, I noticed that she had several fish charms hanging off the zippers.

I watched from a distance while absentmindedly stocking some shelves. Several minutes went by before the woman finally departed, but her smile lingered as she backed away toward the door, and then with a small wave she disappeared. I raced to the counter and Henry's cheeks reddened instantly.

"Who was that?"

"Nobody, Brody."

"So there's a ghost here that I saw you talking to? Or maybe an angel? She was very pretty, Henry."

He gave me a stern look that quickly gave way to a smile. "Her name is Miranda Perry. She's a journalist for one of the fly fishing magazines."

"Which one? I mean, I should probably get familiar with more of these magazines if I'm going to continue working here."

"Very funny, Brody."

"What? I'm serious."

"*American Angler*."

"Cool. Is she writing an article about you or the shop or something?"

"No. She was just chatting."

"I see. Well, I just had a quick question about the inventory."

When the question was answered, I returned to the store room. No sooner had I started sorting through boxes when Henry appeared. "What do you mean, *I see*?"

"I don't know."

"Well you must have thought something."

I shrugged. "Well, are you two an item?"

"No, no," Henry said with a shake of his head. "Why? Did you think…?"

"I don't know. Maybe."

"Well, we're not."

"But you want to be?"

"What? No. I mean, she's cool—a very nice woman," Henry said.

"Very pretty, too. You look a little flustered, Henry, like a hormonal teenager."

"Brody!"

I started laughing. "Are you seeing someone else?"

"No. And yes, she's pretty."

"Are you interested in being with someone?"

"I guess. Maybe. But I'm busy," Henry said.

I offered a quiet smile and returned to the boxes.

"What? That's it? You're not going to say anything else?" he asked.

"I'm busy too, sorting through these boxes."

"Very funny, Brody."

"Henry, it's none of my business. But I will say this. Although I've lived in some weird places, I haven't been under a rock. She's clearly interested in you."

Henry sighed and left the storage room.

That evening when Izzy got home from another ACT study session, she found me in the living room with a stack of fly fishing magazines on the coffee table.

"You're really getting into this, aren't you?" she asked. All I did was nod while I read an interesting article Miranda had written about fly fishing in Maine.

"Should we start looking into a fancy trip or maybe competitive tying?" Izzy asked.

I grabbed another magazine. "Yeah. Maybe…"

"What's your sudden interest in *American Angler*? *Fly Tyer* has way more on actual tying."

"I know, but I have another reason for reading these." I peeled through the issue, searching for another article Miranda had written. Izzy sat down and leaned in close to see what I was reading. Just like always, she put my brain on the fritz, especially when her nose grazed my cheek.

"How are you?" I asked.

"I'm good. Seriously, what's your sudden interest?" she asked.

"Well, Henry had a visit from a lady today, and apparently she writes for this magazine. I was trying to get a better idea of her."

"Ah, Ms. Perry," Izzy said. Her lips formed into a thin, mischievous smile.

"You know her then?"

"Oh yeah. I'm not sure how often she comes in, because usually I only work on the weekends. But I would say I see her once or twice a month."

"She just pops in?"

"Yeah, it's always the same thing, Brody." Izzy flopped her legs across my lap. "Ms. Perry walks in and wanders around like she's going to buy something. Then, when my uncle is free at the counter, she goes up and they chat for a while."

"Listen to you get all excited," I said.

"Well come on, Brody. My whole life, my uncle has just been…my uncle. He's never had a nice lady. I would love for him to have someone, and she seems nice."

"Yeah…" I was already sucked into another article that Miranda had written about fishing for steelhead in the Pere Marquette River.

"What do you think?" Izzy asked. Clearly, this was an important matter to her, but what baffled me more was the fact that she actually cared for my opinion.

"Well, she's definitely a story teller. Her writing is fantastic, and with all the traveling she's done, I'm sure her and Henry have a lot in common, but other than that, I think it's none of my business."

"Uhuh. Then why are you sitting here reading all these magazines?"

"Because I'm curious about that lady."

"But you don't care about helping Henry?"

I let the magazine flop in my lap, now too distracted to

read. "I would love to help Henry, especially after everything he's done for me. But I don't want to overstep my bounds, Izzy. I love working at the fly shop. If Henry gets mad at me, he could fire me."

"He's not going to fire you, Brody. He really likes you. I heard him talking to my mom about you the other night," she said. I inhaled a deep breath and gazed at Izzy for what seemed like a really long time. She stared back and her gaze never faltered. When I finally blinked, she let out a whoop of excitement. "I win!" she said. "Will you please talk to him? Just a little."

"How am I even supposed to bring Miranda up?"

"I don't know. You guys get to share all sorts of *man time* while you're driving for fishing trips."

"*Man time.*"

"Yes, Brody. That's what I said."

I shook my head and picked up the magazine again.

"Please, Brody!" she insisted.

"Just a little. You know, I've never said something so silly, but it would be hard to say no to that smile."

It was early in the morning when I woke suddenly in the darkness of the living room. The house was silent except for the sound of Izzy's gentle breaths as she continued sleeping beside me. I shuddered, still trying to get the horrifyingly vivid images of my monster-like father out of my head. I sat up, leaving Izzy to her dreams.

I could still hear the shouting and cursing in my head like he was standing over me, ready to hit me with his belt. Every time I closed my eyes, all I could see were his venomous expressions perpetuated by the booze he consumed like water. It made me want to scream and cry at the same time.

When I looked at Izzy, I wondered what she dreamed about. She seemed so at peace. Then I remembered the night I saw her praying and I turned my attention to the ceiling. *God, I don't know what I did to deserve this, but thank you for bringing her into my life.* Tears welled in my eyes and when I closed them, my father was gone and all that remained was a calm silence.

Izzy stirred. "You all right, Brody?"

I managed a weak nod and then she nudged my side, exposing a smile.

"Are you sure?"

"I had a bad dream. Just stupid stuff."

"Well, you can tell me about it if you want to." Her voice was just above a whisper and her eyes never left me.

I nodded, but was otherwise silent.

"We do this a lot you know." She paused for a yawn. "Falling asleep on the couch together, I mean."

"I know. I'm sorry." It was an empty apology though. The only thing I was sorry for was waking her up.

"Why are you sorry? It's nice." Izzy tugged gently on my

shirt. "Come here."

I knew it wasn't really possible, but I felt like I was staring at someone I'd known my entire life. When I lay down next to her again, I planted a soft kiss on her warm cheek and silently prayed for good dreams. Within seconds of her running a hand through my hair and along my shoulders, sleep carried me away.

The next day, Henry and I drove a group of prospective fly fishers to a remote part of the Willamette in search of rainbows and cutthroat trout. With Henry's help, I had set up all the dry dropper rigs we needed for the day, and so far the clients were having great luck with the flies I'd selected. Since they were also more familiar with fly fishing than most, Henry and I were able to enjoy some conversation and fishing ourselves.

"You were pretty quiet on the ride out here," Henry said.

"I know. I was thinking," I replied.

"About Izzy?"

"No, not just her. A few other things."

"Anything you care to share?"

"Maybe in a minute. You're going to get a bite."

"How do you know?" Henry asked.

"I saw a rise behind that rock a few minutes ago." Henry had been teaching me all sorts of nifty tricks for finding active fish, and sure enough Henry's line suddenly went tight.

"Oh baby!" he exclaimed.

The folks we were guiding turned in delight to see their instructor begin a promising battle. When the energetic trout exploded from the river, its contortions sent the hook flying.

"Damn! That's rotten luck, Teach!" yelled one of the clients.

"But great inspiration!" yelled the other. They returned to fishing and so did Henry and I.

"You were saying," Henry said.

I was too busy gawking at his seamless casting motion to answer right away. With a final flick of his wrist and little effort, Henry sent twenty yards of line sailing out across the river.

"Yes. So, I was talking to Jack yesterday…"

"Oh, was he telling you about the bug-eating stories?" Henry asked.

"What the…bug eating?"

"Nevermind. I'll tell you about it later. Not something to talk about before lunch."

"Okay. Well, Jack mentioned that you've helped out most of the other employees in one way or another."

"Yeah, I guess. I try doing what I can for people. I told you my sister rubbed off on me."

"It's kind of you. I still thought maybe you felt sorry for me or something, but you really are a good guy."

"Thanks, Brody."

"No problem. I'm switching flies."

"Alright…I'm guessing that's not everything you were thinking about," Henry said.

"Nope." I was confident that appearing distracted while fiddling with the knot would make my next question seem more casual.

"What else?" Henry asked.

"Well, you are a great guy. How come you don't have a lady in your life?"

"I'm busy, like I told you."

Before I could stop myself, the next words flew from my mouth. "That's a lame excuse." I sucked in a breath and glanced at Henry. His shoulders drooped and a low groan sounded out over the river. The line he should have been mending was drifting downstream without his attention. "I'm sorry. I shouldn't have said that. I'm gonna go start heating up lunch."

"Brody—"

"No, I shouldn't have pried. I'm sorry." I started backing out of the river.

"Really, Brody. Just hang on," Henry said, so I paused. "You're probably right."

"I am?"

"Yeah. Would you come back down here so I don't have to shout?"

I waded slowly back into the river.

"There was somebody a long time ago. Close to fifteen years ago actually."

"Oh. Really? What was her name?"

"Cecelia." Henry's cheeks bunched up when he said her name and I could tell it still bothered him.

"Can I ask what happened?"

Henry just gazed at the river, absolutely silent. He drew long lengths of line through the ferrules and restarted his casting motion, but the line snagged on a nearby tree branch. He groaned loudly, and instead of being the patient man I was accustomed to, he yanked the line. A loud, twangy snap filled the air when the leader broke.

"We were going to get married. At least I thought we were going to get married. We weren't much older than you and Izzy. I thought for sure we would, but when I asked, she said no."

"Henry, I'm sorry. I really didn't want to bring up bad feelings."

"Brody, stop worrying so much. It's probably good I talk about this. After we talked about Miranda yesterday, I went home and stared at a bunch of stuff that I still have from when Cecelia and I were together. I still have the ring. How pathetic is that?"

That was when the sad truth dawned on me. "That's why you don't have a family."

He nodded. "First it was Sarah. Then it was Izzy. I'll never forget the day she was born. That first time I held her was so incredible. Izzy was so tiny and beautiful, but I was so jealous of Heather. After our dad died, I moved out here and was all by myself. Heather was pissed at me for leaving. She said I was being selfish. Then they moved here too, and I wasn't sure how I would handle it. But I'll never forget the day Izzy and I first tied flies together and went to the park… Easily, one of best days I've ever had."

I was worried Henry was going to crack and I sort of wanted him to stop, but just when I was about to say something he kept going.

"Now it's you. Getting to teach you all this stuff about fly fishing. You guys are like the kids I never got to have."

"Henry—"

"Cecilia was the daughter of a doctor, and I was the son of a carpenter," Henry said. "You're a smart guy. I think you can see the disparity."

"Yeah, a stupid one." I didn't care if I was being blunt any more because that was something that had always bothered me. My entire life had been a disparity.

"Why? It's true. I was the poor local boy and she was well off. She listened to her father when he told her to get a good education at a respectable institution."

I made a sound of disgust.

"What was that for?"

"How much has your sister told you about me?"

"I don't know, not much really. Just that you've had a rough upbringing."

"And you like me?"

"Of course I like you, Brody. Didn't you hear what I just said? I figured we're pretty good friends."

"Then you should know that 'rough upbringing' is an understatement. My home life was terrible and I was a foster kid by twelve. I've been living on the streets for the last two and a half years—practically homeless. Does that change your opinion of me enough to not want me spending time with your niece?"

Henry swallowed again. "No," he finally said. "I think you're a great guy and I know that you care about her."

"Alright. Well I guess my point is that just because something didn't work out for you a long time ago doesn't make you worthless or a bad person or something. It was her choice to give in and leave. Would you really want to be with her now anyway? You're the owner of a successful business that's given you the chance to meet all these wonderful people since then, including Miranda, so I think maybe you're better off."

"Yeah, maybe you're right, Dr. Phil," Henry said. "Maybe you're right..."

"Who's Dr. Phil?"

Henry laughed and punched me in the arm.

"Seriously—who is he, Henry?"

September had come and gone, and October was flowing swiftly by as well. The closer it got to Halloween, the more Eugene put on a costume of its own, and I loved it. Knobby, colorful gourds and pumpkins adorned the steps and porches of homes throughout the area. The smell of cinnamon and pumpkin spice mixed perfectly with the crisp fall air.

Work one particular day consisted of drinking apple cider and helping Henry put on a fly tying session for one of the local elementary classes. I was having an absolute blast, and although I was still learning the subtleties of tying myself, I knew enough of the basics to help the students with their questions.

"Do you guys do this a lot?" I asked.

Henry stepped back from one of the students, and we both watched as the youngster wrapped a grouse feather around the hook to form a beautiful soft collar on a wet fly.

"Why? Are you having fun?" Henry asked.

"Yeah, this is great."

"Good. We do a lot of these throughout the winter for students and vets. I would love the help."

"Count me in."

A tug on my jacket brought my attention to a young girl. "Can you come help me, Mr. Brody?" she asked. I glanced back to Henry who gave me a sarcastic smile.

"Get back to work!" he ordered.

When the lesson was over we returned to the fly shop, and I spent the rest of the afternoon putting away the practice equipment. By the time I was finished, Izzy was waiting for me at the front counter.

"So, what are you two up to this evening?" Henry asked.

"I don't know," I replied.

"I do," Izzy said. "I've got a surprise for Brody."

"Any chance you can spill the beans?" Henry asked. Izzy grinned at me and leaned across the counter to whisper in her uncle's ear.

"Ha, Brody," Henry said. "I think you're in for a treat."

With a wave goodbye, we hopped in her car and rode on home. When Izzy led me into the kitchen, I noticed the two large pumpkins resting atop the kitchen table as well as an array of utensils for carving.

"Oh my, Izzy."

"How long has it been?" she asked. "I couldn't resist."

"Too long. Are we really doing this?"

"Yeah if you want to."

After shedding our jackets and shoes, we sat down at the table. Izzy dove right in, sketching out a pattern on her pumpkin, and I amused myself by enjoying the concentrated expressions she made.

As much as I wanted to carve pumpkins with her, I couldn't. Every time I lifted up a marker to start sketching, the memory of a Halloween from so many years before cackled at me like an evil warlock.

"Brody? What's wrong? You're not doing anything."

I blinked, realizing that I'd gone cross-eyed staring at the pumpkin.

"Ah, I'm just thinking."

"Sorry, Brody, but I'm not buying that. Tell me." Izzy set down her tools. I groaned and tossed my own tool on the table. The loud clatter rang through the otherwise silent kitchen. Then Izzy ran a hand through my hair. "Hey. What's wrong?"

"Nothing."

"Doesn't seem like nothing."

"Izzy, I haven't carved a pumpkin since I was seven years old."

"Alright. That's okay."

"No it's not, Izzy." My anger swelled. "Carving pumpkins is something special for kids and I never got to do it because my dad was such an asshole!"

Izzy jumped when my fist slammed into the table, but just

as quickly she took my hand in hers. "Tell me what happened."

"Why? What's it matter? It's not going to change any-thing."

"Because I want to carve pumpkins with you. I want you to get this stuff off your chest so you can be happy."

"Fine. Mrs. Murphy got me a pumpkin to carve, and I spent most of the afternoon at her house making this goofy, big-toothed thing that I thought was awesome. I took it back to my dad's, hoping he'd think it was cool, too. But he didn't. He knocked it onto the floor and stomped on it until it was mush. He yelled at me the entire time, telling me to stop wasting my time doing stupid stuff. I started crying but that didn't matter. He just hit me until I cleaned up the mess."

When I looked at Izzy, her bottom lip started to quiver.

"Yeah," I grumbled. "Wonderful."

"I didn't mean to upset you."

"You didn't upset me, Izzy. You're a sweetheart. It's my dad's fault."

Izzy pressed her lips against my cheek. "You can change that right now. Don't let him keep bothering you."

"Easy for you to say. Your dad would never do that."

"No, he wouldn't. But in almost twenty years, I've also only spent a handful of holidays with him." That took the wind from my frustrated sails. Izzy let go of my hand and returned to her pumpkin.

"I'm sorry, Izzy."

"It's okay. Like I said, you get used to it. I just really

wanted to do this with you." Izzy picked up her marker and continued drawing on her pumpkin.

I never would have thought such a sad moment in my life would later become one of the happiest. I leaned over to give her a kiss. "What do you have so far?" I asked.

Izzy's dimples appeared and she eagerly turned her pumpkin to face me. It was a fantastic grinning face that helped me forget all about the crummy memories in my head.

"You don't have to get mad, Brody. He's gone..."

"I know."

"So will you keep going?"

"Definitely. Thanks, Izzy."

"Anytime." Her smile broadened and she handed me a marker. Once we were happy with our designs, we cut off the tops and began piling pulp and seeds on the table. Then it happened.

It all started with the flick of a finger. One quick movement that sent a gooey, wet seed splattering against my cheek. Her insatiable giggles filled the kitchen, but I didn't even look at her. In one swift motion, I sent a clump of sticky pumpkin pulp back in her direction. Only when there was a sharp intake of breath did I finally chance a glance in her direction. The pulp was draped across Izzy's cheek and her expression was somewhere between startled and elated. Orange goo was running toward her chin. A baited silence fell when she flung a much larger chunk of pulp at me, which landed squarely on my chest.

"Are we really gonna do this?" I said, standing up. The

squash fell to the floor with a loud squelch.

Izzy's smile was devious. "Of course."

Then all hell broke loose. Pumpkin guts were flying around the kitchen as we danced around the table, ducking fire and scooping up more ammunition. We were having so much fun that neither of us noticed the front door open. Heather must have heard us laughing and yelping because she wisely paused before entering the kitchen. A glob of pumpkin whizzed by at eye level and she watched in dismay and shock as it slammed into a wall. More orange slime began rolling to the floor. She walked through the doorway and found Izzy on my back trying to rub slime into my face. Her hair was plastered with pulp and seeds and my clothes were covered with huge wet marks. She cleared her throat as loudly as possible without laughing herself.

"Oh shit," Izzy said.

I stopped as well and swallowed my nerves, but made no move to set Izzy on the ground.

"Hi, Momma."

"Hi. What have you two done to my kitchen?"

I opened my mouth, but nothing came out. Instead I heard the gentle plop of pumpkin guts landing somewhere on the floor. There was goo everywhere.

"Well?" Heather asked.

"Brody started it," Izzy said, and pushed the rest of the pulp against my face.

"Did not!" I sputtered. "She flicked a seed at me while we

were carving pumpkins." We both stared at her mother, wondering if she was going to laugh or explode.

"How much spaghetti would you like?" I asked. Izzy snorted in my ear which caused all of us to crack.

"I'll just order take out," Heather said, pulling the phone out of her bag. She took several pictures of us and then turned back the way she came. "This better be cleaned up when I get back."

C risp yellow, orange, gold, red, and purple leaves fluttered in the breeze above me, barely clinging to the dark brown branches that were going dormant for the winter. It was late in the afternoon several days after Halloween, and I was lying in the grass behind Izzy's house. Normally I enjoyed the comforts of her parent's fenced off yard at night while watching the stars. Today, however, I was staring up at the trees. Every now and again a gust of wind would break more of them free, sending a shower of leaves raining down upon me. Each time it made me smile.

"What are you doing, Brody?"

"What? Oh, hey. I didn't hear you come out." I sat up, brushing aside the leaves that had landed on my chest.

"Clearly. You must be thinking pretty hard about something," Izzy replied. "Should I leave you alone for a while?"

"Nah, stay here. I was just poking around in my bag."

"Ha. I haven't seen that in a while."

"Yeah, I was looking for my good pocket knife."

"But you haven't opened it yet, have you?" I shook my head. "Why not?"

"I don't know. Got distracted by the scenery I guess." I motioned to the trees above our heads. Her hair fluttered in the breeze, and when I got a fresh whiff of her perfume, she started giggling.

"You always get a funny look when you smell my perfume."

"It smells good."

She grinned and sat down next to me. Then she prodded the bag. "Is there still much inside?"

"Yeah, a few things. I carried everything in this bag, you know. Whatever I couldn't fit in my pockets went in here," I said. "Food, bus tickets, extra socks, my pocket knife…stuff like that."

"Where'd you get it?"

"The first foster home I had. The foster dad got me a bike and a paper route to keep me out of trouble."

"You were a paperboy?"

"Yeah. Why are you laughing? Do you think it's silly?"

"It's just funny trying to imagine you delivering papers."

"I was the best, like *Maniac Magee* with pedals," I said.

Izzy laughed again. "Well what happened? That sounds

like it could have been a good gig."

"The family had a son that was used to being an only child. He didn't like having me around, so him and his buddies picked on me all the time."

"That's awful."

"Yeah, it was, so I came up with a grand plan of escape. Being a rebellious twelve-year-old, I packed all my stuff in the bag before I put my newspapers in the next day. When I was done with the route, I just kept biking. Everything was going great until the cops picked me up at the bus station trying to buy a ticket." I patted the bag like it was an old friend. "I lost the bike, but I kept the bag. After that I got sent to a different home."

"How many times did you move?"

"By the time everything was all said and done, I think I had ten different homes."

"Seriously?"

"Yep." I lay down again. "It sure is beautiful out here."

When Izzy lay down next to me, a leaf promptly drifted down and landed on her face, which she brushed away with a laugh. "What happened when you moved?"

"I went to court. Well, usually every three months I would go for a mandatory review, which means I'd go hang out with a court attorney for an hour or so and answer all their questions. Then a judge would review the case and decide what happened next."

"Every three months, huh?" Izzy said.

"Like I said, usually. I was in more often than that."

"So you were a badass troublemaker then?"

"Depends. Are you into bad boys?"

She flashed me a seductive expression that made us both laugh. "Just keep going, you dork."

"When I first got into the system everything was okay. I tried to follow all the rules. You know—be good, go to school, listen to your foster parents. After a while though, it just got difficult. Kids at that age can be awful. Some will bury you in useless pity and others will make fun of you for not having a family…"

Izzy slid her fingers into mine, so I kept talking.

"As I got older I didn't like telling people where I was all the time, and that with the combination of foster siblings was just…blah. So I was in court all the time. 'I don't know what we're going to do with you, Mr. Allen.' That's what the judge said to me after my third or fourth trip to see him."

"What's it like?"

"Kind of scary at first, I guess. But in the end it's just frustrating. It was my word against the foster family's, and once you've been stamped with the label 'delinquent,' it makes any credibility you have at the age of fourteen go down the shitter."

"Brody, that's terrible."

"Tell me about it. I mean sure, there are some truly messed up foster kids, but some people will make the assumption that you're messed up to begin with just because you're a foster child. They don't necessarily take into account why you're in that situation in the first place."

"Yeah…What happened? I mean, is there one time that really sticks out?"

"I got sent to a new family after I tried to run away from that first one. It was fine at first. This one had a mom, dad, and a daughter. But there was something off about the daughter. She was a couple years older than me, and she was already hooked on cigarettes. I got home from school one afternoon and I caught her sneaking money out of her mom's purse."

"She begged you not to say anything, didn't she?"

"Oh yeah. I just rolled my eyes and walked away. Then I made the mistake of leaving and going to the library. When I got home, her mom was going off about losing a bunch of cash, and guess who she blamed?"

"You," Izzy said, and I nodded. "Seriously? The daughter set you up?"

"Yeah. She put some of the money she stole under my mattress."

"That's bullshit! Did you say something then?"

"Yeah, absolutely. I told the foster mom that her daughter was stealing money for smokes, but then her mom just gave me the my-daughter-is-an-angel speech. Her husband then chimed in with the classic: 'We gave you a place to live and this is how you repay us?' Child services came to get me the next day, and then I went to court. A few days later I was in another new home."

Izzy looked appalled. "So that first day when you were

here and I said don't steal anything…"

"Don't worry about it, Izzy."

"I had no idea who you were. I was just trying to be cautious."

"Really, Izzy, it didn't bother me. You get used to that sort of thing."

"Yeah, but that's terrible that people jump to that conclusion."

"Yeah, well…" My voice faded away and I closed my eyes. She squeezed my hand and I squeezed back.

"So what happened before you left for good?"

"Well, I spent a lot of time at the library. I don't know what I would have done without the library."

"You could have picked up fly fishing," Izzy blurted out. My eyes flew open and I turned to face her. Our noses were just touching and she was biting her lip, holding back a grin. Then I tickled her. Her laughter rang out across the yard as she rolled about in the grass. Then she tickled me in retaliation until I was laughing so hard I couldn't breathe.

"Where have you been all my life?" I said when she finally relented.

"I've been on a lifelong journey to become a trained fly fisherwoman so I could teach you." We both started laughing again.

"That's it. Everything makes sense now," I said.

Izzy poked me. "Keep going."

"Well most of the annoying kids didn't go to the library,

which was why it was almost always quiet. I would get all my homework done and then I would read. I got tired of people staring at me and judging me all the time. Books don't judge. In fact they love when you peel 'em open and stare at their innards."

Izzy lost it and buried her face in my hoodie. "You're such a dork."

"Thanks, but yeah, I spent as much time as possible at the library. By the time I turned sixteen though, I'd gotten to a point where I was tired of being a burden to people. It was easier just being on my own, so I set up a meeting with the guidance counselor at my high school. She was really cool about everything and got me set up to take the required test. I was really banking on this to work because I planned things out much more carefully this time."

"No runaway bike though." She grinned. "Or did you have another by then?"

"Nope, no bike this time."

"Damn."

"Yeah. I had to wait about a week before I got the results back. I passed though. It was a pretty cool feeling, and that night I left. I waited for the foster parents to go to bed, left them a little note saying thank you for everything, and called a taxi. I hitched a ride on my first long-distance bus trip, and now here I am."

"Do you think they looked for you?"

I shrugged. "Maybe for a while, but it's not like I was an

actual member of their family, and besides, there's so many kids in the system that it's hard to keep track of them all." After that, the questions stopped for a while and we both just stared upward at the trees and the sky.

"Do you think it was selfish of me to leave like that?" I asked.

"I don't know. Do you think it was?"

"Sometimes. The judge was always telling me to be hopeful and that things would work out. He knew lots of foster kids who became cops and other cool things, and for some reason I was determined to make the judge happy. But more and more it just seemed like the odds were stacking up against me. Making the judge happy wasn't necessarily going to make me happy. That last family was probably the most reasonable family I was with, but I was just tired."

"Yeah, well, at the risk of sounding mushy, I'm glad you made it out here." Then Izzy sat up. "Can I peek?"

"Yeah, go ahead." I sat up too, and drew the cloth strap back through the metal clasp. She lifted the flap and peered into the bag. Inside were a couple pairs of socks, a pocket knife, and some pliers. There were also a couple containers of vitamins, a baggie with a toothbrush, toothpaste, and a large pad of paper, which she immediately thumbed through.

"You can draw? You never told me you can draw," Izzy said. I just smiled. "And some of these are really new. I've never seen you drawing."

"Sometimes I draw at night after you and your mom go to

bed." I gave her a sheepish smile.

"They're really good." She came to a page with a dog on it. "You drew Molly?"

"Yeah. I don't know if it's any good, but—"

"I love it! It's perfect." She stared longingly at the picture until I nudged her knee.

"What?" she asked.

"Let me see that." She handed me the pad of paper and before she could say another word, I tore the sheet out.

Izzy gaped at me. "What are you doing?"

"Take it. I drew it for you anyway."

"But—"

"Just take it. I want you to have it." I knew I'd never be able to do enough to thank her for being so amazing.

"Thank you, Brody." I grinned when her lips met my cheek. "There's so much I don't know about you."

"Well, if it makes you feel any better, you know more than anyone else."

Izzy nodded and carefully began putting everything back in the bag. That was when she saw the plain, worn out envelope inside.

"What's this?" she asked.

"Oh." I'd forgotten that envelope was in there. "Um..."

"Do you not want me to look? I won't." She handed the envelope to me.

"No, it's all right. It's just some personal things. Birth certificate and a couple pictures."

"Are you sure you want me to? You look nervous."

I was nervous. My heart was pounding and the breezy sixty degree air suddenly felt stifling, but I handed her the envelope anyway.

"I've never shown anyone the pictures," I said.

"But you're showing me?"

"Yeah. Go ahead."

Very carefully she peeled open the envelope. Just as I said, there were some personal documents, but the special items were the two pictures of a woman.

"Brody…" Her voice grew soft.

"That's my mom." She was young in the picture, with brown hair like Izzy's and blue eyes like mine.

When Izzy set the picture down, there were tears in her eyes. "She's very pretty." I could only imagine the thoughts going through her head, but she stared at the picture for a long time. Of the few pictures I had of my mother, this was by far my favorite. She was laughing about something that made her cheeks bunch up into the best smile I'd ever seen. Often I tried to guess what it might have been—a funny joke, perhaps something my dad had said to her? Whatever it was, the joyful expression that I'd never known in person still helped me to feel some sort of connection to her.

Before Izzy could say anything though, the back door opened on the house.

"Well, look at this! Izzy's with a boy!"

"Oh great." Izzy gave the girl a lazy wave after passing the pictures back to me.

"What?" I whispered. "Who's that?"

"My sister, Sarah," she replied. I nodded and quickly shoved my belongings back in the bag.

"Did you meet a college boy, Izzy? He's cute!" Sarah said. After crossing the lawn, she sat down in the grass beside us. When I glanced at Izzy, she rolled her eyes.

"No," she said.

"My name's Brody. It's nice to meet you." I reached out a hand. When Sarah let go, she stared at us with a mysterious grin on her face. She resembled Izzy in many ways except she was a little taller and her hair carried an auburn tint. Her nose was slightly more pointed and she wore several rings on her fingers.

"What are you doing here?" Izzy asked.

"Well, I had a long weekend at school and I thought I'd come home since I haven't been to visit in a while."

"Cool. I must say, Sarah, you look…very colorful," Izzy said. Under her windbreaker, she had on preppy floral capris and a flowy peach top. She carried a yellow Longchamp bag on her arm as well.

"Thanks. You like it?"

"Yeah. I guess. It looks like the Easter bunny dressed you in its favorite colors." When I tried to hide a snigger behind a cough, Izzy broke out laughing. Sarah gave her a stern frown.

"It's the *in* thing at Notre Dame, Izzy. The winters get long out there, and we need a little color once everything gets dreary in the fall," she said. Izzy raised her eyes and smiled at me.

"Speaking of school, have you decided where you're going yet?" Sarah asked. A handful of leaves crunched beneath me as I shifted uncomfortably where I sat. With all the excitement of the last several weeks, it hadn't really occurred to me until then that Izzy could be leaving the next fall to start a new life somewhere.

"You would like Notre Dame. There are so many fresh faces. The campus is beautiful and the guys have big dorm parties every weekend," Sarah continued. She tried to entice Izzy further by mentioning something about fishing and Lake Michigan, but Izzy wasn't paying attention because she had caught sight of the look on my face. I was doing my best to stay expressionless and pretend like I wasn't paying attention while fiddling with my bag. When I noticed her staring, I masked everything with a smile.

"Um, yeah. That's cool, Sarah. I've been looking, but I haven't picked anything yet," Izzy said.

Sarah nodded and decided to change the subject. "So, has Mom suddenly become lax on her boy policies?"

"I don't know, maybe she likes me more," Izzy said. I couldn't help but chuckle. "Besides, I'm the baby. I learned from your mistakes."

"Oh shut up, Izzy. I never did anything wrong," Sarah said.

Izzy winked at me. "I distinctly remember Sarah getting caught at least three times sneaking out her window to go meet boys in the middle of the night," she said. Izzy and I both laughed when Sarah's jaw dropped.

"I have no idea what you're talking about, Izzy," Sarah retorted.

Izzy leaned into me. "One night, our dad was actually home and I remember waking up to him yelling, 'Would you like me to drive you over there, Sarah? I'm sure Billy's parents would love to see you right now!' I was dying in my room. It was three in the morning." Sarah's cheeks were approaching neon pink as Izzy and I rolled over in the grass laughing.

"I hope she doesn't talk about me that much, Brody," Sarah said.

"Nah, but now I'll be sure to ask," I said. Izzy leaned into my shoulder again.

"Oh, I'm liking this one, Izzy. How did you two meet anyway?"

Izzy gave me another beautiful smile. "He stopped by Uncle Henry's shop one day. We've been hanging out ever since."

"Hmm," Sarah said. "Very cool."

"Are you still with that guy, Clayton?" Izzy asked.

"Nah, we've been done for a while. But I want to know more about Brody." Her amber eyes had a prying quality like a fox. "What do you do? Are you in the same classes as Izzy?"

I exhaled a slow breath. "No. I'm done with school already."

"But you're not in college? There's a bunch here in Eugene."

"I haven't had time. Been kind of busy with other things."

Her eyes narrowed. "Work then?"

"Yeah, that's part of it. I work at the fly shop with your uncle."

"Oh, so he just walks in and Uncle Henry hired him on the spot, huh?" Sarah said.

"Something like that," Izzy said.

"What do you like to do then?" Sarah asked.

"You ask a lot of questions," I replied.

"Well, my sister keeps making googly eyes at you. I want to know you're a good guy." Izzy swatted at her.

"Fair enough," I said.

"So where are you from?" she asked.

"Back east."

"Where abouts? I live out east too. South Bend, Indiana."

"That's the Midwest. I'm from Portland, Maine."

"Oh—way out east." It was like a chess match and the continual back and forth was putting my nerves on edge.

"Yep," I said. "Been traveling a lot."

"How much?" Sarah asked.

"Don't bother, Sarah," Izzy said. "He's got you beat ten to one, easy."

"Alright. Fine. What do you like to do?" Sarah asked.

"Izzy and I go fishing a lot, and she's teaching me how to tie. I like reading and I love to cook."

"And drawing," Izzy added. "He likes to draw." She showed her sister the picture of Molly.

"Wow, Izzy. You're lucky. Clayton couldn't cook worth a shit," she said. I noticed Izzy's fair cheeks were tinged now as well.

"You know what? I think I'll make everyone dinner tonight," I said. "If that's okay with you, Izzy."

"Sounds good to me," Izzy said.

"Me, too," Sarah said. "I'll see you guys inside. I want to go see Momma." We sat in silence, waiting for her to disappear inside.

"Hey, I'm sorry about that. I wasn't expecting her at all," Izzy said.

"It's all right, Izzy. Really."

"Well you handled that really well."

"It's not the first time that's happened to me. Masking my answers isn't that hard for me, sadly."

"Well you don't have to hide anything from me."

I shook my head. "I don't want your sister to bother you though. Do you want me to stay somewhere else tonight?"

"Brody, you're not sleeping on the street somewhere!"

I couldn't help but laugh. "No, I just meant like go to Henry's or something."

"Don't worry about Sarah," Izzy said. "I want you to stay here."

I wished Sarah would stop talking about college. She had mentioned it on and off throughout dinner, and now Sarah and Izzy were sitting in the living room talking about it again. Heather had gone for a shower, and I lingered in the kitchen to do the dishes. I think Izzy was worried that I could hear them talking, because she kept hushing Sarah and telling her not to get so excited. It didn't matter though. I could still hear them.

"Seriously, Izzy, you should see it out there. In the winter the campus looks like something out of *Harry Potter*. All the old, brick buildings are covered with fluffy, white snow. It's so beautiful, Sis." I groaned silently and scrubbed a little harder. The longer I was in Eugene, the more I fell for Izzy. The way she looked at me, the way it felt when we fell asleep on the couch or when we stayed up late talking and tying together. The idea of a fairytale love story was enough to make me laugh, and yet I ached for it. I had stumbled into her life a sick, dirty mess—misunderstood and unfortunate. Yet I hoped that I was the nicest guy she'd ever met, because she was by far the most amazing woman I'd ever known. Her heading off to college had the potential to ruin that.

"That does sound pretty cool, Sarah. I do have to finish some apps and I'll definitely keep them in mind," Izzy said. "I'll be right back."

"Okay," Sarah replied. "I think Mom's done in the shower anyway."

I heard the gentle creak of the couch as Izzy hurried into the kitchen. I was right where she expected me to be—with my hands and forearms covered by long, yellow gloves and elbow deep in suds—scrubbing furiously at food burned onto the casserole dish.

"We have a dishwasher you know," she said.

"I know." I didn't look at her. "I want to make sure these are all cleaned off."

"Uhuh. Or you're avoiding me and my sister. Are you mad at me?"

"No."

"Hey. Look at me."

My hands ached and I finally stopped scrubbing to stare at her. Somehow I managed a smile, but it didn't feel as sincere as it could have been.

"Don't lie to me."

"I'm not mad," I said. "I just don't know what to think I guess."

"Brody, I've hardly thought about school and I know my sister made you uncomfortable. You've been distant ever since she got here."

I shrugged and kept scrubbing the pan. "I really like you, Izzy, but I don't want to hamper your life." I yelped when she prodded me in the ribs. Her eyes were shiny with tears, but her expression was hard.

"You're not hampering my life, Brody."

"I'm sorry. I didn't mean—"

"Don't worry about my sister."

It didn't take long for a smile to creep across my face and I splashed her cheek with a handful of suds. She laughed and leaned into me playfully. "I suppose I could use the dishwasher now," I said.

"Yeah, and then we can go watch our show." Izzy grinned. A few minutes later we were curled up on the couch, ready to watch a television show that Izzy had introduced me to. Heather had also joined us, although she claimed a solo seat in the recliner.

"I don't mean to interrupt, but you two are so cute." There was a sleepy smile on her face as she sipped from her glass of wine. At the sound of footsteps on the stairs, our laughter faded to silence. Sarah appeared in the living room dressed for bed as well.

"What's this? All tucked up on the couch with hot chocolate and a blanket," Sarah said.

"Yeah," Izzy replied. "We're watching *Castle*."

"Best show ever," I added.

"Alright. Move over, Sis," Sarah said. "By the way, thanks for dinner, Brody."

"You're welcome. Glad you liked it."

When the gruesome opening scene unfolded in the living room, Izzy shuddered with disgusted excitement and slowly intertwined a few fingers with mine under the blanket. Sarah decided to speak again when the opening credits came up.

"You really have loosened the reins, Mom. I never got to have boys over like this."

Heather tittered. "Izzy doesn't see the need to sneak out late at night like you did, Sarah."

Sarah's eyes flashed to Izzy. "Did you tell her to say that?"

Izzy was still giggling from her mother's jibe and shook her head.

"Well seriously, when does Brody leave? Does he live here or what?" Sarah asked. Izzy squeezed my fingers a little more as I leaned forward to press pause on the remote. Despite Sarah being a few years older than me and much more confident, the sudden silence was clearly alarming to her. "What?" she stammered. "I'm just asking."

"I was going to make a joke about being a butler or something, but I guess I'll just tell you. I do kind of live here, Sarah."

You would have thought somebody just told the funniest

joke of all time to a person who sucked in a balloon full of helium. Sarah's high-pitched laughter filled the living room as she squirmed about in her seat.

"Now that's hilarious," she panted. "I've really got to come home more often." When she realized none of us were laughing, her head swiveled between her sister and mother for any sort of clarification, but all she received in return were blank stares.

"Yeah right, and I'm pregnant," Sarah said.

"Really?" Izzy asked. Heather made a funny noise into her glass.

"No!" Sarah exclaimed. "And there's no way Mom would let some random dude stay in the house. No offense."

"None taken," I said. "I've heard worse."

"I don't get this. Are you like homeless or something?" Sarah asked.

I scratched my head. "Yeah. I am. Well kinda. Not really any more, I guess. Your sister and mom were kind enough to give me a place to stay."

Sarah's shocked face glanced between the three of us multiple times before coming to rest on her mother. "What's going on, Mom? Are you guys all messing with me? You never let any of my boyfriends live here." Both Izzy and I raised our free hands to protest, but Sarah cut in. "Don't bother denying it. You two are adorable." The tense moment erupted in laughs and Izzy flushed.

"Um, well…" Heather began. I knew she was thinking

about the scars. It was all over her face. "I don't want to mix up any of the details, so I think it would be better if Brody told you."

Sarah's eyes returned to me. "You're homeless?"

"Well, I was until your mom gave the A-OK for me to stay here. I'm a foster kid that left the system and I've been on my own for almost three years," I said.

"Holy crap. That's insane," Sarah said. "Have you told Dad?" Izzy and her mother exchanged nervous glances.

"No," Heather finally said. "I don't want him to worry. He has enough to worry about over in that desert."

"You can't tell him, Sarah," Izzy said.

"But it's Dad," Sarah replied.

"Yes, honey," said her mother, "and he's my husband. I don't want to bother him with this because it's not something that he needs to worry about. Is it, Brody?"

"Nope."

Heather nodded. "He worries about you girls so much and I don't want him to freak out about this. I'm just trying to help Brody get on his feet."

"Please don't tell him, Sarah. I know that you talk to him all the time," Izzy said.

"I won't tell him," she finally said. "I'm kind of jealous honestly. It's like you have a chef living in the house." We all laughed again and I unpaused the show. I could feel Sarah staring at me. About halfway through the episode Sarah broke her silence when the show went to a commercial.

"What's it like?" she asked. "I'm sorry. I just can't stop thinking about this."

"Which part? Not having a home or being a foster kid—because neither one is that great."

"I guess the not having a home part."

I shifted in my seat, trying to lean affectionately into Izzy. Then I smiled gratefully at Heather. "Running into Izzy and meeting your family is easily the best thing that's ever happened to me."

Apparently that was enough for Sarah. At least, I hoped it was.

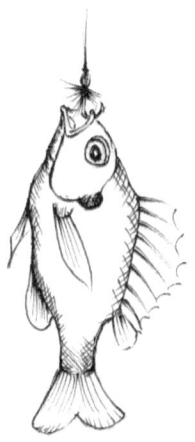

Keep it. Consider it a present for a few belated birthdays. Izzy's words replayed in my head as I squeezed the smooth cork handle while beginning another casting motion. I had gone for years with hardly any belongings. Now I had a handful of new clothes as well as my very own fly rod. The sleek four-weight model and its medium-sized reel were perfect for catching bluegill in the pond.

That afternoon, the sky was blanketed by thick low-hanging clouds threatening rain. Cool rains had already fallen several times that week, which meant there were less people down at the park, even on the days that were sunny. I didn't mind though, especially when I was caught up in my own head, trying not to let negative thoughts get the best of me.

The more attached to Izzy I became, the more I realized

how terrible it would be to lose her. But it was more than that. It was Heather and Henry, too. I sighed and whipped the line back to begin another cast. The lack of disappointment in my life was starting to worry me.

After growing up with my father I'd figured that anywhere beyond his shabby house would be better, but being a foster kid had been just as frustrating, if not more so. Nothing was permanent and there had been few friends to call upon—many whispered jokes at my expense. I was completely detached from the things that other people took for granted every single day.

Izzy wasn't like that though. I knew that with her dad being gone, she saw things differently. Different than anyone else I'd met anyway. But deep down I still worried that she just considered me a misfit and felt sorry for me, because I knew that she could have anyone she wanted.

A cool breeze brushed across my face and the relaxing casting motion set my mind adrift. *Forward…back…forward… back…cast!* Fifteen yards of line went whistling by my ear, carrying my fly out over the pond. As it came to a rest on the surface of the pond, I gave into more daydreams.

Since my awesome lifestyle put such a damper on things, I'd never actually been with a girl before. The passionate kiss we shared in the mountains had admittedly left me wondering what it would be like to have sex with Izzy. I was sure what was beneath her plaid shirts and jeans was truly gorgeous. Yet, as much as I wanted to be with her, I was definitely scared. I didn't want to end up like my father.

Nothing came for my fly, so I whipped the line back and cast out again. One of the things I was most excited for was spending the holidays with Izzy and her family. The thought of being able to enjoy Thanksgiving and Christmas was worth more to me than any gift or amount of money.

A flash of white underneath the water's surface caught my attention, and then something consumed my fly. A battle ensued, and I knew that this fish was the biggest I'd hooked yet at the pond. As the fish tugged and tugged, I felt a struggle in my head as well. Even if we dated seriously, I knew that Izzy would probably head off to college, and then what? I considered moving with her, but the last thing I wanted was to be someone who held her back.

Then of course, there was the issue of her father. Every time I thought about Sarah, I worried about her spilling the beans. I'm sure it was well within the Sarge's capabilities to stick me in the back of a transport plane bound for some unknown place. The fish yanked hard and I worried that it might break my leader. I could only imagine what the Sarge would say when he found out that his daughter was hanging out with a foster kid who was also living in his home. The fish exploded from the water and I grinned with excitement. It was a big fish and definitely not a bluegill. When exhaustion set in, I reeled it to shore.

"Look at that!" I turned to see Izzy strolling toward me, and I held up the fish. "Let me get a picture. That's an awesome smallmouth." In the wake of her smile, the remainder of my stressful thoughts dissipated into a calm oblivion.

"Thanks," I said and gently set the fish back in the water.

"When did you get here?" she asked. "I stopped by the shop to get you."

"Oh, I'm sorry. Henry told me to head out early so I could make something for that trip tomorrow. But I wanted to come practice first."

"Well it looks like you're getting better."

"Ha. How long have you been watching?"

"Long enough. You didn't hook your ear anyway," she said, and I laughed. "Can I help you cook later?"

"Of course. Would you mind if we stopped at the grocery on the way back to your mom's though?"

Izzy didn't answer right away because she was getting her line ready to go. "Nope. That sounds perfect. How about the first person to catch seven fish picks out a dessert?"

"You're on!"

"And no crossing lines with me to slow me down like you did last time."

"Seriously, Izzy? I still have no idea what you're talking about. I'm telling you, it was the wind."

She grinned and shoved me affectionately. After a couple hours of fishing, the tally was six to six. Darkness was settling around us and we were both tired and hungry, but neither of us wanted to admit it. Just before I thought about calling it quits, Izzy hooked her last fish.

"Oh, yeah!" she exclaimed. "I win." I gaped at her. Hanging from her hook was a bluegill so small that it should have been considered a minnow.

"By a technicality," I teased.

"A fish is a fish, Brody," she said, plucking the little bluegill from the hook. "And it's so cute. You should give it a kiss."

"Oh yeah, you weirdo."

Izzy grinned and held the fish up to my face. The bulbous eyes stared at me and the tiny mouth opened and closed as it gulped for air. She gave a little shriek when the fish's lips met mine.

"You're not gonna kiss it?" I asked. She shook her head after setting the fish back in the water, so in one swift motion I picked her up off the ground and planted a fishy kiss on her cheek.

"Brody!"

When I set her down, I noticed a big white truck parked at the far end of the pond. I didn't think much of it until we drove out of the park. I glanced in the mirror and saw the truck's lights—instead of heading out the other park entrance, the truck came the same direction as Izzy and me.

"You okay, Brody?"

"Huh? Yeah. I'm good. You decide on your victory dessert?"

"I was thinking we could make cupcakes if you're up for more cooking."

"Definitely." Normally Izzy's smile made me feel like a champion, but when I looked back to the mirror, I could still see the white truck a few cars back. It made the hairs on my neck stand on end. Something didn't feel right at all.

"You're not going to leave are you?" she blurted out.

"Huh?"

"I noticed that you do that a lot—stare out the window. I know you're thinking, but are you thinking about leaving?"

"No. I love it here. Just a few things on my mind. That's all."

"Well, I hope everything is okay. You know you can talk to me about stuff or whatever."

"Yeah, I know." I considered mentioning the truck behind us, but I didn't see the point in worrying her, especially when she was rocking to the music in the driver's seat. Just before pulling into the grocery store parking lot, I looked in the mirror again. The truck was gone. I breathed a small sigh of relief and followed Izzy inside.

I loved going to the grocery store with her. She made something impossibly mundane into something truly enjoyable. Usually we raced up and down the aisles, dodging the stock boys and grumpy shoppers. Tonight, however, Izzy was standing on the end of the shopping cart I was pushing, singing along to the songs on the grocery store speakers.

Everything was going fine until I noticed something strange. There was a guy staring at us from the far end of the aisle. Not blatantly staring, but casually. Izzy was having too much fun to notice, but when I saw this guy a third time, I was certain he was following us around the store. Something about his face was strangely familiar, but he was always too far away for me to get a good look at him.

"Is this what we need, Brody?" Izzy held up a bag of beans.

"Yeah, that's perfect." She dropped them in the cart and kept singing. When I looked to the end of the aisle, the guy was gone and I never saw him again. By the time we left the store I was excited to make dinner with Izzy. However, when I saw that same white truck leaving the parking lot, the hairs on my neck prickled again.

What I'd been too afraid to tell Izzy was that I thought it was my father, somehow released from prison, trying to track me down. But now I knew it was someone else, and I was positive whoever had been in the store was the same person who was driving that truck.

"You all right, Brody?" Izzy was staring at me again, her hand poised, ready to turn the key in the ignition.

"Yeah. I think so. Just hungry." It wasn't the answer I wanted to give, but she was so happy and cheerful. I couldn't ruin that.

Soon we were back home sautéing meat and onions in the fry pan. A pot of carrots and beans was steaming away on the stove, and the jazz music was playing again. By the time Heather got home, Izzy and I were sitting at the table, spinning deer hair for an order of dry flies that Henry needed. It wasn't easy, but I was getting the hang of it. Heather sniffed hungrily at the delectable aroma that had pervaded the house.

"We saved you a bowl," Izzy said as she focused on her vice. "It's on the counter."

Heather spooned through the hearty chunks of sausage mixed with beans, carrots, onions, and tomatoes.

"What is it?" she asked.

"It's called cassoulet," I said, letting go of the bobbin. "I learned how to make it when I worked down in Louisiana. It's one of my favorites."

Heather eagerly took a bite. She closed her eyes and spun in a slow circle, leaving me to wonder what she was thinking. When she opened them again I was staring at her, waiting with bated breath for her opinion.

"You should open a restaurant, Brody," Heather said.

I let out a sigh of relief and Izzy gave my arm a shove. "I told you she would like it, Brody."

Heather laughed and took another bite. "You know something though, I don't know if those folks out on the river will like this stuff. I think you might have to leave the whole pot here."

Izzy and I both broke out laughing.

"At least leave me another bowl," Heather said.

"We can do that," Izzy said. My heart swelled and I basked in the glow of feeling useful. Then there was a knock at the door.

"I'll get it you guys. Just keep tying!" Heather left the kitchen, carrying her dinner with her. When she returned she looked positively unsettled, and let the bowl come to a rest on the counter with a loud thud.

"Izzy. Can I talk to you?"

"Yeah, sure. Who was at the door?"

"Just come here, sweetheart." Izzy's pale complexion grew whiter still.

"Did something happen to Dad?"

Heather shook her head and disappeared into the living room. Izzy's face scrunched in confusion. When she returned, she looked as distressed as her mother had, although she tried to hide it behind one of her fantastic smiles. I played along until Heather went to bed.

"So, what was that about earlier?"

Izzy was staring blankly at her homework. She shrugged, but said nothing.

"Okay," I said.

"What do you mean 'okay'? You're not gonna say anything else?"

"Izzy, ever since I got here, you've been kind to me and haven't been pushy with me. I'm not going to pry. That being said, you can talk to me about stuff too, you know."

"I know." Izzy leaned over and kissed my cheek. "It was Derek."

"Oh. Really?" Her words were like a bombshell and I pulled away as the fear and anxiety crowded around me on the couch.

"Yeah, but I don't want you to be mad or worried or something."

"I'm not mad. I just…" I sighed. My stomach felt like it was swirling in the drain.

"Brody—"

"What did he want?"

"He wanted to talk to me, but Mom said no. She never liked him. She said he smelled like weed too."

"Weed?"

"Yeah, Brody. Pot. You know, the drug?"

"I know what it is, Izzy."

The humor faded and her face scrunched up as if she'd just eaten something awful. When I didn't say anything, Izzy picked up her pencil and started drawing random lines on her paper. "Mom wasn't happy. She said he was acting weird and looked smug as hell."

"What else did she say?"

"She told me to make sure that if I'm not with Henry or here at home, to make sure I'm with you. My mom likes you, Brody."

"Well that's good."

Izzy slid her fingers into mine. "Brody, I promise you there's nothing going on."

My head moved up and down, but I remained silent. I believed her, but as her eyes searched me again, I realized that I was worried for a completely different reason.

"I think I saw him at the grocery store tonight."

"You're probably being paranoid. That would be nuts."

"I'm not paranoid, Izzy."

The look she gave me said otherwise.

"All right, he's got light brown hair, and he's a little taller than me. Blue and white jacket and trendy looking clothes. Fancy sneakers and a smug expression on his face."

"Holy shit. You saw him. Where was he?"

"I saw him a few times around the grocery store. It seemed like he was following us, but every time I saw him he would look away."

"That doesn't make sense. He's hanging out with Jackie now," Izzy said.

I shrugged. "He drives a white truck doesn't he?"

"Yeah. How did you know that?"

"He was at the pond tonight. He followed us to the store."

"Oh God." The remaining color drained from her cheeks. "You can't tell my mom."

"Why?"

"Because she'll freak out. Listen, Derek was probably high as a kite, chowing on fast food or something."

"Yeah, right," I said, but we both knew it wasn't true.

"Seriously, I hope we're good. I don't want you to leave or something."

"I'm not gonna leave. I believe you, Isabel."

"Good, because we've got other matters to take care of."

"Like what?" I asked, doing my best to put Derek out of my mind.

"It's time to get Henry a date."

Early the following afternoon, I found a spot on the river-bank to heat up our lunch. The fire crackled and popped merrily, sending up thick smoke to join the misty fog that was already drifting through the mountains. It had been a relatively uneventful morning so far, but our clients seemed to be having a great time. Apparently Mac and Henry had been friends since Henry had moved to Oregon. He had brought along his ten-year-old son, Nate, and a coworker who Mac insisted needed a break from the office.

After pulling our drift boats ashore, Nate continued messing around, fishing in the river and sneaking about in the woods. Henry helped get the other two situated in the river before joining me by the fire.

"So, Henry," I began. "We've known each other for a

while now…"

"Yeah we have, buddy, and don't worry—I have no plans to fire you. You've been a great help. And this food you make is amazing!"

"Thanks. That's good to know, but I was getting at something else."

"What's that?"

"I was curious about that lady Miranda. I saw you two talking again the other day. How did you two meet anyway?" I asked.

"We met at a Trout Unlimited function up in Seattle last year."

"That's sweet. Has anything…"

"No, not really." His tone was the complete opposite of the strong, confident fly fishing expert that led newbies in search of a wild river adventure.

"Can I ask why not?"

"I don't know, Brody. I just…I'm so used to fishing and working at the shop."

"You're scared."

The polarized sunglasses made Henry's expression difficult to read. "Maybe," he finally said. "It's complicated."

"Well I think you should go for it. You know she likes you. That's half the battle."

Henry laughed. "All right smarty pants. What should I do?"

"Take her out for coffee or have her over for dinner or something. I don't know. Whatever adults do."

"You're an adult."

"There's varying levels of adults," I countered. "I'm what they would call a *young* adult."

"What does that make me? A senior citizen?"

"No way!"

"Well, what do you and Izzy do together?" he asked.

"Who says we're together?"

"Oh come on, Brody. You realize *no one* would believe you."

I smiled and stirred the contents of the pot. "We tie a lot, watch movies, go fishing, dance, and I'm teaching her how to cook."

"You dance?" Henry stammered.

"I try."

"Fair enough. Let's go with dinner, for example. Would you and Izzy join us if Miranda said yes? Just a really casual, informal thing. You two could give me some moral support and possibly help with dinner."

I bowed my head, hiding another grin. *Our plan worked!* "Done. I'll ask Izzy when we get back tonight. Will you ask Miranda?"

"Yes," Henry said after a deep breath.

"You have to ask her, Henry!"

"I will!"

Then there was a tug on my jacket. "Hey, Mr. Brody. You should come check this out. I found something cool in the woods!" Nate's eyes were brimming with excitement and his curly blonde hair was fluttering in the breeze beneath his winter cap. There was also a tall stick clutched in his hand, giving him the appearance of an avid mountain climber.

"Alright, buddy. Do you mind, Henry?" I asked.

"No, go ahead. I'll stir. Don't be too long though. There might not be any lunch left."

I laughed as Nate and I trotted off down the stony shore.

"You have such a cool job, Mr. Brody," Nate said.

"Yeah, I like it. Are you having fun so far?"

"Definitely! This place is so cool! Did you see the mountains, Mr. Brody?" Several times that morning, heavy gusts of wind had blown aside the thick blanket of fog, exposing the snow-capped mountaintops. Winter was definitely on its way.

"Yeah. It's pretty," I answered. Nate grinned and disappeared into the underbrush. Despite many of the trees having lost their leaves, the forest was filled with thick, fragrant evergreens. Soon we could no longer see the river, and the trees blocked out the sounds of camp. Shadows off in the distance made me think of the bear that Izzy and I had run into.

"Hey, stay close, Nate."

"Okay." He jumped back in front of me, but kept up his excited pace.

"What did you find anyway?"

"A waterfall," he whispered. Our short hike through the woods ended when the narrow trail gave way to a damp, rocky terrace. The misty spray hanging in the air made it feel like we were walking through a cloud.

"Isn't this awesome, Mr. Brody?" I followed him forward, listening to the gurgling river as it rushed over the rocks, tumbling into the greenish-blue pool below.

"Yeah, but be careful, Nate. Those rocks are slippery."

Nate had set aside his walking stick and was climbing on the rocks like a billy goat. "Will you take my picture, Mr. Brody? Please?"

"Yeah, sure." I pulled out my guide camera and stepped back a few feet. "Big grin! You're a superhero!" Nate grinned like hell and lifted his arms up, but in that one split second as I pushed the button, everything changed. A gust of wind howled down the river, and suddenly Nate's face was overcome with terror as he lost his footing on the wet rock. His arms flailed, but there was nothing for him to grasp as he fell back.

"Brody!"

I rushed forward, but it was too late. His small frame kept falling until he collided with the river. There was no sound of him hitting the water—only the roar of the river as the current consumed Nate's body.

"Oh my God." The camera slipped from my grasp, clattering against the rocks. I collapsed to the ground, not feeling the pain as my knees pounded into the hard rocks. I couldn't breathe. My chest heaved as I stared bug-eyed at the current, waiting, hoping for Nate to reappear. But he never did.

I pushed myself to stand and started shouting.

"Henry! Henry! Call for help!" Panic and fear were setting in as I waited for an answer. But there was nothing—just the sound of the waterfall.

"Call for help!" I was yelling as loud as I could, hoping my voice wouldn't be drowned out by the river or blocked by the thick evergreens.

"Brody! What happened?" Henry's voice was far off still and I didn't bother to answer. There wasn't time. I stepped back farther from the waterfall's edge. All I could hear was an eerie wind whistling through the tree branches, urging me to go. *Now!* My heart was pounding like a race horse as I broke into a sprint.

"Brody!" Henry shouted. He was closer now. I could hear him tearing through the woods, his feet crunching dirt and gravel behind me, but I ran faster. "Brody! No!"

I still didn't answer. I didn't look back. The roar of the river had returned and I leaped into the void. The fall lasted for an eternity. The wind whistled by my ears and I could feel every part of my body all at once. Every hair on my body felt electrified under the layers of garments I was wearing. Nate's terrified expression was plastered across my mind, and my heart was beating so fast I was sure I was going to have a heart attack. I wondered if they'd look for me. Surely they'd look for Nate, but I was the kid with no home. A runaway. Whether I really mattered to any of them or not, I had to try. All at once, the forty-foot fall was at its end.

I slammed into the river and was immediately sucked under the waterfall. All I could hear was a muffled roar as the icy, frothing water engulfed my face and body, leaving me horribly confused and disoriented. It was a battle in itself not to open my mouth and swallow half the river.

You have to get to Nate. I kicked my legs, but the waterfall kept pushing me deeper into the pool. Just when I thought I was surely a goner, the pressure vanished. My lungs were on fire, but I kicked my legs as hard as I could, and soon I was caught in the river current. When I finally broke the surface, the waterfall had to have been at least fifty yards behind me.

I scanned the river, but there was nothing. The water was pushing me along so fast that it made it difficult to focus on anything. I tried to remember what color jacket Nate had on, but the water was so cold. My brain was already slowing down.

Think! Think! The river swept me along and I tried my hardest to remember. We'd parked for lunch, so everyone had taken off their life jackets. *His coat was…green! yellow! stripes!* At that moment, there was a flash of an arm. For an instant, I glimpsed Nate rolling over in the river, but he didn't appear to be fighting the current. I blinked, trying to get the water out of my eyes, and Nate was gone again.

Oh my goodness. Please don't be dead. Swimming with the current should have been easy, but my clothes were filling with water as I tried to propel myself forward. I was like an awkward piece of driftwood completely out of control.

Come on! It didn't help that I was getting colder. My muscles burned as I tried to kick and swim faster, but we zoomed into another set of rapids and I got sucked under. The current pummeled my body and I feared that I would soon collide with a rock or get skewered by a submerged branch. Somehow though I didn't, and when I finally popped up again Nate was drifting toward the edge of an eddy. I frantically paddled closer.

Gotcha! I grabbed the sleeve of his jacket and then his whole arm just as we slipped back into the current. The river was like an icy python engulfing us, strangling us until we could no longer fight back. The numbing coldness was stripping away the remaining strength of my fingers, and I feared I was going to lose my grip soon.

"Nate," I croaked, but the boy was unconscious if not worse, and his face had gone snow white. I tried to swim toward an edge, but Nate's added weight made it nearly impossible. It didn't help matters that the river also seemed to be picking up speed. I kept my free hand outstretched, trying to get a hold of something. Anything. Finally my arm and leg slammed into something. A rock. Probably a boulder.

"Ahhh!" My yelp of pain was quickly silenced by a face full of water, but there was no ignoring the crunch of bone. The pain that seared through my body was so severe I nearly let go of Nate. Somehow though it slowed us down, and we drifted into a shallower stretch of river. I treaded water until I got us closer to shore; by the time we reached the edge, Nate's skin was picking up a ghostly blue tint. It took every last bit of energy to crawl from the water and heave Nate onto dry ground.

His hat was gone and the curly locks were matted to his face. When I brushed them aside to listen for a breath, my hand came away red. Then I noticed blood oozing onto the rocks beneath his head.

"Oh God. No, no, no…" I listened for a pulse, but Nate was quiet as a tomb. I tried desperately to remember the CPR lessons.

One, two, three. After pressing on his chest, I plugged his nose and blew into his mouth.

"Come on, buddy! You're a superhero. Remember?" But there was no response.

One, two, three. I pressed, but my compressions were getting weaker. Again, I blew into his lungs. The cold was setting in on me faster and faster. Never had I been so cold in my life.

One, two, three. Once again, I pressed and blew into Nate's mouth, and just when my own strength left me I heard him cough and sputter. I collapsed onto my back, terrified at what was about to happen, but there was nothing I could do.

My breathing was raspy, and I watched my chest heave while my burning lungs tried to pull oxygen from the air. They were shutting down, too cold to function properly. The sound of my pounding heart faded from my ears when my head thudded back against the ground, too heavy to lift. My trembling hands went still, frozen to the bone. A darkness creeped in around the edge of my eyes, and with each blink I saw less and less. I could hear that eerie whistle through the evergreens again.

Then she was there, leaning over me like an angel. Everything about her made me feel at peace. Her beautiful brown hair, her kind green eyes, and her moonlit complexion.

"Izzy…" My eyelids closed one last time, too heavy to keep open, and I was consumed by a frosty darkness…

I didn't like bees at all, but I was surrounded by them. I could hear the constant drone of their little wings as they buzzed loudly around my ears. For some reason I couldn't open my eyes. In fact, I couldn't move anything.

You died. Remember? Some other part of my mind stirred to enlighten me of that depressing fact. *Well, maybe I'm in hell, surrounded by bees. Maybe I don't want to open my eyes.* Then everything slowed down again, even the bees. I could hear every discernible beat of their wings. *Thump, thump, thump, thump, thump…* But the noise didn't last—just as quickly as it came, the sound was gone and silence returned once more. When I finally woke, there was another noise.

Beep…beep…beep… But there was something more. Hushed whispers. The more I came to, the more I could hear…

and feel. Someone squeezed my hand and I squeezed back.

"Momma, he's awake." Izzy's voice. Adrenaline surged into my bloodstream and I was finally able to open my eyes. Her spring green irises were all that I could see, and I knew life was rushing back into me.

"I'll tell the nurse." Heather's blurry form hurried from the room.

"Hi, Brody." Izzy's voice was barely above a whisper, and there were tears in her eyes. She leaned over and kissed my forehead. Her lips were so warm.

"Hey, cutie," I croaked. "You're so beautiful."

She giggled. "You're high."

"Tell me about it. There were so many bees. I didn't think they came out this time of year."

"Bees?"

"Yeah. They were all…bzzzzzzz…and then everything slowed down, but they were still fast. Thump, thump, thump…" I hoped she would laugh at my drugged up goofiness, but the serious expression stayed.

"There were no bees, Brody. That was probably the helicopter."

"Helicopter?"

"Yeah, you were airlifted out of the mountains."

After several blinks, Izzy came into better focus and I saw that her eyes were puffy from crying. "I was in a helicopter…"

Before she could say anything, the nurse hustled into the room. She quickly scanned the monitors alongside the IV unit and whipped out a flashlight to check my eyes. "How are you feeling?" she asked.

"Fine I guess…I was in a helicopter?"

"Yes," said the nurse. "You were airlifted out of the national park yesterday afternoon. You nearly died from a bronchospasm—dry drowning." It was like someone hit fast forward in my brain, and I clamped my eyes shut when everything started flashing in my mind. *We were on a long weekend trip on the Deschutes. We were drifting boats down the river. We had stopped for lunch. The waterfall. Nate.*

Nate! My eyes flew open again and the heart monitor went crazy as I tried to sit up. "What happened to Nate! He didn't die, did he? Did he?"

"Relax, Brody," said the nurse. "You need to lie back." I glanced at Heather and Izzy, hoping for an answer that wasn't devastating. Even the nurse appeared distressed.

"No," she finally said. "You saved his life. I'll be back to check on him later, Heather. Everything looks all right so far, but you need to rest." She left the room and I sank back into the pillow, turning my attention back to Izzy and her mother.

"I'm really glad you're okay, Brody," Heather said. "I'm going to get Henry. He'll want to see you." She left the room again, but I never took my gaze off Izzy.

"Why are you smiling?"

"Because," she said.

"Because why?"

Izzy sat down on the bed beside me and ran her fingers

through my hair. Then she gave me a kiss. I will never forget how warm her lips were. "You finally made it to Portland," she whispered.

Despite my body aching, I chuckled. "You're kidding…"

"Nope."

I closed my eyes. She giggled when I tried to lift my hand in triumph. "We should go out for a celebratory dinner," I mumbled.

"Yeah maybe." Her eyes were getting watery again and she scooted a little closer.

"What happened, Izzy?"

"I don't know, Brody. I was so scared. I guess Henry was able to call for help, and then he called my mom. I was in the middle of history class trying to pay attention to a lesson about the Louisiana Purchase, but I kept thinking about that drag queen story."

"Oh those drag queens—such a distraction."

Izzy laughed despite the tears starting to run down her cheeks. "I got the most worried and nauseous feeling ever. It felt like I was getting drenched with ice water. I knew something terrible had happened."

I wanted to tell her to stop, but she kept going. "Then the teacher's phone rang—and the teacher's phone never rings, Brody—but I knew it was for me. The other kids started whispering while they watched me packing my bag, and I was out the door before the teacher was even off the phone. Mom was waiting for me at the office, and we drove up here as fast as possible." I closed my eyes again and she ran her hands through my hair. "Brody, please don't ever scare me like that again."

"I didn't mean to."

"I know. I just—"

"I'm sorry, Izzy." I wasn't used to someone caring so much about my well-being.

Then she kissed my forehead again. "You saved him, Brody. You saved that little kid."

I shrugged, not knowing what else to say. "You're not gonna leave are you?"

"Nope. I brought my homework," Izzy said.

"Good. I'll help you if I can."

"You need to rest, Brody."

"Okay." She squeezed my hand and then I drifted off to sleep. When I woke, Izzy was sound asleep, but Henry was wide awake in the chair beside her. There were heavy bags under his eyes, and his hair was even messier than usual.

"You got any water?" I asked.

"Oh, that's really funny, Brody," Henry replied. "How are you feeling?"

"I'm all right. Just sore. Is Nate okay?"

"Yeah. Thanks to you, you crazy bastard." He squeezed his ball cap like he was wringing out a rag. "I can't believe you jumped in after him."

"You should have seen him, Henry. He was so happy, and then so scared..." I shuddered as the vivid images flashed in front of me again. All of a sudden I felt restless, trapped by the bedsheets. The pearly white pillow was hot against my neck and my knuckles went white as I clenched a handful of sheets.

"Hey. It's all right. You're both okay," Henry said. "He really wants to see you, but the nurse won't let him out of bed yet. They think he got a minor concussion, so they don't really want him running around the hospital."

I closed my eyes and took several deep breaths. When I opened them again, Henry gave me a reassuring smile. "So, a dislocated shoulder and a sprained ankle. When are you coming back to work?"

"Is that all? Give me a week," I said.

Henry tried to laugh, but nothing could take the grave expression from his face. "My God, Brody. You were like a damn ice cube when we found you guys. Nate was coming to, but you were out cold. You were so blue, and your clothes were full of water."

"Yeah. Well, it's not exactly summer up there in the mountains."

Henry managed a weak chuckle. "You've got balls, Brody. What were you thinking?"

It was hard to tell if he was reprimanding me or praising me, so I shook my head.

"Come on, Brody. Tell me."

"You have no idea, Henry. Getting to see Nate with his dad... Nobody's ever taken me fishing or done anything fun with me. All he wanted was a picture. He was so happy. I had to try."

"Brody…"

"Are you mad, Henry?"

"What? No. I just…I don't know if I could have done what you did. You'd known Nate for what—four hours? And you nearly gave up your life for him."

"I had to try. I guess you guys rubbed off on me. Those CPR lessons worked too, by the way."

"Well, believe me. We're all glad you did. Especially Nate and his family." Henry made a weird noise and I thought I saw a few tears in his eyes, but then he turned away.

"Good," I whispered. "How are they doing?"

"Really shook up, but they're all right. They came to see you, but you've been asleep for a while." I nodded into the pillow. "You should probably keep sleeping. Let me know if you need anything."

"I can think of one thing."

"What's that?"

"When I get out of here, we gotta have that dinner. No excuses."

"Done," Henry said. "No excuses."

As soon as I closed my eyes, sleep consumed me. However, there was no peace to be found in my dreams. My father was there, yelling and cursing as he chased me through the woods. Then I fell. I plunged into the river again and I was scrambling, trying to swim upward. But it was dark and I couldn't tell which direction was up. The river was spinning me every direction and I was running out of air. I knew if I opened my mouth my lungs would fill with water and I would drown. I would cease to exist. Then there was something. A warmth. On my hand. It squeezed and I squeezed back, and then I was free of the river. I could breathe. My eyes darted around the room before coming to rest on Izzy. She was sitting next to me on the bed again.

"You're okay," she whispered. "You're okay. It's just a bad dream."

My eyes closed again and my chest heaved. The dream had felt so real. Then her fingers brushed through my hair. "You're okay," she repeated. "Just relax."

"I don't need any more bad dreams, Izzy."

"I know. They probably won't last that long. Just try to focus your thoughts on something happier. Think about me."

I smiled gratefully at her.

"Do you need anything?" she asked.

"A couch."

"A couch?"

"Yeah. I miss the couch at your mom's. I miss lying with you." My eyelids were getting heavy again. "Thank you for staying. That's really nice of you…"

"You're welcome, Brody. I wish we were back on the couch, too."

I held onto her smile as I drifted off to sleep once again.

Two more days passed before I was allowed to be discharged from the hospital. I was freshly dressed, sitting with Izzy on my bed while the nurse ran a stethoscope across my back to make sure my breathing had returned to normal. Then I heard Heather clear her throat.

Izzy and I turned at the sound, and that was when we caught sight of Nate. I will never be able to put into words the sense of relief I felt seeing him standing in the doorway. His curly blonde hair was flopping against his cheeks, doing nothing to hide the huge grin on his face.

"You're ready to go, Brody," said the nurse. "Make sure you keep that ankle brace on as much as possible, and just be gentle."

"Sounds good," I said. "Thank you." I eased off the bed and Izzy helped to keep me steady while I got situated with a pair of crutches.

"Hey, Mr. Brody," Nate said.

"How's it going, buddy?"

"Eh, I've been better." Nate gingerly touched the white bandage covering the wound on his head.

"Me too," I replied. Without another word, Nate rushed forward and hugged me so hard that it nearly sent me toppling back onto the bed. Heather started crying, and when Nate's parents walked in they both succumbed to tears as well.

"Thanks, Mr. Brody," Nate said.

"You're welcome, buddy. I'm glad you're okay. You ready to get out of here?"

"Yeah!" he said.

"How about you guys?" I asked the rest of them.

Everyone except Nate's mother nodded eagerly. "We'll be along. You go walk with him for a bit. He's been really excited to see you," she said.

"Alright," I replied.

"Are you okay to walk?" Izzy asked.

"Yeah. I'm good I think. Thanks. If I fall over, just laugh at me."

"Alright." Her eyes were sparkling. I gave her the most thankful smile I could muster and hobbled out of the room with Nate.

"So," I said.

"Thanks for saving me," Nate blurted out.

"No problem."

"Can I ask you something, Mr. Brody?"

"Sure."

"Does all this make you my brother now?"

"I don't know." It was the honest truth. I had no siblings. "Does it?"

"I don't know either. It seems like something a dad or a big brother would do," Nate said.

"Makes sense, except if I were your big brother, then you wouldn't have to call me Mr. Brody any more. Just Brody."

"Can I just call you Brody then?"

"Sure."

"Did you know we rode in a helicopter, Brody?"

"Sort of. What happened anyway?"

Nate shrugged. "I don't know. It was weird. I just remember falling and hitting the water really hard. I started coughing really bad after you brought me back to life. My whole body hurt and I couldn't see and my ears were ringing, but then my vision got better. You were all cold and blue. I thought you were dead because I couldn't wake you up."

"Yeah, I was freezing."

"Yeah, then my dad showed up a little bit later. He came running out of the woods and wrapped me in his coat. Then a few minutes later this huge helicopter showed up. I've never seen something so big. It was all white and orange, but they couldn't land though, so this guy came down in a basket and they brought you back to life too, and then they lifted you up into the helicopter. Then he came down again to get me and my dad. I wish you could have seen it up there, Brody. It was so amazing, but you were asleep on the floor."

"Yeah. What did it look like?"

"Everything was so tiny. It was like being on top of the world. But we were going so fast. They were really worried about you. They kept saying they didn't have a lot of time."

"Wow. What happened to Henry?"

"I think he went back to the camp. Him and my dad's friend must have packed up all our stuff and drove back."

It was overwhelming for sure, and I didn't know what else

to say. When I glanced at Nate dimples appeared in his cheeks and he nudged me with his elbow. "Who's that girl, Brody?"

"Her name is Izzy," I replied, glancing behind us.

"She's really pretty," he whispered.

"Yeah, she's beautiful." I was happy to see her cheeks flush.

"Is she your girlfriend?"

I couldn't help but glance again, because I knew she could hear us. "I think so," I said.

"That's good." Nate pushed open the door at the end of the hallway. "Well, I think she likes you."

"Really? How do you know?"

"She keeps smiling at you."

Nate's parents treated us all to an early dinner at this great little restaurant and brewery not too far from the hospital. Everyone sitting around the table had a glow about them—this fantastic aura that I didn't know people could have. By the end of the meal, Nate was falling asleep in his chair and I wasn't far behind. My entire body ached, and I just wanted to go back to Heather's house. Thankfully, the ride home was peaceful and quiet.

Izzy sat in the back of Heather's car with me, rubbing my head. Every few minutes, Heather glanced at us in the mirror, but I was too tired to say anything. After a while, I fell asleep against Izzy's shoulder. When we got home, Izzy helped me inside and Heather went for a shower. Before calling it a night though, I made Heather a cup of tea, which I left on the kitchen counter alongside a thank you note.

Henry asked me to stay home to make sure I got as much rest as possible, so I spent a lot of time sleeping and tying flies. It was rejuvenating, but I had a sneaking suspicion he didn't want me accidentally knocking things over with my crutches. Izzy was amazing as usual, helping me around the house and sitting with me on the couch, but it was Heather who really surprised me.

Since Izzy had to continue with her classes at school, Heather made an extra effort to check on me. Normally she took her lunch to work, but for nearly a week she came home to talk with me in the kitchen while we ate peanut butter and jelly sandwiches. Several times I caught her staring at me with her kind eyes and a soft smile. Before returning to work she would do something very motherly, like rub my back or give me a sideways hug. One time she even kissed my head and ruffled my hair. Every time I said thank you she would just smile and give me a simple nod. I think she wanted to cry, too.

When I was finally feeling well enough I crutched myself to the shop, which took much longer than I anticipated, but I was anxious to keep working. I missed seeing the organized clutter of the shop and hearing the jingle of Molly's collar. Henry was hesitant at first, but I think he knew deep down I wouldn't take no for an answer, especially when I pulled ten bags of freshly tied flies from my backpack.

The first get well card came the day after I returned to work. I was sitting in the store room boxing up orders when

Henry tapped me on the shoulder.

"Here you go, buddy," he said.

"What's this? I don't ever get mail."

"Well there's a first time for everything." He left me to stare at the thick envelope with my name scribbled across the front. Aside from my GED results, I couldn't remember ever getting any mail. It was something so simple, and yet I didn't know what it felt like to have something personally addressed to me. I flipped the envelope over in my hands several times, wondering what was inside, and finally I peeled open the letter. Inside was a cheery get well card from Mac and his wife. I didn't know what to say, and over the next couple of days several more cards appeared, leaving me a little overwhelmed.

"What's going on?"

Henry looked up at me from behind the counter. "It looks like you're getting some get well cards."

"I know, but how do they know?"

"The fly fishing community is pretty tight knit, Brody. Words gets around."

The weekend after the accident, I had another surprise. Nate and his father walked in early on Saturday morning while Izzy and I were stocking shelves. Apparently Nate had been pestering his father for another chance to come visit the shop, and since Mac had a conference at one of the universities, he brought Nate along.

When Henry showed up, he found all three of us in the store room. Nate was having a blast racing up and down the ladder, getting new articles of clothing or fresh fly tying materials from their bins so he could help package the online orders. When that was finished, Nate helped Izzy and me stock the shelves out front, then we started teaching Nate how to tie. Henry couldn't get enough of it, so in between customers he was always sneaking over to take our picture.

It was definitely a morning that made me stop and think about how fragile life is. We had both nearly died, and yet here we were, tying flies together in Henry's shop. Nate was incredibly attentive, and he watched Izzy's instruction like the best student. However, I often found him staring at me with his lively, brown eyes, waiting for my approval. Knowing that I mattered to him is something that I'll carry with me forever.

When Izzy and I went home after work, neither of us mentioned the morning with Nate. I think Izzy knew it embarrassed me slightly—having anything to do with the spotlight—but when we lay down on the couch before bed, she finally broke her silence after giving me a long kiss.

"You were wonderful with him today."

"Nate's a good kid," I said. "I'm glad he's okay and I hope he had fun today."

"He had a blast, Brody. He was using the storage room like a jungle gym."

I nodded but didn't say anything. My mind was racing down that river again.

"Hey, look at me. Is everything all right?" Izzy asked.

The world seemed to slip away as we stared at each other.

It was just me and her. I wanted to say so much more to her. I wanted to tell her about how I saw her standing over me before I went unconscious. I wanted to tell her that I was absolutely head over heels for her, but I held back. "Yeah, there's just a lot on my mind," I said instead.

"Well, I'm really glad that you're all right," she said. I ran my hand across her cheek and gave her another kiss.

"Thanks." I hugged her tightly under the blanket, and that evening we fell asleep watching *A River Runs Through It*.

"You're serious? Henry really said this date is really going to happen?" Izzy asked for the umpteenth time.

"Yes," I said.

"*My* Uncle Henry?"

"Yes, I think so. He's the guy that we work for right?"

Izzy laughed. After breakfast she had hustled me into the car so we could go somewhere. She was extra giddy because I'd finally gotten word from Henry that the date with Miranda was scheduled.

"It probably would have happened earlier if it weren't for me nearly dying," I added.

"It doesn't matter how long it took. I'm just glad you're okay."

"Thanks. Where are you taking me anyway?"

"We're going to get you a nice shirt and maybe some

pants. We need to be presentable."

"You're enjoying this so much, aren't you?"

"I am. Welcome to the *mall*." The car came to a stop and I glanced nervously at the large shopping center looming in front of us.

"You really don't have to do this you know."

"Sure I do," she said. "Come on. Are you going to be all right to walk?"

I slid out of the car and put some weight on my ankle. The brace had been doing wonders, but my ankle still ached and I had no intentions of hurting it further. "I think I'll need the crutches."

"Alright. One sec." Before I could protest, Izzy rushed to the back seat to retrieve them.

"Thank you, Isabel. I hope you know I'm going to dance with you like crazy when I can walk again."

"I'm looking forward to it. Maybe in the meantime you can sing with me."

"If you want to see glass shatter, then sure."

Izzy's laughter lasted much of the way across the parking lot. When we finally crossed the entrance to the mall, my chest tightened. I couldn't recall anything so full of people. I figured that being an actual part of society again would make the discomfort from being around so many people go away, but it still made me nervous.

I had no intention of letting Izzy down, so I subconsciously gritted my teeth and focused on the bright smile that never seemed to leave her face. We wandered around to a few of the stores Izzy liked. After a while I realized I was actually enjoying myself, but unfortunately our fun date was about to have a rude interruption.

"Izzy! O-M-G. Is that you?" It was by far the most annoying voice I'd ever heard.

"People actually talk like that?" I mumbled.

Izzy snorted into my hoodie, but regained her composure in an instant. "Hi Jackie," she said. "Fancy seeing you here."

"Oh this place rocks, girlfriend. So many good deals!" Jackie said. "Who's the cutie on crutches?" When our eyes met I knew at once that I'd seen her before.

"This is Brody," Izzy said. "He just moved here a couple months ago."

"Oh, this is the guy you brought to that party." She flipped back her bleach-blonde hair, and I recalled the woman dry humping Derek on the ratty recliner.

"Yeah, that's me. It's nice to meet you, Jackie," I managed.

"You too. What happened to you?"

"Um—I sprained my ankle while I was out fishing last weekend."

"Oh, you poor thing. But at least with the crutches your shoulders will get a good workout. Gotta stay positive!" Before I could stop her, she gave my arm a gentle squeeze. It probably would have made most guys wet their pants, but all I wanted to do was go home and take a shower. Izzy didn't look happy either. Her eyes were simmering with disgust and the smile on her face was a fake one.

"Right," I said.

"Jackie, I just remembered I totally saw the best sale at Abercrombie when we walked in. They put up a ton of fifty-percent-off fliers." Izzy was lying through her teeth. When I asked about that store her exact words were "that store is a day ruiner because it smells like high school and rejection."

"Seriously? I was just heading over there!" Jackie exclaimed.

Izzy nodded and I fought back a grin.

"Well thanks for the tip!" She turned to leave and then stopped in the doorway of the store.

"Oh, by the way. You should totally bring Brody out and about more! He's good to look at. Later, girlfriend." We listened to Jackie's heels clicking as she hurried off for the imaginary sale after flashing us a porcelain smile.

"Izzy?" I said once Jackie was out of ear shot, "Would you totally hate me for wanting to trip her with my crutches?"

"No." Izzy laughed.

"So that's Jackie, huh?"

"Yep. That's Jackie Jacobs. The snarky cheerleading captain at school. She's snooty and irritating and she's always on the prowl for a new boy toy."

"Which right now is Derek?"

"As far as I know."

"I see." I hobbled my way to another clothing rack, praying that was truly the case.

288

"Do you think she's pretty?" Izzy blurted out.

"Huh?" I paused my search for the perfect shirt to see Izzy shake her head and turn her attention to a rack of belts.

"I'm sorry. I was just wondering. I probably shouldn't have asked. I mean, if you think she's pretty that's totally fine. She is pretty—"

"Izzy, that Jackie girl doesn't come close to how pretty you are. You are beautiful to me in ways that she never could be." I gave her a bright smile and resumed sorting through shirts.

"Well alright then."

A few minutes later, I stepped out of the dressing room wearing the last new button-down I picked out. It was a thicker, dark burgundy and Izzy immediately smiled.

"What do you think?" I asked.

"I think…" Her sentence fell away as she fussed with the collar.

I raised my eyebrows. "Not good?"

"No, you look very handsome. I really like this one."

I couldn't help my cheeks getting hot as I stepped back in the dressing room to get redressed. When I came out we went to pay for our items, but by the time we were through the checkout line, I didn't feel gwell. There were so many people crowded around us and it was hard to think with all the talking. Izzy nudged my stomach.

"What's wrong?" she asked. "If you're worried about money, I can help you out—"

"It's not that." I shook my head and my voice fell to a whisper. "It's all the people."

"Oh, I'm sorry. I didn't even think—"

"Don't be. I didn't either. Would you care if we ate somewhere else for lunch?"

"Nope. I've got just the place."

"I'm sorry to be such a pain. It's just a little overwhelming."

"I don't care," Izzy said. "Just means we can hang out somewhere quieter."

We spent the afternoon driving around, and Izzy took me up the river to an out of the way restaurant called the Rustic Skillet. We squeezed into a corner booth and got drinks ordered before Izzy asked a question that had apparently been nagging her all afternoon.

"What did you do about clothes before?"

Something between a sigh and a chuckle escaped me.

"What was that?" she asked.

"Nothing. It's just—you tend to ask questions that I never considered answering for anyone."

"Well, you told me I could ask them."

"I know. Uh, socks and undies were a must, obviously," I said, and she laughed. "So I would save up money from work and buy those brand new at whatever store was around."

Izzy nodded silently as she sipped from her glass.

"But everything else I would buy secondhand since it was way cheaper. I usually had a couple outfits, and I would wear them out before buying anything else. When I needed to wash, I would go to the laundromat and clean everything."

She wrapped an arm around mine. "What about showering?"

I chuckled and shook my head.

"Come on, Brody. Tell me."

"I had my ways."

"Tell me, Brody!" Her intoxicating grin easily coaxed the embarrassing memory from my brain. "Well, I found a few public places to shower. Those were nice because sometimes I could get hot water. Otherwise, I was faced with the chilly alternative."

"Which was?" Izzy was biting her lip, eager to hear the answer.

"You're really gonna make me say?"

"Of course. It's a condition of you staying in my mother's home," she teased.

"Uhuh. Very funny." Thankfully, I was spared for another minute when the waitress appeared to take our orders. As soon as the waitress was gone, Izzy scooted closer and started grinning again.

"So...you gonna tell me?"

I peered at her from behind my drink. "Will you tell me something you're scared of?"

"Are you going to laugh at me?" I shook my head. "Okay. I once found a spider in my bed, and I couldn't sleep for three days, so now every night I whip back the sheets to make sure there aren't any. Your turn."

"Wait, wait, wait. The outdoorsy girl is scared of spiders?"

"Don't push it, Brody."

"I just…I mean…We saw a bear!"

"Yeah. A mama bear, with two cuddly cubs! Not some little, eight-legged…arachnid…that could crawl into your ear and lay eggs in your brain!"

"Fine. That's a fair point. Well, sometimes you gotta do what you gotta do," I said. "The farther west I came, the smaller and more spread out the towns got, and I had to figure out a different way to stay clean. So several times I've made the early morning jaunt to a nearby river or creek…"

Izzy was dying in her seat, probably imagining my bare white ass racing in and out of a freezing cold river. "Oh my goodness, Brody. So, in addition to your fantastic stage singing career, you're like a professional skinny dipper!"

"Stop, Izzy."

As if the story wasn't embarrassing enough, she kept prodding me in the stomach, making me laugh even more. "So jumping in that river last week was no big deal then?"

"Nope. It was rather refreshing. No shower could ever match that."

Her laughter eventually faded to silence as she aimlessly fiddled with her straw.

"What?" I asked.

"Would you save me if I fell in the river?"

There had been so much on my mind since getting back

from the hospital. I knew that something like this could have happened just as easily while Izzy and I were out fishing. The thought of losing her made it hard to focus, and yet it was easy to see myself angry and bitter, having neglected to express my true feelings. I took her hand under the table and gave it a gentle squeeze.

"Isabel, you have no idea how much it means to me—all the stuff you've done for me, and waking up to your smiling face in the hospital. I would do everything I could to save you if you fell in the river."

"Alright then."

I was beginning to notice that something was bothering Izzy. Her normally calm, subtle sass and cheeriness had been mixed up with nerves and jitters. She'd taken the ACT already, so I wondered if maybe Jackie had said something to her at school. Either way, the worry was never anything permanent, and when she looked at me it would disappear behind a smile.

A couple days after our run-in with Jackie at the mall, Izzy, Henry, and I spent the hour before closing planning trip schedules for the next couple months. When everything was situated to Henry's liking, Izzy and I said goodnight and headed home.

Since I had missed out on the later part of high school, Izzy had been enlightening me on the social oddities of that time. This included stories about strange teachers, funny moments with the band kids, stupid things the jocks and cheerleaders did, and of course trying to dissect what some of the school lunches were really made from. I particularly enjoyed Izzy's suspicions of Jackie falling asleep in her cheerleading uniform while binging on powdered donuts.

But not even our raucous laughter could drown out the steady rumble of Derek's truck. I wasn't sure at first, but when Izzy stopped talking, I knew it was because she was looking. I decided to glance as well. There he was in the driver's seat, looking smug as ever—much like my father. I could just hear him calling the truck his "baby," knowing it was probably paid for by his father's pocketbook.

Then it hit me. That's why she was nervous. Something had happened. Whether it was good or bad I had no idea, but when she turned her attention back to me, there was an extra brightness in her smile. She slid her arm around mine and the truck engine roared as Derek sped away. We kept on walking. Izzy never looked back.

It had been almost two weeks since the accident, and most everything had healed up aside from the throbbing in my ankle. I was standing in the spare room upstairs, trying to get ready, but part of me felt insanely out of place. I'd been wearing the same variation of clothes for years. Tonight, however, I was wearing an entirely new outfit, and I wasn't sure what to think. My hair was freshly trimmed courtesy of Izzy, and as I stared at myself in the mirror I couldn't help but notice that my eyes seemed bluer than normal, like they were full of life again.

A gentle knock on the door behind me brought my attention to Izzy, who walked in with Heather behind her—both smiling. Izzy had curled her hair and left it hanging loosely over the thin scarf that was draped around her neck. She had on jeans like me, and was wearing one of the new shirts Heather got her for her birthday. Izzy's eyes were as kind as I'd ever seen them, and I couldn't stop staring. Eventually I laughed and looked away.

"Hi, Brody," she said.

"Hi, Isabel."

Heather blotted her eyes with the sleeve of her sweater. "Wow. If only you'd been here for prom last year, Brody. It would have been way more exciting."

"Mom," Izzy said, and I chuckled again.

"You two look adorable. I'm glad you're doing this for Henry. I want a picture before you leave."

"Okay," we said in unison. Heather left the room laughing.

"You clean up good, Brody," Izzy said, stepping closer. I was glad she was the one to move—my legs were getting rubbery. *Do girls' legs ever get wobbly? My goodness...*

"Thanks. You look really pretty," I said.

"Thanks. You look very handsome." She adjusted my collar.

"Are we good to go?" I asked.

"Yeah, definitely. I mean, besides the picture." I could barely breathe. "You all right?"

"You look...incredible." I didn't know what else to say as she slid a hand into mine.

"Come on, you dork."

We went to find her mother, who insisted on taking picture after picture due to a camera malfunction. We finally escaped to Izzy's car and started the short drive across town to Henry's home. Then her phone started jingling.

"Will you get that, Brody?"

"Sure." I grabbed her phone from the console and read the message to Izzy: "'Are you two sure about this?'"

"Oh, Henry better not get cold feet," she said.

"He won't." I typed a reply: *Yes, we are. See you soon.*

The phone jingled again.

"He says, 'Good. OK. Me too. I need help with dinner.'"

Izzy's laughter filled the car. "Just tell him to relax. We'll be there in a minute." Before I finished the message, the car slowed and we pulled into Henry's driveway.

"Alright, Brody. You remember the plan. First, we'll keep things casual."

"Two, we'll make jokes."

"And when things heat up—"

"We exit," I finished. Izzy grinned and eagerly hopped from the car. I followed her up to the porch, wishing I had asked her one more question, but the front door opened and the question was driven from my mind. Molly skittered onto the porch and began nudging our legs with her nose and paws.

"Oh, I'm so glad you guys got here first," Henry stammered. "I'm a little nervous." Nervous was an understatement. There were actually beads of sweat collecting under his messy hairline.

"Relax, Uncle Henry," Izzy said. "Everything's going to be fine. Trust me."

"Yeah. Right. Hi, Brody."

"Hey," I replied. "You want us to get cooking?"

"Is that all right if I ask you guys to help with that?"

"Are you kidding?" Izzy said. "We would love to!" Izzy and I both laughed when Henry let out an epically long-winded sigh of relief. He stepped back from the door and we crossed the threshold. I offered to hang up our coats so Izzy could try to calm his nerves, and I quickly lost track of their conversation when something on the wall caught my attention.

At first glance, there seemed to be nothing out of the ordinary about the coat rack, but I couldn't have been more wrong. A series of sturdy metal hooks adorned the bottom of this five-foot-long piece of richly grained hardwood. The remainder of the headboard had been carved into a mesmerizing display of flies, various species of trout, mountains, and rivers. It was so ornate that it looked like it was alive. Whoever made this had literally captured a moment in time.

I let my fingers graze across the wood, picking up the subtle indentations and chisel marks that made the trees on the mountains, the swooping cuts of river currents, the delicate strokes that made the fins on the fish. It was unbelievable. Then I noticed that someone had inscribed a quote along the bottom:

Many men go fishing all of their lives without knowing
that it is not fish they are truly after. – HDT

"What do you think, Brody?" Henry was standing beside me, waiting for my opinion.

"It's incredible," I said. "I've never seen anything like this before."

"I can't imagine you would have. My dad made it. I'm

glad you like it."

Izzy gave me a half smile and wrapped an arm around Henry. "Come on, Uncle Henry," she whispered. He wiped his brow and mumbled something about needing another shower. I chuckled as they left me to peruse the carvings on the coat rack. When I finally headed for the kitchen, I realized the coat rack was just the beginning.

Henry's house was like something out of a dream. It was an outdoorsman's paradise. Everything about it felt natural. The walls were painted in simple, natural colors: pale greens, blues, and tans. Where there wasn't paint, there was rustic knotty pine. Even the banisters and rungs were fashioned from treated tree limbs.

Like Izzy's home, there were also paintings and photography on the walls, although many of them were related to fly fishing. There were, however, very few pictures of his family, and it wasn't until I wandered into the living room that I found a picture of Henry with an older gentleman. Henry had an arm clasped around the older man's shoulder, and they were each holding up a beautiful trout.

"That's my papa." Izzy had snuck up beside me without making a sound.

"It's a great picture," I said. My eyes drifted to another picture on the fireplace mantle. A tiny plaque on the frame read: "The Fly Shop Family." It was a Christmas portrait with all the employees at the fly shop.

"You'll be in that this year," Izzy said. It was a wonderful thought, but before I could say anything else, she wrapped her arm around mine. "We should probably get cooking. Miranda will be here soon."

I gave one last glance to the picture of Henry and his father. When we got to the kitchen, Henry was poring over some cookbooks.

"Henry, your house is amazing," I said.

"Thanks. It's been a work in progress for a long time. Izzy can vouch for that one."

"Yeah," she replied. "He had just bought this house when we moved to Eugene. I was just a little kid, but he's been working on it ever since." I nodded and kept staring around the dazzling kitchen.

"So what are you thinking, Brody?" Henry asked.

"I know what he's going to say, Henry," Izzy cut in. "Something fun and easy."

"I like fun and easy. That sounds good," Henry said. "I don't want to burn the house down because I'm too nervous." We all laughed and Izzy glanced at me with a bright smile.

"Fun and easy," I repeated. "I'm thinking pizza, a salad of some kind, and maybe some of that smoked fish and crackers if you have any of that still."

"Definitely!" Henry said. "Fridge is stocked." When Izzy opened the fridge to peer inside, her hand flew to her face. I couldn't help but look as well.

"What in the world? Henry, are you prepping for Armageddon?" I asked.

"I probably should have asked what to get before you guys showed up, huh?" he said.

"It looks like you bought the entire refrigerated section of the supermarket," Izzy exclaimed.

Henry groaned. "Oh goodness. I'm hopeless."

"No you're not. Go shower, Uncle Henry. We'll get things going," she said.

"Yeah? Are you sure?" he asked.

"Just go," Izzy insisted.

"You know something—you two are great together." With one last grateful smile, Henry dashed upstairs.

"I'll be right back," Izzy said. She disappeared into the living room while I fished ingredients from the fridge and cupboards. Then the music came on. Happy, carefree notes were dancing through the house, and when I closed the fridge door Izzy was leaning against the counter, biting her lip.

"He said we look good together," I blurted out.

"I know," she said. I stepped closer and slid my arm around her waist. Everything became a colorful blur as we spun around the kitchen.

"Alright, alright," Izzy finally said. "We should probably make something."

"Yeah, right. Pizza," I said. After mixing up two boxes of dough, Izzy and I decorated the pizzas with all the popular toppings. Just as we slid the pies into the oven, a flurry of feet on the stairs announced Henry's return.

"Miranda's going to be here soon," Henry said. "Wow,

what's that smell?"

"Pizza," Izzy said. "You're looking good, Uncle Henry."

"You think so?" Henry glanced down at himself. "Are you sure? Because I already changed my shirt three times."

"Definitely. Miranda's going to love it," I said, and I was sure she would. Normally Henry was decorated in his worn out khakis or jeans and swag provided by some fly-tying company. Tonight, however, he had on brand new jeans and a classy dark green polo, and his beard was neatly trimmed.

"You two are my saviors," Henry replied. While he transferred some of the extra food to a spare fridge in the garage, Izzy and I finished the salad and plate of appetizers. Then came a knock on the front door. Like a judge's gavel, the sound echoed through the house and the color drained from Henry's cheeks.

"It's going to be great, Henry," I said.

"Take Molly!" Izzy added. We gave him a reassuring thumbs up, and Henry went to let Miranda in. I glanced at Izzy, who gave me a hopeful shrug. Then to our delight excited laughter carried through the house. Molly reappeared, trotting proudly in front of Henry and Miranda like a hostess leading them to their table. Miranda looked much different than the other times I'd seen her. Her bomber jacket and jeans had been replaced with a chunky knit sweater and leggings. The rugged hiking boots were swapped out for a simple pair of moccasins, and despite appearing windswept and mildly exhausted, she had a glowing complexion that shined brighter every time Henry said something to her.

"Miranda, this is my niece, Isabel, and her...boyfriend, Brody," Henry said. From the corner of my eye, I noticed Izzy's cheeks were a touch pink, but we both said hello and exchanged a handshake.

"It's nice to officially meet you guys. I've seen you two before—you both work at Henry's shop," Miranda said. We nodded.

"Do you like it? I think Henry's shop is fantastic," Miranda said.

"Yeah, it is," Izzy said. I just kept nodding. Henry and his shop had changed my life forever. Conversation flowed well between everyone, and as dinner finished cooking Henry began to relax.

"Wow, you guys really outdid yourselves," Miranda said when we set the hot pizzas on the counter.

"I, uh—asked them to help me out a little bit tonight," Henry confessed. Izzy and I watched with bated breath, waiting for her reaction. To our surprise and delight her smile only got broader.

"If we would have had dinner at my place, Henry, I would have done the exact same thing—my little brother and his girlfriend." Miranda laughed again at Henry's blatant sigh of relief. I winked at Izzy. When I moved to the fridge to get out the salad, she squeezed in beside me.

"Give it another hour. When dinner's done, we're out of here." Her whisper broke into a quiet giggle. "I've never talk-

ed covertly with someone in the fridge before." When I started laughing, my head knocked against the roof of the fridge.
Izzy's giggles filled the kitchen.

When we finally sat down to eat, Miranda shared stories
of her travels for the magazine and interviews with stubborn
old fly tyers throughout the country. But no matter how stubborn or reclusive the tyer, many of the stories ended the same.
Miranda ended up being treated like family even in the most
remote places with the most random people. It reverberated in
the depths of my soul. That was the same heartfelt treatment
I'd received from Izzy's family and everyone I'd met through
the fly shop.

"Thank you all for dinner," Miranda said after setting
down her glass of wine. "It was delicious. Let me know if
there's anything I can do to help clean up."

"No way," Izzy said. "You two go hang out. We'll clean
up." Henry gave us a thankful smile as he guided Miranda away
to the living room.

"My goodness, Brody!" Izzy squealed. "This is so exciting!"

"Tell me about it. I don't want to joke about this, but seriously—you and me starting a match making service sounds
like an amazing idea."

"Yes! Something like eHarmony. How about flyfisherson-
ly.com?" The idea made me laugh, but I was confused.

"What's eHarmony?"

"Oh, Brody." Izzy laughed and wrapped me in a warm

embrace. "Can you make some sort of dessert?"

"What? Are we leaving already?"

"Yep! I'm gonna fill the dishwasher quick and then we're gonna split!"

"Banana split!"

"Do it!" I was overcome by a moment of pure wonder as I stared at Izzy. All she cared about was making people happy. I spun her around the kitchen and gave her one last smile before yanking open the freezer door. After finding the toppings and sweets to make dessert, I set to work. By the time Izzy finished loading the dishwasher and putting the extra food away, I had assembled a banana split that was so romantic, I think it made Izzy's heart flutter.

"Wow, Brody. I want one." I leaned into her and we stared at the cold treat resting on the counter with one frosty spoon stabbed into it. Before we slipped away to the entryway to grab our coats, Izzy proudly put a finishing touch on the dessert: a single lit candle.

"Ready?" I whispered, and Izzy nodded.

"Hey, Uncle Henry!" she called. "We have dessert in the kitchen!" And like two church mice, Izzy and I slipped from the house without making a sound. We ran to her car, laughing and cheering, and it didn't stop until we were halfway back to Heather's.

"Brody! That was amazing!" Izzy exclaimed. "We need dessert now!"

"There's that dessert shop by the park."

She nodded and continued singing along to songs on the radio. My eyes drifted to the window. The street lights flashed by and I felt myself slipping into a daze. Something was wrong. I knew that I should have been having more fun, but there was a mysterious feeling creeping about inside of me. It was like something in the darkness was stalking me, and I had no idea what it was.

All I knew was that everything about this Friday night had been fantastic and I wanted it to stay that way. Yet, I knew it was coming to a close. The ice cream tasted so good, and Izzy was so radiant and stunning, but I was helpless to stop the darkness from consuming me.

She was the first person to ever break the lock on my heart and soul. I know that sounds corny, but I'd spent six years trying everything to keep horrendous memories buried and locked away. Becoming emotionally attached to her meant letting my guard down and exposing those nerves that might never heal. In that moment of weakness, the flashbacks started.

I was eight years old again, and I'd only been home from school ten minutes. My father was already drunk and angry with me because the dishes weren't getting done fast enough. I wished desperately for the yelling to stop, but it only got louder and I tried to scrub faster. My father slapped me in the face so hard that my lip split. I could see the blood dripping into the sink—red drops swirling with the diminishing bubbles...

I shuddered when a series of red and blue lights filled Izzy's car as a police car went whizzing by on the street.

...My father yelled again and pushed me off the stool I was using. My arm smacked into the counter as I fell. I was turned awkwardly now, leaving my other arm to take all my weight as I collided with the floor. The break was instantaneous. I yelped in pain, but not from the break. My father gave me several more swift kicks before realizing the break was so severe that blood was smearing all over the kitchen floor....

"So my mom wants us to grab her something, too. Apparently her final exam went really well and she says she deserves a special treat." When Izzy dropped her phone and turned to me, my face was pale and clammy.

"Brody, what's wrong?"

Without another word, I got out of the car and started walking off into the darkness.

"Brody, where are you going? It's starting to rain!"

I didn't answer. I just kept walking, welcoming the icy drops that were pelting my face. Eventually I heard a door slam, but the flashbacks were getting worse. I tripped on something and fell into a puddle. When Izzy found me back in an alley, I was slumped against the side of a building with my head buried in my hands, trembling uncontrollably. When Izzy's hand touched my shoulder, I pulled away like a scared dog.

"Hey," she said. "What's wrong?"

"Go away, Izzy."

"Brody—"

"Go away," I said. "You don't understand. You have no idea what I've been through." The siren of another police car could be heard out on the street. I shuddered again and turned away.

"You're such a useless piece of shit, Brody! Why couldn't you have died?" I didn't say anything and just waited for the shove that sent me hurtling into my dresser. I lifted my arms, trying to deflect the belt that he whipped across my body, but it hardly did anything. I fell to the ground and he kept going. Only when the welts broke open, staining my shirt with blood, did he finally stumble out of my room.

I hid under my bed, trying to fight back the salty tears that were burning my cheeks. I waited and waited, hoping it would just end. I just wanted it to end. Then there was the explosion of the door breaking and the police shouting as they came into the house...

"Look at me," she said. "Please..." But I didn't budge, so she did the only thing she could. Izzy knelt down between my legs and took my face in her hands. They were so warm despite it being so cold out. "Look at me, Brody."

Tears were still running down my face, mixing with the cold rain that was falling harder by the second. My world was shattered. Broken. There were bits and pieces of brightness. That was Izzy. I could see her in front of me, but I could also see the evil man who was my father. "Why are you here?" I mumbled.

"Because I'm not leaving you."

"Everybody leaves, Izzy."

"I'm not leaving you, Brody. We were hanging out. Remember? We hitched up my uncle with Miranda. We were having fun I thought."

Another sob escaped me. "Me too…"

"Well, tell me what's wrong so I can help."

"You can't help me, Izzy."

"I can if you let me. Come on, Brody, you can tell me. You don't have to hide any more. What's wrong?" This time when our eyes met, I knew all she could see in me was fear and uncertainty.

"My life has been nothing but a fucked up mess, Izzy. My stupid-ass dad. Me bouncing from family to family, job to job, just trying to get enough to eat and stay warm, sleeping on porches and in trucker cabs. I don't even remember the last time I had ice cream or went to a mall. Doing all this with you—this is what it's like for normal kids, normal people who have families and real lives, and I don't feel like I deserve any of it." More tears poured down my cheeks.

"Hey…"

"Can you imagine being ten years old and seeing your dad shooting up heroin after beating the pulp out of you? My dad was a monster! He ruined everything!"

She broke then. Tears ran down her cheeks and she just

kept staring at me, unsure of what to say.

"You. Your family. You're all so kind and awesome," I said. "I don't want to lose that. I've never had this before."

"Who says you're going to lose it?"

"I always lose anything good. I've lost everything!" As I succumbed to more sobs, I bowed my head and didn't look at her again until she put a finger under my chin.

"You haven't lost me, Brody," she whispered. "What you don't deserve is to have lived the life you have."

"Well I did, and I don't want you to spend time with me just because you feel sorry for me. I don't want to lose you, Izzy." The frigid drops of rain were starting to soak into my clothes. My hands began to shake again, and when I closed my eyes it was like I was stuck in the river again, running out of breath.

"I'm not going anywhere, Brody."

"How do you know? I've heard that line before, Izzy. Foster parents say that, but gradually they realize you're not a good fit, while you're realizing the same thing, and then they just cut you loose. I'm so scared, Izzy."

She leaned in closer and put her forehead against mine. "I'm not some foster parent, Brody Allen. I promise: I'm not leaving you. This is your life now, Brody. Yours. You're a fly fishing guide now, and no one can take that away from you— not even your dad."

My head sank to my chest, but Izzy quickly picked it up again.

"I want to be a part of your life, and so does Henry and my mom. I would like my dad to meet you too."

"Why? So he can ship me off to Timbuktu?"

"No, but maybe a session of boot camp in the back yard." Izzy managed a half smile, and a teary sob escaped me that time. "Promise me you won't leave."

I shook my head. "Izzy, what if I don't belong here? I'm just a nobody."

"You're not a nobody!" She let go of my hand and punched my arm. "Did you feel that?"

"Yes, but why—"

Before I could finish she grabbed my face and kissed me. "Did you feel that?"

"Yes, Izzy—"

"You're not a nobody, Brody. You're my boyfriend, and I don't want to lose you either! So, promise me!" The rain continued to pound the pavement, drenching us both to the bone, but Izzy never looked away. "Promise me, Brody!"

"I promise." I'll never forget that kiss we shared in the alleyway. Her tender lips tasted like strawberries, and her warm hands were the best thing my cheeks had ever felt. Izzy backed away only after giving my forehead one last kiss.

"Sorry I punched your arm."

"It's all right. I'll live."

"Good. So let's get my mom her treat, then we can go home and I can tease you while you attempt to make flies."

When I wiped away the tears and blinked a few times,

everything had returned to normal. My father was gone and the awful sense of despair was washing away with the rain. I stared at the raindrops running off Izzy's nose.

"What do you say?" she asked.

"Okay."

She took my hand to lead me from the alley, but I held my ground. When she looked back, I wrapped her in the best hug I could muster. Her sopping wet locks stuck to my cheeks, but I didn't care because she smelled like home. Not long after, we were falling asleep on the couch and my question from earlier that evening popped back into my head.

"I was going to ask you earlier tonight if this could have been, you know, like some sort of first date or something." Izzy was sitting on the couch the same way she always did when we were together—at the end seat with her legs across my lap.

"If it was, it was the best first date I've ever had," she said.

"I hope so."

"Yeah. But honestly, I think we've probably had three or four first dates by now." I turned to face her, and in the darkness of the living room the light from the television danced across her face.

"So that kiss in the library…" I began.

"I'm still pissed that janitor showed up," Izzy finished.

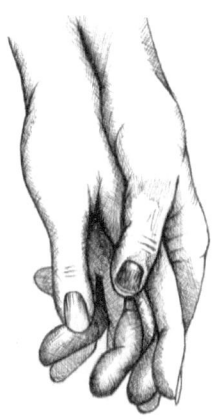

‌I wasn't usually one to break down in front of people. I'd grown accustomed to accepting the pain and frustration of being alone. I'd learned to accept disappointment, and always had a foot out the door. When something went wrong or didn't feel right, I left. That's the way it had been for years. But now things had changed, and I wondered if my episode in the alley would make things awkward between Izzy and me. No one had ever seen me so vulnerable. But in all actuality, it brought us closer together.

Our nights spent tying together became long hours of discussion, with both of us recounting frustrating times in our past. I elaborated on times with other foster families, and Izzy alluded to the marriage troubles that her parents had gone through while she was growing up. There was a level of trust between us now that neither had ever experienced before, and that trust was growing exponentially.

A few weeks before Christmas, Izzy and I spent another Saturday fishing up in the mountains. It was a chilly day, and throughout the morning we caught a few glimpses of the sun, but often it was hidden behind blustery clouds—the weather couldn't seem to make up its mind.

By the middle of the afternoon the clouds had grown menacing and were swirling angrily above the mountaintops. The fish must have sensed the coming storm as well and were no longer biting, so Izzy and I headed for shore. As we stood underneath the evergreen boughs, amongst the stones and drift-wood, the sounds of the river diminished to a gentle gurgle. Then the rain came.

The fat drops plunked in the river and splattered against the rocks, echoing through the river valley. It was like a symphony that only Mother Nature could play. Izzy and I grinned at one another and started down the trail. When a clap of thunder boomed over our heads, the downpour was unleashed. We ran hand in hand back to her car.

"It's really coming down," I said. "Do you think we should just call it a day and head back?"

"No, not yet," she replied. "It's probably safer to just wait it out. The roads up here can get kind of hairy when it rains this hard."

"Alright." I leaned the seat back and closed my eyes. My chest was still heaving slightly from our sprint back to the car.

She found my hand and gave it a gentle squeeze, but before I could squeeze back, Izzy let go and turned on the radio. Then she climbed into the back seat.

"What are you doing?" I asked.

"I'm changing. If you haven't noticed, Brody, we're soaked." Her mischievous grin set my body on fire.

"Oh. Alright. I'll, uh, just try not to peek." Izzy laughed while I sat there watching the windows fog up. Then there was a tap on my shoulder.

"You should change too."

"Oh, I don't have any extra stuff—" I don't think I could have stopped staring if I wanted to. She was down to her shorts and a t-shirt now, and the car was filling with the smell of her perfume. It was making my brain go nuts.

"I brought you some. Come here."

I climbed into a space that Izzy had cleared of all our fishing gear. When I was finally free of my waders, Izzy scooted forward and gave me a kiss. I kept nudging her closer.

"Brody," she whispered as I lifted off my sweater, "you should probably know that I've had a thing for you since the day we met."

"Likewise." I smiled and closed my eyes for a few seconds. The only sounds I could hear were the rain drumming steadily on the roof of the car and her breathing gently against my face. When I opened them again, Izzy's fingers danced around my waist as she started to help me out of my shirt. Part of me wanted to stop her because I was scared of what she was about to see, but her fingers felt too good.

For a few moments, it was pure bliss. She tossed my shirt aside and our lips met again. From her seat on my lap, Izzy delicately kissed and caressed my neck and shoulders. It was indescribably beautiful. Then she felt the scars.

There were no words. Just a solemn few minutes as her fingers traced the nicks and gashes along my back and arms that had since become pink fleshy bumps. Each scar seemed to tingle as her finger grazed past, and part of me wondered if Izzy could make them all disappear. The rain came down harder outside and she gazed at me with watery eyes. Then our foreheads touched as I gently pulled her close again.

"I'm so sorry, Brody," she whispered.

"It's okay. You saved me." Our lips met again. Then I was helping her slide off the tank top she had on under her hoodie.

"You are the most amazing woman I've ever seen, Isabel Cooper." She giggled as my hands brushed across her bare skin that was getting hotter by the second. "If I'm going to be stuck in the mountains, I'm so glad it's with you."

Izzy grinned. "Likewise. I have one question for you, Brody."

"What's that?"

"You still think fly fishing is complicated?"

"Nope. It's elegant and beautiful."

Izzy and I were laying on the couch, enjoying a pre-Christmas episode of some show, when a question popped into my head. I rubbed her back and she looked up at me with one of her beautiful smiles.

"What's up?" she asked.

"Do you ever wish your life was different?"

Izzy shrugged and her smile faded. "I don't like that question, Brody."

Before I could say anything else, she got off the couch and headed for the kitchen. It left me feeling restless and worried, especially after sharing such an intimate afternoon together. Then I heard Izzy groan from the kitchen, and something clattered on the counter. When I came into the kitchen, she looked exasperated as she took a long drink from a glass of water.

"Are you mad at me?" I asked. The glass thudded loudly on the counter.

"No, I'm not mad at you, Brody."

"Well you seem mad. It was just a question."

"I know it was just a question, but you don't get it, Brody. I've spent a lot of time wishing my life was different. I wished I hadn't moved so much. I wished that I had more friends. Sometimes I wish that my dad didn't serve so that my parents could be together more. I don't even know if he's going to be home for Christmas—but I realized a while ago that I just need to appreciate what I have in my life. I'm healthy. I have my mom and Uncle Henry here. We live in a beautiful part of the country where we can go hiking and fishing all the time."

"I know…"

"Why do you think I spend so much time with you? With my mom? I know stuff has been rough for you and rougher than anyone should have to deal with, but I hope that you don't spend too much time wishing for so much. You've got to stop living in the past and appreciate what you have right in front of you, because had your life gone differently we might never have met, and in my opinion that would suck!" Her speech came to a close and Izzy headed upstairs without another word.

Then the phone on the counter jingled. Even though it was Izzy's, I picked it up without a second thought. It was bad enough that Izzy seemed mad at me, but when I read the message my heart and stomach sunk even further. I headed for the entryway and slid into my boots and sweater.

"Where are you going, Brody?" Heather's face was etched with worry. Clearly she'd heard everything, since she'd been in the other room reading.

"I don't know. I think Izzy…" I could barely form words as I motioned back toward the kitchen.

"Brody. Don't go. She's just frustrated. Let me go talk to her."

I wanted to give in and let Heather work some sort of motherly magic, but this wasn't necessarily something she could fix. Nothing could erase the repulsive text message from Derek that was seared into my brain.

"Brody, please." Heather stepped forward, but I shook my head and walked out the door, letting it shut silently behind me.

I counted the lines in the sidewalk as best I could in the ever-growing darkness. I felt terrible for violating Izzy's privacy and peeking at her phone. When I saw Derek's name pop up on the screen though, I couldn't help myself. Now I wished I hadn't even looked. My heart knew that everything was probably okay, but neither my head nor gut could make up their mind. There was still a part of me that was unchanged—that hadn't adapted to my new lifestyle—and in that moment when disappointment seemed inevitable, I ran.

The key clicked in the lock and I stepped inside Henry's shop, potentially for the last time. It seemed like only yesterday that Izzy had been prodding me awake on the back porch. The fly shop was a special place, but once again I was facing the subtle realization that maybe I didn't belong.

I absentmindedly wandered to the back room and sat down at the counter. I stared at the vice where I'd spent so much time making flies for Izzy's birthday. I could see that smile on her face all over again. We had spent so much precious time together. I closed my eyes and took several deep breaths.

I won't leave you, Brody. Her words replayed in my head, and I could almost feel her forehead against mine, her hands on my cheeks. Izzy was right. Running wasn't the answer any more. I needed to quit living in the past. It had been stupid to leave without asking her about the message. She was probably worried about me. When I opened my eyes, there was a flash of light out in the parking lot. Not long after, another pair of headlights danced across the room.

Izzy is the only person who knows me so well. That left me wondering who the other headlights belonged to. *Henry perhaps?* I shut off the lamp, but lingered in the back room for several minutes before heading for the back door. I was nervous that she was going to be even more frustrated with me. But when my fingers finally grasped the door knob, the hairs on my neck were standing on end.

I opened the back door halfway, expecting Izzy or Henry to be racing up the back steps of the porch, but there was nothing—just a cold, damp, dark alley. Then I heard the distinct rumbling of a large truck engine, and I knew Derek must have been there in the lot.

After locking the door behind me, I hurried down the steps and half sprinted the length of the alley. When I reached the edge of the building I paused, catching sight of Izzy talking to the same guy I'd seen following us through the grocery store. He was several inches taller than her, with dirty blonde hair, and in the light of the street lamp it was easy to see his flushed cheeks. There was also a swagger to his step, and in an instant I knew he was drunk.

"You followed me here?" she asked.

"I guess. Yeah. I just really wanted to talk to you," he said. "You're not answering my calls or texts."

"Yeah, I know. I don't want to talk to you."

"Why not?"

"Because I'm done with you. I've been done with you for a long time, so get lost."

"You going to find your new boyfriend then?"

"Derek, just get out of here. Go play with Jackie or who-ever you're messing around with these days!" She turned for the shop, but then his hand was around her arm.

"But I wanna talk." Before she could do anything, he swung her around and pushed her up against the side of his truck. A loud gasp of air flew from her lungs. "Everything changed so fast and I don't know why."

"I told you why. I wasn't interested."

"Yeah, not interested. You didn't say you were cheating on me."

"I never cheated on you. We weren't even dating!"

Derek made a sound of disgust and used a free hand to try and undo the zipper on her coat.

"Derek! Stop! What are you doing?"

"Shut up, Isabel! Let's just have some fun." From a distance I watched as he tried to kiss her. My anger flared and I started making my way across the parking lot.

"Derek, you're drunk! I don't want to do that with you! Ever!" I broke into a sprint when I heard her cries as his hands groped at her body.

"I think you do! I think you want it just as bad as I do!" Derek said.

"Fuck you, Derek! Get off me!" She tried to shove her knee between his legs, but Derek just laughed and slammed her up against the truck again.

"Just shut up, okay? It will be fun!"

"No! I don't want to, Derek! Stop!" But her sounds were muffled when he put a hand over her mouth. Izzy retaliated, and a scream of pain flew across the parking lot as she bit down on one of his fingers.

"You bitch!"

Izzy cringed when his large hand blocked out the light from a nearby street lamp. But the blow never came. In a flash of shadows I caught Derek's arm with one hand and buried my other fist into his lower back as hard as I could. His anger became a painful groan instead.

"You should just leave, Derek, and don't ever talk to her

again," I said.

Derek turned in a fit of drunken fury, already swinging a clenched fist at me. Suddenly time slowed to a complete stop and it was my father in front of me, drunken spittle flying from his mouth as he cursed at me. The hand flying toward my face would surely leave behind a bruise or broken lip—if not something worse—and I stood frozen like the twelve-year-old kid I used to be...

"Brody!" Izzy's voice snapped me back to reality. I deflected his hand with ease, and when my fist collided with the front of Derek's face, there was a sickening crunch as his nose broke and blood spurted everywhere. But I didn't stop there. I yanked a stunned Derek away from Isabel and laid several more blows into his ribs and a kick to the leg that would leave him limping for days.

In seconds it was over and Derek slumped to the damp ground with bloody drool running onto his sweater. I held out my hand for Isabel, but she didn't take it until she also gave Derek a swift kick between the legs. Needless to say, he passed out from the pain.

"Asshole!" she yelled.

"Come on. Let's get you out of here." I led her away from Derek's truck, but something was still wrong. Her breathing was frantic and when I opened the door to her Jeep, she stopped in her tracks. Her wide-eyed gaze shifted nervously between me and the dark interior of the car.

"Izzy, we're going home," I said. But she shook her head

and backed away from me. There was a look of terror in her eyes. I stepped closer and slowly put a hand on her shoulder.

"Go away!" she yelled. Before I knew it, she was trying to punch me.

"Hey," I said, catching her hands. "It's all right. You're okay, Izzy. Look at me. It's just me, Izzy."

Her eyes finally focused on me. Then she collapsed into my arms. Tears were streaming down her cheeks and her entire body was shaking. "Don't leave, Brody. I'm sorry. Please don't leave."

"I'm not going anywhere," I said. Her cold, trembling hands ran across the light stubble on my face. I gingerly brushed aside the warm tears still pouring down her cheeks. Then she leaned closer and her soft lips found mine. Each kiss was like a promise to one another, delicate and beautiful, yet full of passion and excitement. When her arms slid around my neck, I hugged her as hard as possible, wanting her to know that I didn't ever want to lose her. Eventually we parted, but she stayed close and the shaking continued.

"Are you okay?" I asked.

"Thanks to you I am. You were…"

"Isabel, I wasn't going to let him hurt you. I'm sorry about what I did though."

"I'm not. He deserved it. Please don't leave, Brody. He's been pestering me for a couple weeks, but we weren't doing anything. I'm sorry if I worried you."

"It's okay."

"No, it's not. I should have said something, because I didn't want you to get worried and leave, and that's exactly what happened. You're the best part of my life, Brody."

"Don't worry about it." I pulled her into another hug and rubbed her back until the shaking subsided.

"Would you mind? I don't really feel like driving," Izzy said, handing me the keys.

"Sure." We left Derek drooling and unconscious on the ground and started for home. It wasn't long, though, before she started crying again.

"Brody, you realize that if you hadn't been there, something awful could have happened."

"No, Izzy. Don't even think about it. It didn't happen." I reached over in the darkness and she took hold of my hand. Both of us fell silent until we were nearly to her house.

"Did it hurt—punching him?" Her fingers grazed the tops of my knuckles, which were swollen and covered with flecks of blood.

"Not really. I mean it aches a little now, but the last thing I was worried about was my hand hurting—just wanted to make sure you were okay."

When Izzy didn't reply, I looked over to find her staring wide-eyed out the window. I didn't bother to ask why because as we turned into her driveway, the headlights lit up a black SUV with military plates.

"My dad's here."

I sucked in a breath. "Should I go stay at Henry's or

something?"

"No. I want you to stay with me. Come on." As soon as the front door closed behind us, a flurry of feet rushed to greet us—one the soft clap of slippers and the other the hard thunk of combat boots. Izzy was starting to shake again from nerves, so I squeezed her hand and she squeezed back.

"Izzy. What's wrong?" Heather asked, rushing forward to comfort her daughter. I was having a hard time not staring at her father. He was a big man, and his combat attire made him look even more intimidating.

"Did he hurt you, sweetheart?" asked her father. I knew he meant me. It was evident in the way he was glaring at me, but when Izzy's eyes flashed to her father, his stern expression relented.

"No, Dad, *he* didn't hurt me—and his name is Brody. It was that dumbass Derek. He caught up with me in the parking lot when I went to get Brody. Now, if you guys don't mind, I'm going to shower." In a swift motion, Izzy let go of my hand and pushed past her parents, heading for her bedroom. Her footsteps echoed throughout the house as the three of us lingered in the entryway.

"I'm glad you're back, Brody. This is my husband, Eric. Don't let the uniform intimidate you. He's a big softy." Heather gave me one last smile before rushing after Izzy.

"Very funny, honey," Eric said. "Come here, Brody."

"Where are we going?"

"The kitchen."

"You're not kicking me out?"

"No." Eric walked off to the kitchen. I followed tentatively, but lingered in the doorway. "I said come here, Brody." With each step I took toward the counter, my heart pounded harder. When Eric started digging in the freezer, I thought for sure my life was over. He was going to finish me off with some secret weapon he kept on ice.

"There were are." Eric tossed a bag of frozen peas on the counter. "For your hand."

At once the panic subsided. I nodded gratefully, but remained silent.

"It's been an incredibly stressful couple days and I just want some answers."

"Where should I start?" I asked.

"I would like to know what happened tonight."

"Izzy might not want me to say anything."

"Yes, well, I guarantee you Izzy will tell Heather everything, so I want to know what happened, Brody."

"That Derek guy followed her to Henry's shop when she came to look for me," I said.

"Why was she looking for you?"

"Because he sent her some stupid message on her phone that I saw, and I got upset, so I left."

"That's what Heather said," Eric continued. "He tried to force himself on her, didn't he? Heather said he's been sneaking around. If he raped her, Brody—"

"Boy, you military folks don't beat around the bush at all,

327

do you?" My attempt at lightening the mood was moot. Eric's eyes were brimming with a protective rage.

"We don't have time for that in the field and I don't consider this much different of a situation at the moment."

"Mr. Cooper, I didn't let anything happen to her. Nothing happened to Izzy. She's just scared. She actually gave him a nice kick when I was done with him."

All at once the fury evaporated into a sheepish smile. Then his shoulders sagged in defeat. "I hate being gone all the time."

"She misses you, sir. A lot."

Eric snorted. "Brody, don't give me any *sir* business. I get that enough already. Where's Derek?"

"He's probably still lying next to his truck at the shop if you want to talk to him."

"You didn't kill him did you?"

"No. I don't think so. Just made him sorry for touching Izzy."

In one swift movement, Eric's hand clapped down on my shoulder much faster and harder than I expected. "Thank you for keeping her safe, Brody."

"You're welcome." I sucked in a breath as Eric fell silent and took a seat beside me.

"Heather's been explaining your situation to me. Actually, she and Sarah told me some things," Eric said.

"I'm sure they did. Like I told Mrs. Cooper, if you don't want me to stay, I'll go."

"Nobody said anything about you leaving. Brody, Heather has been like a cocoon the last couple months, and I was worried I was losing her all over again, but it turns out that it's you who's been worrying her."

I bowed my head. "I'm sorry, sir."

"Look at me, Brody." Our eyes met and the sharp jawline slackened. "She has been worried sick about you. The only reason Heather didn't tell me was that she was afraid I'd send you packing. I'll admit I was a little hot when I found out about you, but that was only because she'd held out on me."

"Mr. Cooper—"

"Brody, I don't think I was here five minutes and she broke down. I've never seen Heather cry like that. She told me you don't have a mom and that your father…"

I shifted uncomfortably in my seat and instinctively tugged on my sleeves, making sure that none of the scars were showing. Eric's expression grew even softer and he just nodded.

"I said I was sorry, but Heather just kept crying. She's been having a hard time sleeping and she comes down at night to check on you all the time. Then she told me you almost died trying to save one of Henry's clients."

I didn't know what to say. "Yeah. That was—"

"Pretty amazing as I hear it."

"Yeah. Something like that. I'm glad the kid's okay."

Eric nodded. "Heather also mentioned that you and Izzy tie together and fish together all the time, and you two managed to match Henry up with a nice lady."

"That was a good night," I laughed.

"It sure sounded like it. You and my little girl seem pretty good together."

"Mr. Cooper…" I was starting to feel overwhelmed again.

"Brody, I don't want you to ever feel like you have to leave. You're welcome to stay here as long as you like."

"Really?"

"Yes. Besides, I don't think Izzy would be too happy if you left." The long breath I'd been holding finally escaped me. Not long after, Heather and Izzy reappeared; before anything else, she gave her father a hug that was long overdue.

"I'm glad you're home, Daddy," she said.

"Me, too. Are you all right, sweetheart?" he asked.

"Yeah," she said. Izzy ran a hand through my hair and planted a warm kiss on my cheek. "Any chance you could make us one of those giant ice cream sundae things?"

"I suppose," I said. Her parents laughed and moved to get ingredients from the freezer and cupboards, leaving us to stare at each other. Everything about Izzy was home to me. As I got lost in her green eyes, I slid an arm around her waist, urging her closer. She leaned in to kiss my cheek again, but this time she didn't pull away.

"I love you, Brody." Her voice was just a whisper in my ear, but it was clear as a bell. I held her close.

"I love you too, Izzy," I whispered. "I've never said that to anyone before."

She giggled. "I hope not."

Eight Months Later

So, here I am enjoying an early spring day on the river-bank, because the fish aren't biting. It sure is amazing what can happen in a year. It's actually been a year to the day since Isabel Cooper found me behind her uncle's shop on the verge of catching pneumonia.

After that infamous night with Derek, everything sort of fell into place, oddly enough. I got to celebrate a real Christmas with Isabel's family, as well as my birthday a few weeks later. When I mentioned to Heather how many birthdays I'd missed, she insisted on covering the cake with probably three dozen candles. Needless to say, it was the best birthday ever.

I kept up with my guide work, and it wasn't long before Henry was sending me out to guide my own trips. The months flew by, and when June arrived it was time for Isabel's graduation. Seeing her celebrate a once in a lifetime moment was something truly beautiful, but Henry had plans to make that night even more memorable.

He and Miranda's relationship had flourished, and after Izzy's graduation they told everyone about their child on the way, marriage prospects, and the fly fishing lodge they had purchased down in New Zealand. The icing on the cake was that Izzy and I would be spending our summer there, guiding, exploring, and fishing.

It took us the better part of a day to go from the States to New Zealand's south island, and then another five hours west of Christchurch to get to the lodge. Nestled in a grove of hardwoods and evergreen trees, the lodge is bordered by a functional cattle farm, a breathtaking river, and a chain of mountains that make up the edge of Mount Aspiring National Park. Winter was just getting started when we got here, but that made it no less captivating. The snow-capped mountains and winding rivers looked like something out of a fantasy novel.

The fishing has been unreal, and some of our haunts are so remote that we have to use a helicopter to get there. I can't wait to show Nate the pictures. During our stay, Izzy and I became friends with most of the clients, many of whom came from all over the world just to fish in New Zealand's crystal clear waters. We also became good friends with a lady named Grace and her dog Lily. She's one of the locals who lives and works at the lodge during the week. When we had a free weekend, she took Izzy and me exploring and even brought us back to her hometown for dinner with her family. It was incredible.

Most evenings after the clients have retired from a day of heavy fishing, Izzy and I take a walk through the valley. Sometimes we fish until dark, but more often than not we just enjoy a long walk, and Izzy feeds the cows through the fence.

We're starting to miss Eugene, though. Henry and Miranda spent most of the summer building a nursery, and they send us pictures every few days. Izzy's getting anxious to start her college classes in Eugene. She encouraged me to apply as well, and I actually got in, so maybe we'll get to have a few classes together. To top it off, Izzy's father finally got reassigned to the States.

After everything that's happened, I finally feel like I belong—like I have a home. Here comes Izzy, making her way down the riverbank. Her hair is fluttering in the breeze and she's rocking a pair of polarized blue aviators she found at a shop down here, and let me tell you: they look damn good on her.

"You ready to go fishing one last time?" she asks. "A hatch is starting up the river." I grin when she slides her hand into mine.

"You're so beautiful," I say, and she plants a kiss on my cheek. I will never be able to thank her enough for giving me a chance and changing my life. When you find that person who knows how to make you feel loved, and at the same time makes you want to do everything in your power to make them feel loved—that's your person. I will do my best to love Izzy and take care of her forever.

"First to seven picks out dessert tonight," I say.

Izzy laughs and whips her pole in front of my face. "No crossing my line."

THE END

ABOUT THE AUTHOR

R.K. BLESSING

R.K. Blessing loves the outdoors and goes fly fishing when he gets the chance. Along with tying flies he also enjoys writing, cooking, drawing, and binging on a good television series when one presents itself. He lives and works in Michigan's lower peninsula.